# I LOVE YOU I HATE YOU!

## G.A.HAUSER

G. A. HAUSER

I LOVE YOU I HATE YOU!

Copyright © G.A. Hauser, 2013

Cover photograph by Dennis Dean

Cover design by Mark Antonious Richfield

Edited by Stacey Rhodes

ISBN Trade paperback: 978-1482-3922-4-1

The G.A. Hauser Collection LLC

First The G.A. Hauser Collection LLC publication:
© February 2013

WARNING:
"The unauthorized reproduction or distribution of this
copyrighted work is illegal. Criminal copyright infringement,
including infringement without monetary gain, is
investigated by the FBI and is punishable by up to 5 years
in federal prison and a fine of $250,000."

## Dennis Dean Images

Award-winning photographer Dennis Dean continues to make his mark as an internationally known photographer. He is credited for his creative abilities, strong composition, and dramatic lighting. Dennis specializes in state of the art digital photography for fitness, fashion, and fine art.

Dennis published his first art book, "Within Reach" to rave reviews, which led to his work being showcased in a plethora of art publications, fitness magazines, calendars, greeting cards, as well as countless exhibitions, including two in London at the Adonis Art Gallery.

He is the founder of Dennis Dean Images and creative director and photographer of Five Star Monkey's Ruff Riders and Live Free Be Strong brands. He is also the editorial photographer for *Mark* and *Passport Magazines*, having shot countless covers and fashion layouts.

Dennis is proud to be partnering with Fort Lauderdale's Royal Palms Resort & Spa showcasing his work in all the rooms, bar and grill, the spa and fitness center. Stop by the resort to see Dennis' work, or make an appointment for a photo session at 954-240-8307.

Be sure and check out www.DennisDean.com & www.RoyalPalms.com.

## CHAPTER 1

Parker Douglas tried not to listen in on the conversation that was occurring right near his desk.

"Dack, just give him these roses and write him a card. Here. I've written what you need to write in it." Henry Sheen, the art director, handed flowers and a card to Dack Torington, who was a photographer and lifestyle editor for their magazine.

The first week at a new job was never easy for Parker, and being hired to work for *Judas' Rainbow,* an LGBT magazine based out of Los Angeles, was like finding the proverbial pot of gold. Parker had worked hard for years, since graduating college with a BA in journalism from NYU, and finally knew he'd found a perfect fit. He just didn't want to fuck it up.

Typing his sex and lifestyle column on the computer, his fingers paused over the keyboard. Yeah, he was eavesdropping. How could he not? The men were right beside his desk.

"Roses? Are you kidding me? Henry, I am not giving Mason roses."

*Mason.*

Parker peeked across the large office space, free of dividers and loaded with employees working, and no doubt, listening as well, and trying not to look as if they were.

*Mason Bloomfield?*

5

Parker couldn't imagine it being anyone else, considering there was only one 'Mason' working with them on the magazine.

Gorgeous, mature Mason Bloomfield—a tall, dark and handsome macho man with brown hair and light eyes. Were they blue or green? Parker didn't know yet, but when the senior editor Sigourney Edina had shown Parker around and introduced him to the staff, Parker had been smitten…no, not smitten. Enamored? No. Attracted! Yes. Attracted to the stunner who was the group advertising manager.

Mason had his own office, as did a few top salaried employees at the magazine. Parker peeked in the direction of Mason's office, behind his back, but his door was closed.

"You messed up, Dack. Don't screw it up worse. It's Valentine's Day tomorrow. You have a chance to apologize." Little, balding, bespeckled Henry seemed so concerned.

Parker tried not to make it obvious he was listening, writing his column about men and their sexual needs, health issues, and even some love advice thrown in for good measure.

Dack shoved the roses at Henry, making the petals scatter. "I hate Valentine's Day and I'm not giving him flowers."

Parker actually winced at the act, seeing poor Henry pick up the stems, holding the card, and walk away to his end of the office. If Henry was trying to fix or salvage a relationship between Dack and Mason, he may have been wasting his time. And why Henry was intervening? Giving an attempt at the role of peace-maker between the two men? Parker had no clue. Since he was so new to the group, he could only assume either Henry had set the two men up, had a vested interest in them getting along, or just felt concerned and wanted to help.

Learning office politics was par for the course for a newbie. Not only did Parker have to do his work and do it well, he needed to be aware of landmines and keep clear of internal battles.

He made the mistake of meeting Dack's gaze right after the confrontation. The man was imposing, at least six foot tall and built like a muscle-bound-god. He had 'hurt' written all over him, and Parker could see how men would fall for a man like that. How many gay guys were into muscle worship and got stomped on when they actually thought a relationship was possible with one of these pretty egomaniacs?

To Parker's surprise, instead of a leer or glare, Dack smiled at him with a slightly flirty curl of the lip. "Mm."

"Huh?" Parker pretended he hadn't heard every word that had been said between Dack and Henry.

Dack ran his hand over his shaggy brown hair, showing off a large biceps and broad forearm bulging through his business attire. "Hey."

"Uh. Hey?" Parker laughed, trying to be sympathetic and not sarcastic.

Dack strutted off, as if he were too sexy for his pants, glancing back at Parker like he was fresh meat. The stunning man entered the employee lounge, vanishing from Parker's field of vision.

Dixie Thorpe, the fashion editor, walked closer to Parker, as if trying to appease the new guy after he witnessed the first office drama. She said, "I assume you write most of your columns about stuff like that. You know, *Sex in the City* meets *Queer as Folk*."

"I do. Have you read them?"

"No. I haven't had the pleasure yet. But I will when you need help with proofing them." She looked back at the employee lounge, but Dack hadn't emerged yet. "Sigourney does all the hiring and firing. Her and Chester Elgin the deputy editor. I'm just a peon who makes sure things look good on paper."

Parker thought Dack looked good, and that's why he was so much trouble to become involved with.

"Oh well. Don't worry about Mason and Dack. They're fine."

Parker wasn't worried, but nodded to show he could have been. He went back to his work and noticed Dack, holding bottle of water, returning to his desk, which was right beside Parker's. Dack scooted in his chair and tapped computer keys.

Soon after, the door right behind them opened. Parker tried to keep typing. Since they worked a month's issue in advance, he was writing March's column for their '*Sex and Spring Style*' issue.

Out of the corner of his eye Parker caught Mason Bloomfield walking to the employee lounge. Mason and Dack exchanged not so amiable glances.

Dack blew out a breath and said, "I'm in the doghouse. May as well get on my knees and beg."

"Good luck." Parker watched Dack follow Mason to the lounge, staring at his broad shoulders and tight slacks. *Buddy, you are trouble on a stick.*

Parker assumed he knew the type. Self-absorbed and couldn't keep his cock in his trouser if the zipper were soldered shut.

He went back to typing and always found new inspiration for his columns from the activity he encountered every day.

~

Mason used the espresso machine to make hazelnut coffee for himself. As he loaded a small packet into the machine he noticed Dack enter, closing the door behind him.

"Leave it open." Mason knew Dack's tactics. He'd been dealing with them for nearly six months.

"Baby, don't be like that." Dack drew close, close enough so Mason could feel his body heat on his back. "I'll make it up to you."

Mason didn't know how any man could make up for standing him up—and cheating—but somehow he allowed Dack to do just that, repeatedly.

The espresso machine stopped and steam rose from the cup. Mason removed it and knew it would be scalding hot. He set it on the counter and added flavored creamer.

When he spun around there was Dack-the-rat, looking hotter than hell, giving him his 'forgive me, baby' eyes.

"Where were you last night?" Mason used a wooden stir stick to mix his coffee.

"Just out with friends. You know. I only intended on spending an hour, but I had a few drinks..." Dack leaned in to kiss Mason's neck, sending chills through Mason's body.

How many times did Mason hear that same excuse? "And you couldn't call? Couldn't return a text message to tell me you weren't coming?"

"Time got away from me." Dack pushed his cock into Mason's hip. "Yoseph was buying shots. Ya know. I was too drunk to—"

"Not here. Not at work." Mason nudged him away, sick of the same sad story every time Dack didn't show up.

Dack stepped back and held Mason's belt loops, rocking him side to side while their crotches met. "Let me make it up to you."

Why did Mason always forgive this man?

Dack glanced back at the closed door. "Tomorrow is Valentine's Day. I'll book us a room for two at your favorite hotel."

"What's my favorite hotel?" Picking up the cup, Mason blew on the hot coffee. He didn't have a favorite hotel but that didn't stop Dack from pretending he did.

Dack appeared to think hard about it. "Whatever hotel you want. Name it. Dinner for two? Candlelight? Huh? What do ya say?"

What could Mason say? He wanted Dack. "Okay."

Dack pecked Mason's cheek and scooted off, as if he were through with his 'forgive me, baby' ritual and could get back to being his rotten self.

~

Parker tried not to appear obvious that he was being nosy. Dack exited the lounge first, smug and full of himself. Since only five minutes had passed since the two men were in the lounge together Parker assumed Dack hadn't given Mason a make-up BJ. But whatever magic Dack had cast on Mason, the spell seemed to have worked.

Before Mason emerged from the employee lounge, Dack snatched one of the long stemmed red roses from Henry's desk and rushed to sit at his own.

Mason exited the break room a moment later, holding a cup of coffee, looking smart in his business suit. In Parker's estimation, Mason Bloomfield had to be in his late thirties, maybe early forties, was nearing six feet tall, maybe a skosh under, and was trim and well put together from his brown full head of hair to his bright hazel, yes, they were hazel eyes, to his expensive Italian leather shoes.

Though Dack was the type of stud gay men drooled over, the candy on your arm type of lover, Parker went for men like Mason. Handsome, mature, bright, trim and not stinking of ego and heartbreak.

When Dack presented the rose to Mason as Mason walked past, Parker stifled a sneer and roll of his eyes at the pathetic gesture.

Mason fell for it, appeared to melt, and sniffed the rose. He gave Dack a wicked smile and once again vanished into his office.

Dack grinned at Parker, as if Parker was in on the conspiracy to woo a man who had been...what? Cheated on? Parker didn't know but he had managed to win back the affections of a good man, even though he was most likely a cad.

Parker gave Dack a tight smile and went back to his column.

'...*Wolves in sheep's clothing. How to spot Mr Wrong!*'

~

Mason carried the rose into his office, sniffing the fragrance. He was a sucker for romance and having a man like Dack woo him was pure flattery. Yeah, they'd had some ups and downs, but Mason had a forgiving heart. He gently rested the flower across the desk, sipped and set his coffee aside, and resumed his working on getting advertising for his magazine. He was lucky to have some clients who were regular contributors and was always sniffing out the new blood.

*Judas' Rainbow* was a gay and lesbian monthly magazine which alternated between men's and women's issues but normally addressed them both, which was unusual for one magazine to do. Most magazines catered to one sex or the other.

Mason thought Senior Editor Sigourney Edina was a pioneer and though she was tough, outspoken and 'loud' when she was annoyed, he admired her. She began this magazine on her own, on line, and it grew until they had a few million glossy issues in circulation across the world, in many different languages. It was then a share of her company had been purchased by a huge media conglomerate, keeping her and her staff intact, but no doubt, paying Sigourney a tidy sum.

Mason had worked with her for three years and had seen many employees come and go, men and women not up to Sigourney's high standards of productivity, or personality clashes. Either way, if you lost respect from Sigourney, you were out of a job.

He began typing on his keyboard, going through his list of steady clients who shelled out for their big two-page ads first, then he'd hit up the smaller companies until he determined what space was left to fill. It was then he wheeled and dealed with the smaller, lower income clients who were grateful to get an ad in their gorgeous hot-selling magazine for under a grand.

His instant messenger pop-up box opened, one from the internal email group. It was from Dack. It read, '*got us a suite at your favorite—the Wilner Hotel!*'

Mason narrowed his eyes. That was not only *not* his favorite hotel, he had never heard of it. He looked it up on line and was immediately disappointed not only with the two star rating but the reviews. "You gotta be kidding. My condo is nicer than this place."

Instead of reacting in annoyance, like he wanted to, Mason ignored the instant message, picked up the rose, and snapped it in half, tossing it into the garbage pail by his desk. He felt a sting and looked at his finger, which was bleeding from a thorn. He sucked it in his mouth and muttered through his finger, "Injured by a prick. How appropriate." He shook his head in annoyance.

~

'...*men who perpetrate a cycle of torture,*' Parker typed, trying not to stare at Dack as Dack texted on his phone, rocked in his chair and did everything but appear to actually work.

'...*by begging forgiveness from their partner, even though they have done something quite unforgivable. Are we all insecure, or just love the underlying BDSM themes? Could we want to be treated like a doormat? Is that the new fetish?*'

Parker stared into space thinking about what to write, and then noticed Dack put his phone down, and begin working on his computer again.

There were fifteen employees actually present in the LA office; except the big wig who owned other companies including the one who bought a share of this up and coming magazine, and freelance contributors and photographers, as well. But in reality, that brought the total of employees in this downtown LA office

12

to only a whopping twenty. The rest of their staff was freelance and worked outside the building.

Though the job did pay well, and if Parker was honest with himself, he liked the ideals of the magazine and everything about its content. But…inter-office love affairs? Gossip? He had a feeling this place was rife.

He kept writing, '*…have we learned to love the cycle? Wash-rinse-repeat? Or is there hope that good men who finish last, at least have a decent orgasm?*

'*…as a man in his thirties, has my generation and the ones that came before me, left single to fend for themselves, allowed the decomposition of their own self-respect? Do we lower our standards in ways that become sinister? Or are we still suckers for the pretty faces, and bods?*

'*…if a man is not looking to hookup on a nightly basis and craves a real partner, how low can we go? Are we willing to sacrifice so much just for a warm body? Or do we draw the line and decide, better alone than a doormat?*

'*…The Cycle of Torture…it may sound like some S&M contraption to titillate, but for those of us in our mid-thirties and older, are we really getting off on something (may God give me anything!), rather than nothing?*'

Parker re-read the whole article and hoped it didn't reek of cynicism nor become obvious that he had detected a vicious love cycle in his midst.

The article fit his allowed word count. He took another look at Dack, who appeared to be working, finally, since it was nearing five and the end of the day on this Thursday in February, a day before Valentine's Day.

Sigourney emerged from her office, which was located at the far end of the open space, opposite from where Parker was situated. He was glad, because if he was honest with himself, the woman scared him a little.

13

She was short and slightly rotund, hair cropped like a boy's and dressed in a pantsuit and flat heels. Parker knew her reputation in the industry, and although he admired her, strong women terrified him.

"Are we making deadline, people?" she yelled.

Parker sat up and immediately sent his column to his editor and Sigourney simultaneously, never knowing if he'd get a sneer or a pat on the back for his content. But they had seen his previous work and hired him, so he had to keep his confidence high.

"What's this?" Sigourney picked up the now limp, long stemmed roses from Henry's desk. "You're a day early." She sniffed the buds. "Right? Today is the thirteenth, not fourteenth."

Dixie, who had her desk directly outside Sigourney's office, nodded. "Yup. Today's the thirteenth."

Sigourney took a moment to stare at the roses. "There are eleven here. Ya got ripped off." She put them back on Henry's desk. "Meeting tomorrow morning in the conference room, eight sharp. You're late, you buy everyone drinks at the *Dive on Inn* bar tomorrow night."

Parker chuckled and heard a door open behind him.

Mason had stepped out, obviously hearing her talking to the staff.

"Mr Bloomfield!" she yelled across the room. "Give me good news."

"Got a new client and their car company ad. Now, after years of holding out, they claim to be gay friendly."

"Oh? How did they do that, pray tell?"

Parker rocked in his leather, swivel chair, trying to take in all the information among employees—who liked whom, who was afraid of whom, and everything in between.

"They are using Mark Richfield as their model. Sent me a copy of the full two page spread."

"Oh?" Sigourney's eyebrows raised in interest. "We already have the ads with him nearly naked in *Dangereux* Cologne. How are they going to top that?"

"They got him lounging across one of their newest sports car's front seat 'sporting'"—he used his fingers as quotation marks—"a huge erection."

Parker tried to cover his laugh but everyone in the room chuckled without fear or ridicule.

"Can't do an x-rated ad." Sigourney didn't react the way the men in the room did.

"Nope. Not exposed, but goddamn...huge under his tight black slacks."

"I wanna see that." Dack pointed to Mason and then to his computer. "Send it, will ya?"

Under his breath, Parker muttered, "Figured you'd be the first to ask for it," but no one heard him.

"Still gotta pass the big guy's approval." Sigourney began to head back to her office.

"It's tastefully done," Mason said.

She flapped her hand dismissively, said, "Send it to me now," and closed the door to her office behind her.

Parker breathed a sigh of relief at her exit and spotted Henry trying to gather the stems Sigourney had scattered across his desk. He quickly looked back at Mason, who couldn't help but notice. Mason approached Henry, who didn't look up, remaining sheepish and fussing with the thorny stems.

"Roses?" Mason spun around to look at Dack before addressing the balding older man. "Where did you get them, Henry? Were they a gift?"

"Uh. No. I uh, I just picked them up on the way to work." Henry held the bundle in two fists, but they were unwieldy and kept falling out of his hands from the sharp thorns.

Dixie, a sly smile on her lips, because she knew what had happened behind Mason's back earlier, said, "Don't count them, Mason. There are only eleven."

Parker immediately took note of the look Mason gave to Dack. Mason said nothing about the information, but spun on his heels and returned to his office, closing the door.

"Oh, boy," Parker said, rubbing his hands on his thighs nervously. "I'm amazed he didn't slam it."

Dack didn't react to anything—not his lover's displeasure, nor the fact that everyone around him knew what had transpired. Like a true narcissist, Dack sat oblivious, tapping keys on his keyboard with his focus on the screen. "Hot damn! I found that ad! Holy crap, that guy has a big dick!"

Parker shook his head in amazement and had no idea why decent guys fell for jerks. But Mason wouldn't be the first, or the last.

*Well, if anything, this drama is going to make working here like gossip central.*

A picture popped up on Parker's screen. The top model in the new ad. Parker may have been curious, but certainly wasn't chomping at the bit to see it. The photo attachment was from Dack, sent to all parties in the office. Dack was grinning wickedly, staring at Parker as if waiting for his reaction.

Parker nodded. "Yup, big dick," then deleted it, not wanting to ogle the pretty model at work.

"I'd fuck it." Dack laughed, and rocked in his chair as he stared at the image on his own computer screen. "Making that my screen saver. Damn."

*I have no doubt you'd fuck anything.*

Parker started brainstorming new ideas for the weekly meeting in the morning, wondering what his readers wanted to know about love, life, and health.

He glanced at Dack, who was busy typing, most likely sending the image to his friends and obviously not working.

On his list of possible columns, Parker added, '*Jerks at work. Ya got 'em, how do ya avoid them?*'

## CHAPTER 2

Mason drove through the heavy Thursday night traffic to his condo off Wilshire Boulevard. Using his visor remote, he opened the gate which drew back to the underground parking area of his home. Slowly moving down the steep grade so his Audi didn't scrape bottom, he pulled into his numbered space and shut the engine off. Before he exited the car he checked his phone. Nothing. No missed messages, no texts.

Grabbing his suit jacket, Mason left his car to walk to the elevator, pushing the call button as he inspected the slice on his finger from the rose thorn. It was small but still stung. He entered the elevator and depressed number six on the panel, deep in thought—work related and relationship related as well. He was wondering which required more energy at the moment.

The door opened only at his floor, which surprised him since the building held hundreds of tenants and it was after five. He walked down the carpeted hall, hearing some muted noise of music and voices from behind closed doors. The huddled masses with their own lives and problems, he was surrounded by humanity. But he was a city boy, and not interested in living anywhere else. Which is why he paid a ridiculous amount of money for a two bedroom-two bathroom space of air. Over four hundred grand and most of that mortgaged.

Location. Of course. He was close to the downtown core and his one thousand and thirty square feet of living space was adequate for two. Which was what he had hoped for when he went out of his comfort zone on price and had bought it. Two incomes.

That never happened.

He wasn't ready for foreclosure, but he wasn't splurging on clothing or electronic gadgets at the moment either.

After opening his front door and removing his shoes, he could see through the large open space from the entrance right to the kitchen with a window with a view of the skyline of Los Angeles. Mason entered his bedroom, hung up his jacket and removed his tie, placing both in a large walk-in closet. He undressed out of his business attire and considered a workout in the complex's gym. Was he too tired? That was the question. He did, at the minimum, three nights a week on week days, and worked out both days on the weekends.

Down to his briefs, Mason stood at his bathroom sink to splash his face and make a decision between cooking dinner or changing into his workout gear.

He met his own eyes, water running down his skin. He didn't like what he saw in them. Unhappiness.

Using a towel to dry his face and hands, Mason thought about Dack's crappy attempt at an apology after standing him up last night. The arrangement had been for Dack to meet a couple of his friends, friends Dack claimed Mason would not like—for what reason, Mason didn't know—and then Dack was supposed to come here for an evening together.

Although Mason had cleaned the condo, made cosmos and groomed to perfection, he sat…paced…grew angry. He then texted and called Dack repeatedly until midnight, before he gave up, undressed and went to bed, steaming mad.

Was it the first time Dack had stood him up?

*I wish.*

Mason didn't know why he tolerated it. He wasn't insecure, knew he could probably get another guy if he chose, but didn't want to make the effort. Finding a decent guy in LA was not easy. Most were like Dack. So he figured, what was he going to gain? He and Dack had decent sex and Dack was a nice guy. Wasn't he? Deep down? Dack was just young. He was only twenty-six. The guy wasn't ready to settle down, and had told Mason that.

Yeah, once in a while Dack would forget they had a date, or not call, but they saw each other at work all week. Maybe Mason was being too needy. But taking one of the roses Henry had bought? Presenting it to him like it was some romantic gesture? That was pretty damn low, even for Dack.

Mason met his own hazel eyes in the mirror and decided a good long workout was exactly what he needed. Shutting the bathroom light, Mason headed to a dresser drawer to find his gym shorts and a T-shirt.

~

It took Parker nearly forty minutes to drive less than ten miles. The temptation to take a bicycle to work was great, but arriving sweaty with no place to shower, and dodging the same mad congestion on two wheels he did on four, wasn't a sane option. At least not for him. So he, like all people who lived and worked in the Los Angeles metropolitan area, dealt with it.

He was born and raised in Manhattan, and one would think he would be immune to the chaos. But he'd taken mass transit in the Big Apple. No such luck here.

He parked in his covered parking spot in the upscale apartment building with rent terrifyingly close to his monthly net pay, but he dealt with it. He loved the apartment with its efficient floor plan—kitchen/dining area, open to the living room with a fireplace he would never use, and access to a balcony overlooking the courtyard from his fourth, and top, floor. He did his best to maintain a minimal décor look, since a mere seven hundred square feet of living area was all he had.

But.

All of WeHo was his playground, and coming from New York, New York, a place so good you have to say it twice, he had to admit, ogling glistening go-go boys at night was pretty dang nice. But...he was not into casual sex. Never had been. Well, not often.

He had just gotten out of a bad relationship with Lee, who he was with for five years. Why he had broken it off with Lee? Infidelity. What a novel concept.

He wished he could detach his feelings for a night and just fuck for the sake of fucking, but it wasn't his style. He was one of the dumb schmucks who got attached and held expectations. So he didn't date, never surfed the net, cruising, and never went into a bar with the intent on getting laid.

Ogling pecs? Sure.

But in West Hollywood, that usually meant twinks or twenty year olds. He didn't want a boy. He wanted a man.

Older? Same age? Somewhere in the realm of mid-thirty to fifty. And living in the town of youth and vanity wasn't helping his quest.

He used the apartment's back stairs, always opting for a physical way of burning calories, and removed his key from his pocket. His phone showed missed messages, and as he stood in front of his apartment door he scrolled through the list.

"Oh, come on..." Parker made a noise of annoyance in his throat. He had automatically forwarded his work email to his phone so he kept up to date on anything important. That didn't mean the staff's responses to Dack sending the lewd advertisements from the top model to his email box.

Parker opened the door and took off his jacket, hanging it up and removing his shoes. He set the phone on the kitchen counter and headed to the bedroom to change into comfortable clothing.

By the time he returned to the kitchen to decide what to do for dinner, more emails were piling up. It appeared Dack had fans in the office who enjoyed his 'naughty' banter. Personally, Parker thought that kind of thing should be avoided in the workplace, but wasn't the type to complain or make any sort of disparaging remark. He was new. He didn't need a room full of enemies.

And being on the staff of a LGBT magazine, there would never be slams to his sexuality. It was one of the things he enjoyed about being hired in a gay friendly workplace. Not that he would ever work somewhere that was not. New York, like LA, was cosmopolitan and accepting in its views on same sex couples. After all, New York had approved gay marriage and California was still in the dark ages. No way Parker could have imagined that happening.

All his life he had been under the impression California was the land of pot-smoking hippies, not gun toting Republicans. Live and learn.

He hunted for something to eat, his attention inside the refrigerator, as his phone hummed and vibrated during the exchange of thoughts and quips about the size of Mark Richfield's dick.

Finding leftover pizza, Parker gave it an inspection, then unwrapped the plastic wrap and set it on a plate, putting it into the microwave. While he waited, he kept reading the forwarded emails.

*'...that ain't real. 2 big!'*
*'why did he get a hard-on in a car?'*
*'has he sunk to a new low?'*
*'I prefer his cologne ads with his son.'*

Though it was tempting to add his two cents, Parker kept out. The last thing he wanted was to be misinterpreted on an email and alienate a staff member. Once he got to know them all on a deeper level, he'd cave and give his opinion, which was—Mark Richfield was too good looking for anyone's good. And showing him with a hard-on for a car ad was just begging for life-sized posters, ravenous fans, and of course blatant sex-sells sales.

*Smart fuckers.*

Parker figured the conventional car company would have an enormous boost in revenue from the gay men with the high disposable incomes, and, of course, straight women.

He picked up the phone to look once more at the email attachment, staring at the ad again. "That company will get sales almost as big as your cock, Richfield." Parker shook his head. "That's gotta be fake. No one's got a dick that big."

~

Mason returned from his workout, dabbing his sweat with his shirt and headed to his kitchen for a bottle of water. He guzzled it down as he cooled off and spotted his mobile phone on the counter where he'd left it. He peeked at it and noticed missed messages. Immediately he assumed Dack would be making excuses as to why he couldn't see him tomorrow for Valentine's Day.

What he found instead was a running commentary on the ad Dack had attached to his email. Everyone in the office seemed to have something to say about it.

Just before he tossed the phone down to go to the shower, he looked again at who had responded. Sigourney did not, nor did any of the senior staff. Most of the messages were from Dack, Henry, the interns, Milly and Saul, as well as Dixie and a sub-editor, Del.

Parker had not responded.

"Smart man." Mason set the phone down and stripped his sweaty clothing as he went. Not involving himself in office banter when you've only worked in a place for one week was not only a sign of intelligence, it was a sign of maturity.

Something Dack lacked.

Naked, Mason held his hand under the spray waiting for it to heat up. He stepped in and wet down, still hot from his hour workout but cooling down quickly.

He thought about Parker and wondered if he was in a relationship or not. It wasn't any of Mason's business and he would never ask. He assumed the man was gay judging by his sex columns.

He envisioned Parker, his dark hair and light eyes—blue or green, Mason didn't know. But he did think Parker was decent looking, certainly not ugly.

Mason scrubbed up in the shower, his mind running in too many directions, one of those being, why Valentine's Day had turned into such a downer.

It was the opposite of a love holiday. The unreasonable expectations and commercial crush to get your 'lover' something romantic—i.e. candy, flowers, dinner out…

As far as Mason was concerned it was leftover Christmas merchandizing, continuing to push consumers to buy, spend, and pretend to have either a happy family or a loving relationship. Most of the people Mason knew had neither, and the whole illusion that life was one big Norman Rockwell painting drove people to therapy.

He did not speak to his family.

From a small town in North Carolina, with a church on every corner, and no one walking away from a conversation without saying, "God Bless You"—and not because you sneezed— Mason had been rejected by those who had brought him up.

He was treated like a leper with an incurable disease and couldn't even carry a conversation on with them. They misquoted Bible doctrine as fact, and closed down when Mason tried to continue reasonable conversations, which became screaming matches in seconds.

He left.

Soon after he came out, right after he graduated college with a degree in journalism, Mason fled. Fled to the opposite end of the country, and would have moved even farther if he could.

But his journey west came to a halt once he hit Los Angeles and breathed a sigh of relief to find a sense of self.

Though his career began with writing freelance stories about the close minded sections of a country based on freedom and civil rights, Mason soon gave up on what he deemed useless, self-indulgent ranting. Not only that, he was starving since it didn't pay well, and was living in a closet labeled an efficiency apartment. He survived on cup-o-noodles and cereal. The bad ole days.

It was then that he tried his hand at being a modeling agent, under his own name, as owner and operator. Heck, the town was loaded with gorgeous men and he had found a way to meet them. But that didn't work either.

After months of applying for work, Mason was hired on at *Judas' Rainbow* to sell advertising, and that suited him fine, boosting his salary to an amazing rate.

The political battles exhausted him and years of screaming at his family had not changed a thing. It only gave him a migraine.

He shut off the water and stared down his body to his cock, the water running on his tanned skin, chest and pubic hair. The workout, though he had enjoyed it, began to make him weary. After grabbing a towel and drying off, Mason dressed in a pair of sweats and a T-shirt he had customized by cropping off the short sleeves and making it a mid-riff. It had a silkscreen of the cartoon superman on it—flying, cape whipping behind him—and was soft and cozy. Besides, it made him feel young.

He headed to the kitchen and opened the freezer, removing a ready meal simply because he was too tired to cook. He peeled back the lid and popped it into the microwave. As he waited, drinking water, he stared at his phone. Dack seemed to have all the time in the world to text and email the staff, but not one email came to him directly.

~

Parker shut off his phone, growing sick of it buzzing and then finding only the stupid exchange going on about the ad—still!

*Get a life, people*!

He sat on his sectional sofa, his feet propped up on the hassock and pointed the remote at the television. After checking the time on this Thursday night before Big Cupid's Romance Day, Parker scanned the channels on the idiot box and finally found one show he did like. *Forever Young*. Not only did he enjoy it for its gay content, he liked the fact the lead characters were in their thirties, and not twinks. He was sick to death of the teenybopper shows and couldn't tolerate reality programs.

He sunk into the cushions to watch, and when he noticed two new characters—both *young*—he threw up his hands. "Come on. Not here too!" Parker grumbled but watched the show anyway, instantly disliking the new additions to the gay cable drama, and wishing Carl Bronson and Keith O'Leary's plot included killing the two new brats off.

## CHAPTER 3

Parker got to work slightly early so he could sit at his desk and continue to brainstorm for the morning meeting. Wearing a freshly dry-cleaned gray suit, crisp white shirt, maroon tie, and his freshly-shined shoes, Parker felt sharp and ready. Last night while he lay in bed, he made a list of concepts for columns in his head, as well as themes for new magazine issues, if he was asked for input.

After parking in a company reserved spot, he stood in the elevator. An arm with a dark business suit sleeve and white cuff, come through at the last minute, trying to hold back the doors. Parker reacted and opened the doors by pushing the button. They drew back and Mason, appearing disheveled, joined him.

"Hi, Mason."

"Hi, Parker." Mason ran his hand through his hair and stepped back in case anyone else boarded as they rode up to the tenth floor.

The silence was uncomfortable to Parker. "So…a meeting for new ideas."

"Yeah. Sigourney has them once a week. On Fridays."

"Right." Parker nodded and gave Mason a once-over discreetly. They guy was hot. Totally Parker's type. Parker noticed Mason check his mobile phone device. In order to make conversation he said, "A lot of banter over that ad last night."

Mason blew out a breath which sounded like annoyance. "I know. Christ, sometimes they act like they're in high school."

"I used to be that way when I was in my early twenties."

Mason turned to meet Parker's eyes. "How old are you?"

"Thirty-five."

The door opened to their floor and they walked out together.

"You?" Parker wasn't going to let that opportunity pass.

"Forty. Just turned..." Mason said it as if it were a bad thing and opened the door to their office, greeting the receptionist with a nod as he walked by.

The conversation was over, but not in a rude way. Parker knew how busy Mason was and with the meeting looming, he understood.

Parker stood near his desk, looking around the room as employees arrived, milled around to chat, checked their computers, or dazed off, rocking in their desk chair before the meeting began.

Parker glanced down at his desk. A small envelope was on it, pink in color. He opened it and read *Be Mine*. It was a child's Valentine card, one which would come in a package of a dozen, and unsigned. He looked around to see if anyone noticed he'd picked it up, but no one had.

Sigourney appeared in her smart slacks and blazer, an empty mug in one hand and her paperwork in the other. "Troops, amass!"

Parker dropped the card on his desk, grabbed a legal pad and pen and walked across the office to the conference room.

Inside the well lit space was a rectangular table that had approximately a dozen chairs placed around it, with water bottles, coffee mugs, two coffee urns, and a plate of muffins and doughnuts on either end.

The room was cleanly designed with a small décor-only type table at one side, holding a vase with fake palm stems, and the other end had a wet bar with a mirrored back and sink.

It was cool in the room, as if the heat hadn't kicked on from overnight. Parker was comfortable in his suit jacket and waited to see where he was supposed to sit, in case people had customary positions.

Sigourney claimed the head, at the window side of the room, with Mason on her left, and Chester on her right.

The two interns, Milly and Saul, sat side by side at the foot, crammed slightly but not seeming to mind.

Mason tilted his head to Parker, indicating to take the seat immediately to his left, so Parker did. Beside Parker sat Henry, then Del. Opposite Mason was Chester, and then an empty seat across from Parker. Going down the line beside the empty chair was Morris, and then finally Dixie, who completed the circle next to Milly.

Sigourney pointed to the vacant chair and asked Mason, "Where's Dack?"

All eyes turned to Mason, obviously Dack's 'keeper'.

"He should be in." But Parker had a feeling Mason honestly did not know.

"He was up late, I know that." Dixie poured a cup of coffee from the carafe into her cup. "He was texting me—drunk out of his head—more pictures of that model that he found on the internet."

Parker looked directly at Mason, who flinched—visibly *flinched* but tried so hard to pretend it didn't sting.

"Then he's hung over"—Sigourney flipped through her notepad—"and he's buying the drinks tonight."

Mason shifted and touched the knot in his tie.

Parker watched him. *If that was my boyfriend, I'd dump him, dude.*

29

Sigourney poured coffee as she read from her pad, multitasking and impressing Parker that she didn't spill a drop. "April issue...we don't do Easter eggs or chocolate bunnies, so talk to me, people."

"Darn," Morris laughed as he said, "That leaves out my deviled egg recipes."

Parker noticed Mason continually check his watch.

Henry held up a little pink envelope. "Who left this on my desk?"

"Me." Milly appeared shy.

Henry looked downright disappointed. "Oh. I thought I had a secret Valentine's Day admirer."

Parker had thought the same thing, and that threw his hopes of Mason stalking him right out the window. He checked the items he'd scribbled on his pad. "I was thinking of doing a column on hope...you know, like in spring and renewal."

"Listening." Sigourney sipped her cup of coffee.

"A column on letting go some of our old baggage, and setting our sights on something we may have thought was unattainable."

"We could do a new spring style line to accompany it," Dixie said, taking a doughnut on a napkin. "Like bright colors. Way bright! Yellow, hot pink, lime green!"

Henry said, "We could link it to the new spring movie and book releases, do a rainbow that leads to the book covers. You know, find *ROY G. BIV* in the ebook world out there."

Parker and Mason exchanged confused looks. "Roy G. Biv?" Parker asked, hoping he wasn't the only idiot who had no idea what that was.

Henry explained, "The rainbow colors—red, orange, yellow, green, blue, indigo, and violet."

"Duh!" Dixie cracked up.

"Did you know that?" Parker asked Mason.

30

"Not a clue." Mason checked his watch and his mobile device, appearing completely distracted.

Sigourney told Mason, "See if you can nudge your advertisers on board. Either get them to send us ads with rainbows in them, or use Roy…Biv…whatever, as color codes in the backgrounds. Let's make the whole issue feel festive without bunnies and dyed eggs."

"Or matzo balls," said Del, who had remained quiet until then. "Passover?"

Parker reread his list of ideas, thrilled his had gone over well.

"No religion!" Sigourney waved her hand and didn't seem affected either way. "Okay, newbie. What else ya got?"

"What else?" Dixie said, "He's just single handedly done our whole April issue."

A commotion at the door made everyone look up.

Dack—appearing unshaven, holding an extra large cup from the local coffee shop, his tie undone and hanging low on his neck, his shirt collar unbuttoned, and his demeanor…slightly annoyed—entered the conference room and took his seat beside Mason.

Parker struggled to determine if Dack was in the same clothing as the day before, but just didn't remember. Dack didn't offer an apology and instead, held up a tiny purple envelope in front of Mason's face and said, "This is it? I get you a rose and a night at a hotel and dinner tonight and all you get me is this?"

In agony for Mason, Parker rubbed his eyes and shifted in his seat.

"That's not from me." Mason was calm. Calmer than Parker would have been in his place.

Dack set his coffee down and removed the tiny card, showing Mason as if he needed to see it. "It says 'Be My Valentine'. It's gotta be from you. You're that corny."

Parker's face heated up out of empathy for Mason. How the poor man endured it was beyond him.

"It's from Milly," Sigourney said, reading her paperwork. "Nice of you to show up for work, Mr Torington. You pay for drinks tonight and do the first karaoke song."

Parker tried not to stare at Dack, let alone poor Mason.

"Milly," Dack puckered flirtatiously at her. "Sorry, but I'm gay."

"She gave one to all of us," Henry said, also looking uncomfortable. Only Mason seemed to be unaffected, but Parker knew, he was tolerating the worst of it...internally.

"Anyway!" Sigourney poured more coffee into her cup. "Okay, Parker-my-man...what else?"

"Uh...Do you want more for April or shall I take a stab at May?"

"Stab it." Sigourney kept scribbling notes. "For my staff columnist you're hitting homeruns outta the park."

Parker caught Dack texting, sipping his latte, and Mason appearing stiff as if he were irritated.

"Okay," Parker said, reading more of his scribbles. "I also had a thought on the months leading up to summer. May is like the springboard to getting into shorts and T-shirts and putting your winter cashmere in storage."

"Love!" Chester perked up, his wireframe glasses round and small on his pudgy pleasant face. "I do that every change of season."

Dixie added, "We can go all out on a women's style month, Sig. I mean, do strappy sandals and capris. Lesbian chic!"

"Hair and nails!" Milly said, "Textured and loads of patterns."

"Pics of great storage ideas," Henry said, "scads of bright colored plastic portable and shelving bins."

"And sex."

Everyone looked at Dack who couldn't stop texting. "Sex," he repeated. "Duh. Why do you think we have readers? Ya have to do articles on the latest summer G-strings and cum-flavored lube."

Parker coughed but covered his mouth to shut up.

"Okay, Dack..." Sigourney replied, "You're in charge of the sexing up of the issues with pics of G-strings."

"I'm on it. Getting the UK mag to release the nude centerfold they did of Richfield eons ago."

"Can't do nude. We'll stick a black rectangle over his man-stick. Class dismissed." Sigourney stood, her cup to her lips, her arms loaded with paperwork.

Dack left, his face in his phone, leaving the tiny Valentine's card on the table. One by one the employees filed out, taking cups of coffee and doughnuts with them, chatting about the new ideas in excitement.

Parker stared at Mason. The man did not look happy. Quite the contrary.

After he was left alone in the room, Parker slouched in the seat, staring at the plate of sweet treats he knew would be devoured by day's end from the staff picking and noshing on it.

Did he want to go to a bar and listen to Dack sing karaoke?

*Only if you suck!*

Parker stood up and took a cup of coffee with him to his desk.

~

Mason set his coffee and note pad on his desk and poked his head out of his office. He walked behind Dack and already spotted him surfing the UK magazine website for contact information.

Dack asked Mason without looking back at him, "What time is it in London?"

Mason checked his watch. "Five p.m. They're eight hours ahead of us."

33

"Crap." Mason could see Dack emailing the editor, Adrian Mackenzie.

"Uh, Dack?" Mason checked to see if anyone was eavesdropping. Parker was typing on his computer close by, so Mason lowered down behind Dack to speak softly into his ear. "What time did you get home last night?"

"Dunno." Dack clicked keys, writing up an email asking the editor of the gay magazine to release the nude photo of the American model.

"You're in the same suit as yesterday. And you smell like cigarettes and booze."

Dack sniffed his sleeve. "I showered so it's just the jacket."

Mason tried to think. "You showered but you didn't change? Where did you shower?"

Deliberately not answering, Dack picked up his phone and dialed, holding up one finger to Mason to make him wait.

"We still on for the Wilner tonight?" Mason felt like a needy partner.

Nodding, Dack said into the phone, "Hey, Chester, how much are we willing to shell out for a pic of Mark Richfield in bondage gear?"

Mason gave up and turned on his heels to head back to his office. He caught sympathy in Parker's light eyes, then Parker quickly turned away to continue writing on his computer.

Embarrassment didn't describe how Mason felt. He closed himself into his office, removed his jacket to hang on a hook behind the door, and got busy trying to find clients who had ads that corresponded to *Roy G. Biv*. He was about to lose his mind.

~

Parker overheard Dack going over how much the magazine was willing to shell out for a risqué picture of the man whose ads were lighting LA on fire.

34

He glanced at Mason's closed office door and then went back to his keyboard. His last column was approved with only minor punctuation edits, and Parker prided himself in putting out a quality product that didn't need deep edits, and little more than a proofreader.

Both his editor and Sigourney sent him the 'okay', so he powered on to the next issue where he hoped to gain a few fans, and even be highlighted in the letters to the editor section.

*"To err is human, to forgive divine.' Alexander Pope said this in the seventeenth century, but in the twenty-first, has divinity taken a backseat to the iPhone? If we all make mistakes, do we expect forgiveness? Or is truly getting an 'I'm sorry' a text that never is sent?'*

Parker thought about it and then kept writing. *'Testing -Im srry. Just doesn't have the same impact as the spoken word. Can we cut and paste our way into someone's good graces or has all human decency left with the age of the computer? We have so many ways to bully and torment people, is it unfortunate we can't use this same technology to apologize?*

*'And if we do forgive, and find out our forgiveness was not divine, but merely fodder for an ego, are we fools instead of angels?*

*'Where does humanity end and humiliation begin?'*

Parker glanced over at Dack, who now had his shoe heels on his desk, reclining in his leather chair, his phone to his ear, laughing and having a grand ole time.

Parker picked up the tiny Valentine's Day envelope and removed the little card again. It did make him smile even though it was from Milly. He propped it up against his pencil holder, and kept writing. It was going to be the only Valentine's Day card he was going to get.

~

Mason knew he had nothing to be angry about. Last night he and Dack did not have plans, and Dack had done nothing wrong. Or had he?

*Do we have a relationship that's exclusive?*

Mason was honoring that…as yet…unspoken agreement, but Dack had never stated he was 'only'. Was that honest or nasty?

Mason paced inside his office after he had completed a few phone calls and emails, all ending in getting money transferred into his magazine's coffers, and splashy rainbow inclusive or matching prism colored ads. Yeah, he had a few that were sure things. So it wasn't that hard to get them to shell out.

*You smell like booze and cigarettes.*

*Showered but didn't change your clothing? If you were in workout gear I'd believe it was the gym! Where the hell did you shower if you didn't get to change clothing?*

*You fucked someone! You stayed overnight! Am I out of my mind?*

Mason counted to ten to calm his rage.

Dack was a decade and a half younger than he was and hotter than a fucking gay go-go-boy muscle god.

Mason cracked open his door to peek. Dack, feet on his desk, phone to his ear, the picture of the naked model in a mask and bondage gear was on his computer screen, and Dack was laughing. Laughing!

Closing the door, Mason wished he had a shot of booze to calm his nerves. He walked to the window and stared out at the smoggy skyline and hills beyond downtown.

*Okay. You and Dack have dinner and hotel plans tonight. Take a deep breath!*

Mason did. In and out. He calmed down. What did he get for Dack for their special Valentine's evening? A fucking Bosca Italian made leather wallet!

"Calm down." He sat at his desk and straightened his tie. His choice. It was Mason's choice to buy Dack a gift. His choice to date him. His.

His alone.

Being fourteen years older than Dack had drawbacks. Huge ones. Mason could not compete with Dack's contemporaries. He was not a dipshit who talked about bad television and celebrity gossip. He preferred intellectual conversation but when he mentioned politics or foreign affairs, Dack got a bored faraway look in his eyes. So that was usually when Mason grabbed Dack for a kiss. Then Dack's attention was in high gear. The sex. They had that. It wasn't top notch, but sex from a man who looked as good as Dack? It was a huge ego boost.

*Am I that shallow? Is this relationship based on the fact that I can fuck an amazingly handsome young muscleman?*

"Yeah. So what? Fuck it." Mason picked up the phone and called another client for a big two page spread in the coming magazine.

## CHAPTER 4

At five p.m., Parker shut down his computer and straightened his desk.

Dixie and Milly were giggling excitedly as they put their jackets on and shouldered their designer purses. Henry had his cell phone to his ear, standing near them, and Chester was at Sigourney's open door, looking like he was waiting for her.

A smell of dank booze and cigarettes coming from behind him made Parker step back and look over his shoulder.

Dack asked him, "You are coming to Dive on Inn, right? Do you do karaoke?"

Before Parker answered, Mason stepped out of his office, putting his suit jacket on, but loosening his tie.

"Yes, I'm coming. No, I don't do karaoke." As Parker ogled Mason, he salivated. Mason Bloomfield was his ideal man.

"Uh uh. The newbie has to sing." Dack patted Parker's back and he and Mason walked out of the office together. Parker watched in misery but didn't show it.

Del, Saul, and Morris headed to the exit together, laughing as if, not only were the morning meetings tradition, but the Friday night drinks and bad singing may be as well.

"Mr Douglas?" Sigourney called over the expanse of room, "Are you joining us?"

"Yes." Parker pushed the chair under his desk and was last leaving with the group who were laughing like a pack of college kids about to hit a kegger.

As they headed into the elevator, squashing in, cracking up and making lewd jokes on the way down, Parker thought this kind of comradery at work was a myth. Kind of the *Ally McBeal* afterhours silliness where everyone likes one another and has that evening drink to unwind and bond. He'd never been part of an office group that did this. He liked it. Sort of.

Seeing Dack nuzzling Mason in the back corner was slightly upsetting. Jealous? Hell yeah, he was. But he wasn't jealous of Mason being able to play and flirt with a twenty-something stud. He was jealous of Dack having a handsome, mature, intelligent man like Mason to talk to.

He wasn't a big fan of the green-eyed monster, so Parker adjusted his attitude and figured his day, and man, would come.

A quick breezy stroll down 7$^{th}$ Avenue and their group stopped at a door, so-unobtrusive-you'd-walk-right-past-it-if-you-didn't-look, kind of bar. They bypassed the restaurant and hotel reception desk on the first floor and as a herd, a literal herd of noisy cattle, headed down underground to a poorly lit dive-ish bar, obscenely loud with its laughter and yakking, with someone singing Madonna's *Like a Virgin* over the din...and not singing it very well.

On first glance Parker knew this was not a gay club, not by a long shot, and he was fine with that since he didn't have a man to swap spit with anyway. And mingling with straight friends was high on his 'like' list.

Since it was just after five, Sigourney commandeered a large table and two smaller tables were pushed together as chairs were counted and gathered for their group.

The room smelled of a mix of air freshener and dusty mold and neon advertising signs and spotlights lit the bar and stage but the rest of the room was in near darkness. Flattering light in case you were too drunk to say no? Most likely.

Seeing Dack already claiming a chair at the conjoined tables, and Mason ordering drinks at the bar, Parker didn't know what to do, where to sit or how to order.

Having no idea which chair to take and not, once again, infringe on rights of ownership, Parker stood behind Mason at the bar and when he noticed Mason shelling out cash, he said, loud enough to be heard in the bad music, "I thought Dack had the first round for being late."

Mason gave Parker a slight roll of the eyes as Mason was handed what looked like a shot of something strong as well as a sweet mixed drink. "Maybe he'll get the next round." Mason asked Parker, "What do you want?"

"I can get it. Why should you pay for my drink?" Parker took out his wallet and leaned towards the bartender while Mason brought the glasses back to the table, returning for more.

Once Parker had a draft beer in his hand he made his way to the group, seeing a similar seating arrangement as they had in the conference room. He sat beside Mason on a free chair and looked for Dack. Dack was near the stage, laughing with the young man working the karaoke machine, appearing to have made a friend...or worse. Flirting.

Parker sipped his beer and noticed since it was very loud in the room at the moment, small factions had begun to form at the table leaving him on his own.

The ladies sat at one end, already laughing hysterically for reasons Parker did not know, and hoped that it wasn't about him, and Chester, Morris, and Henry were exchanging ideas, using exaggerated hand gestures and raised eyebrows to prove their point.

Even quiet Saul and Del were seated together, drinks now in hand, chatting as a server brought out appetizers and flatware.

Parker looked towards Mason. Mason held a shot of something brown to his lips and was staring at Dack. Dack, although he may have only had to hand a slip of paper to the young DJ, was now laughing, holding his mixed cocktail, looking as if he were about to hookup. Which had to be absurd, right? Was Dack a man magnet and found the only gay man in the room besides the few seated around their oblong table?

Parker cleared his throat and his agony for Mason grew. *But that's what happens when you chase a man fourteen years your junior.* Or at least that was the cliché Parker heard happened.

His tastes were that of slightly older men. *Mason.* His taste was Mason.

"Pick a song." Sigourney handed Parker the list.

"Oh no. You definitely do not want to hear me sing." Parker not only shook his head adamantly, he pushed the laminated list away.

"It's Valentine's Day," she said, "And I'm the boss. Pick a love song."

"Oh God." Parker gulped more beer and caught Mason watching the exchange.

Mason leaned closer to Parker and asked, "Do you have someone in your life?"

"No. I mean…friends. Yes. But a boyfriend?" Parker felt like an idiot as he shook his head no. He was boiling hot suddenly and felt as if he were rambling. He loosened his tie to hang around his neck and unbuttoned his shirt collar.

Mason's gaze went towards Dack. Dack appeared behind Mason looking puffed up and full of himself, as if he had either just been voted best looking man in the room, or had made a date with the DJ. He stood on the other side of Mason, removed his jacket and rolled up his sleeves before he sat down. He no longer had his drink, probably because he had finished it and left it behind somewhere.

41

G. A. HAUSER

The moment Dack was in the chair and turned his knees towards Mason, in a total attempt of owning him and getting his attention, Parker physically moved away and focused on his beer.

Henry nudged him. "What are you singing?"

"Huh?" Parker wasn't going to be caught dead singing in public. He handed Henry the list.

"Did you pick? You have to pick something. Sigourney won't let you sit here without singing at least one song."

"Believe me. You don't want to hear me sing." Parker avoided everyone's eye and had never felt like more of an outsider. Was everyone having a great time but him?

He peeked at Mason. Dack had his large hand on Mason's leg. Parker looked away and finished his beer.

"So do you even like any of the choices?" Henry asked, pointing to the different artists on the list.

"Huh? No. Henry, I can't sing."

"You don't have to sing. It's karaoke, not Pop Idol."

"What are you singing?" Since Henry was nice enough to talk to him, Parker tried to engage him.

"My usual."

"Which is?"

"*Love Shack*. It's kind of romantic."

"Oh God." Parker rubbed his face in agony at the thought.

"If you want, I can sing something with you. Do you like Billy Joel?"

"I love Billy Joel, that doesn't mean I want to butcher his lyrics." Parker peeked down at Mason's lap again. It was impossible not to. Dack's hand was running down Mason's inseam sensually.

Parker moaned and closed his eyes, turning in his chair so his back was to Mason and he had to stop looking. But Henry was

42

already handing the list to Del and they were head to head picking out their favorites.

"Oh, Mr Douglas?" Sigourney sang sarcastically. "Did you pick a song?"

Parker checked his watch. "I...I can't stay long. I have...uh..."

"A date?" Dixie asked eagerly. "Do you have a Valentine's sweetie who is taking you out later?"

Was he going to lie? To his boss? On his first employee get together. "Uh..."

Dixie held out her hand to him. "Come on! Sing with me!"

"Oh God no." Parker cringed. Hands came out of nowhere pushing him to his feet. When he peeked down, two of those on his ass were Mason's. He was so distracted he forgot why he was standing.

Dixie gripped his wrist and began to drag him.

"I'm not drunk enough!" Parker dug in his heels.

"Come on! Initiation time into *Judas' Rainbow* Friday nights!" Little Dixie hauled his big dumb jock body up to the stage. The small crowd had turned into a mob as the after five o'clock crowd swelled.

Parker's hands went clammy and he began to sweat. He took off his suit jacket and tie and Dixie actually rushed back to their table to hand them off.

As Parker rolled up his sleeves, he asked in terror, "What did you pick?"

"Bonnie Tyler, *Total Eclipse of the Heart*."

Slightly relieved because not only did he know that song, he liked it, Parker nodded and began dabbing at the drops of perspiration at his temple as he went into panic mode.

Words appeared on a screen in front of him and Dixie, and she held onto his waist as the music began. She belted out the words enthusiastically with a decent voice, nudging Parker to join her.

He did, softly, trying not to be heard but Dixie made sure he was heard. She shook him until he made eye contact with her and between lyrics she mouthed, '*Sing to me*'.

That helped.

Singing with more confidence, Parker kept his eye on the scrolling lyrics and in between the stanzas, Dixie's smile. Dixie's voice was wonderful and strong and he didn't sound half bad in low harmony. By the time the chorus came up, and his nerves had calmed he sang louder. It wasn't until he looked up at the table of his co-workers that he realized he was singing solo. Dixie had shut up to give him his opportunity, and there was nothing Parker could do but struggle through.

~

"Wow, he's got a great voice."

Mason was mesmerized by Parker and almost didn't acknowledge Dack's comment. He nodded.

Dack said, "Why was he so scared to get up there? He's fucking great."

Sigourney replied, something to the effect of "people have stage fright and that's why they write." Mason didn't really hear it or believe it. With Dack's hand heating up his inner thigh, Mason watched Parker hit all the notes perfectly and Dixie looking up at his five foot eleven inch height in awe and pride.

The song ended and Parker got a standing ovation including hoots and whistles as he high-fived Dixie and they walked off the stage together.

Parker leaned towards their table to say, "I'm drenched in sweat. Getting another drink. Anyone need one?"

Immediately Dack said, "Yes! Cran and vodka!"

Parker waited but no one else was ready for a refill. He nodded and left, headed to the bar.

Dixie sat back down and sipped her wine. "He's amazing! I really expected the worst. But damn!"

Mason stared at Parker from behind, his long legs and the way the dress slacks fit snugly around his bottom. Parker was fanning his shirt as he waited for his drink, trying to cool down.

"Dack?" the DJ called his name. "You're up!"

"I was supposed to go first!" Dack clapped his hands loudly once, and stood. "Wish me luck." He dipped low and pecked Mason on the lips boldly, then strutted like a celebrity to the stage. Just as he did, Mason saw Parker spy the kiss.

Mason felt embarrassed by it but had no reason to. He wiped his mouth with the back of his hand out of nerves as Parker placed Dack's drink down on the table in front of Dack's empty chair. Mason removed a twenty from his wallet and handed it to Parker, who was obviously still overheated from his little 'number' and gulping ice water.

He held up his hand. "No. I got it. It's okay."

"You don't need to pay for Dack. Bad enough I am." He put the twenty near Parker.

"I'll use it for your next round."

Tom Jones' *It's Not Unusual* was belted out loudly.

Mason cringed and glanced up. Dack was doing all the 'moves' and pointing to the crowd, gyrating his hips as if he were the Welsh singer, or Elvis, and appearing so full of ego Mason was slightly humiliated by it.

The rest of the group was used to Dack's theatrics and were whooping it up and cheering.

Mason glanced at Parker. He had finished his water to the ice and was staring at Dack as he performed. Mason would give his eyeteeth to know what Parker was thinking.

~

*What a fucking A-hole!* Parker watched Dack do an impersonation of Tom Jones that failed miserably. Dack's voice was not horrible.

*But a Tom Jones he ain't.*

If Parker did not know how self-absorbed Dack was, he wondered if he would view this little act differently. It was a crowd pleaser, no doubt. The women were yelling as if Mr Jones himself were up there gyrating for them.

To show he was a good sport, and not a jealous fiend, Parker leaned towards Mason and said, "He's good."

Mason gave him a tight smile back. "He's confident."

"Oh, hell yeah. Very confident." Parker tried to read between the lines but even if he did, what good would it do him? He couldn't compete with the looks, youth or body of the man belting out a song as if he were indeed a star.

He felt a pat on the arm. Sigourney smiled sweetly at Parker. "You did very well. You have a wonderful voice. I wonder why you're so reluctant to do this. You will from now on. On your own!" She pointed in warning.

Parker gave her a smile though he winced inside. *Just shoot me.*

Dack finished with a flourish, sliding on his knees and pumping his fist, maybe lost in some Tom Jones-esque daydream. He looked ridiculous to Parker but he got a huge reaction from the crowd and pure encouragement.

Parker began to wonder if his jealousy was indeed coloring his attitude, so he clapped enthusiastically and even whistled.

Dack took many bows, and he too appeared boiling hot. But instead of sweating like a man, Dack took off his shirt like a stripper. The women went out of their minds and Parker's jaw dropped at the sight of Dack's ripped wall of muscles, hairless and perfect.

He couldn't help it. He leaned against Mason's shoulder and said, "You lucky dog."

Mason clapped for his man, but not enthusiastically—more a slow cadence. He smiled at the compliment and he too stared at the gorgeous fucker as he approached their table, holding his shirt in his hand. Dack reached for his drink and drank it down.

"Wow." Henry laughed and said, "Dack, you look amazing."

"Yeah?" Dack flexed his chest muscles and admired himself.

Parker tore his eyes away from the sight and had to do something to put space between him and what was happening. He stood, nearly tripping, said, "Be back," to no one in particular and headed to the restroom.

After locating it, Parker placed both his hands on a sink and stared at his face in the mirror. "Fuck! You have to be kidding me? He fucks that?" Parker moaned and threw up his hands in defeat, standing at a urinal and suddenly thinking his dick was really small.

~

Mason watched Parker leave.

After downing the booze, Dack leaned a hand on the back of each chair he stood behind, Dixie's and Henry's. He laughed and looked over the selection of songs, deciding on his next one.

Sigourney nudged Mason. "What are you singing tonight? Something for your man for V-Day?"

Mason glanced at the short list of possibilities he had made but still not submitted to the DJ.

"Ya have to," Sigourney said, "If I have to, you have to!"

"What did you pick?"

"Lady Gaga, *You and I*."

Nodding, Mason looked up again at Dack. What would he sing to the guy if he really loved him? *Do I love him?*

Dack flexed each of his chest muscles for his adoring fans, making his tits dance.

*Or do I hate him?*

"Mason?" Sigourney asked.

"Huh? I got one. You'll see." He wrote it down on the little request ticket and headed up to the DJ, handing it to him. "How long do I have to wait?"

"Ya got ten in front of ya. Wanna go next?" The DJ rubbed his thumb and index finger together in a gesture of money.

"Yeah. Why not?" He handed the man a twenty.

The DJ looked at Mason's selection. "Kind of sad for Valentine's Day, dude."

"Just play it."

The DJ held up his hands defensively. "You got it."

~

Parker had cooled off finally and washed his hands and face. He tucked his shirt into his pants and stood tall. He wasn't ugly, just not Dack Torington, that's all. But how many guys looked like that? *Christ.*

Parker left the men's room, since he couldn't hang out in there all night—this was not a gay bar, so lingering was a no-no.

Just outside the ring of his co-workers he stopped short. A sweet male voice was making the goose bumps on his skin rise and the room was so quiet he was in awe.

There, on stage, was the spectacular Mason Bloomfield singing, *Yesterday*, from the Beatles. The contrast between his modest manner and his boyfriend's outlandish display was like comparing Kiss to John Denver. And the worst part of it?

Parker did not see Dack at the table. When he searched the room, Dack was leaning over the bar, laughing with the bartender as he held yet another drink to his lips.

*Wonder who paid for that one?* Parker shook his head and stood as close as he could to his chair, his gaze riveted to the amazing man singing so sweetly and sadly, Parker was nearly driven to tears.

When the song ended, Mason got a standing ovation but because of its sad message and he chose this particular day on which to sing it, no hoots or over the top screaming.

Mason bowed his head and walked off the stage back to his seat. Parker waited as he did, allowing Mason to sit first. "Damn." Parker met his eyes. Hazel eyes. Yes, he now knew they were hazel now for sure. "You are an amazing man. I hope Dack knows what he has."

Before Mason could answer that question, Dack appeared, drunk, and said to Mason, "Time to go. I wanna suck you."

"How romantic." Dixie rolled her eyes, but her words were Parker's thoughts.

"We booked reservations for a room." Dack picked up his shirt and put it back on. "Gonna"—he pumped his hips in a sexual gesture—"all night."

Parker studied Mason's expression as he stoically collected his suit jacket and made sure he had his phone in his pocket.

As Mason met Dack near the end of the table, Parker heard Dack ask, "Why did you sing such a sappy song? Jesus, Mason. You're such a downer."

Parker watched them leave, sitting down in his seat, acutely feeling the vacant one Mason had occupied.

"Oh no." Sigourney said, "My turn. Get ready to cover your ears." Their little group clapped for her in encouragement.

Henry asked Parker, "You okay?"

"Huh? Yeah. Fine." He smiled for Henry and stared at the empty drinking glasses beside him at the table.

~

Mason walked out the exit with Dack, feeling the cool evening air, a contrast from the stuffy dank bar. They headed back towards the office parking lot and Mason asked, "Where did you make dinner reservations?"

"Oh. I thought we'd just call for room service. Ya know." Dack rubbed shoulders with Mason as they walked.

"Okay. That's fine." Mason took his keys out of his pocket.

"I have to stop home first." Dack checked his phone as he walked. "I need a change of clothes and my toiletries."

"Didn't you bring them? You know, anticipating our hotel date?"

"Nope. So." Dack stopped at his cherry red Dodge Charger and kept reading his phone. "Meet you in the room in...what? An hour?"

Mason was speechless that Dack was not prepared for their evening, but he shouldn't have been. "Okay. What room are we in?"

"Dunno. Ask at the desk. I put the reservations in your name."

"My name? Didn't you need a credit card to reserve it?"

Dack gave Mason a sexy smile. "I have your credit card info, babe. You gave it to me ages ago." He went for Mason's lips and pushed Mason roughly against the car fender.

Dack's tongue swirled inside Mason's mouth, making Mason's dick swell. The coarse unshaven skin of Dack's jaw was scratching Mason's face and the last thing he wanted was beard burn. He slowed his man down and caressed his hair. They met gazes. Mason knew he loved this guy, though it was insane to even think about it.

"Can you live without me for an hour?" Dack ran his hand between Mason's legs and traced where he'd grown hard in his slacks.

"One hour. Maximum. Right?" Mason glanced around but no one was in the immediate area.

Dack pressed his lips against Mason's. "You're so hot when you miss me."

50

Mason's cock got a good squeeze and stimulating friction, turning him into an inferno. Dack gave him a parting kiss, climbed into his fancy red car, backed out and waved.

As he recovered from the kiss and grope, Mason caught his breath and walked to his car. He sat behind the wheel of his Audi and took a moment to think. "I'll be lucky if you show up at all."

He started the car and drove to the hotel, wondering if this night was going to be another disappointment. But he tried to keep his faith in Dack. After all, he was making an effort, and this was Valentine's Day. As he pulled in front of the hotel, listening to an audio book, the biography of Winston Churchill, he looked for a valet. There was none in sight. He couldn't see into the lobby from the outside, and noticed a public parking garage close by. In frustration, he returned to the office parking lot and left his car in his reserved spot, taking his overnight shoulder bag with him as he walked back to ground level, and the few blocks to the outside of the hotel's main entrance. Inside it appeared the lobby had been remodeled and was decent.

It wasn't the Desert Palm in Dubai but it was certainly adequate for Dack's modest salary and Mason was happy he had at least made an effort.

He knew his income far exceeded Dack's so he didn't expect unreasonable things from him. Actually, Mason couldn't care less about material gifts, and would rather have been given loyalty and punctuality. He stood at the desk and was greeted by the clerk. "Can I help you?"

"Hi, my name is Mason Bloomfield and a reservation was made in my name."

"Yes. One moment." The man behind the desk tapped keys. He handed Mason a slip of paper and said, "I'll need a credit card and identification."

Mason set his bag on the floor and handed over both, assuming in the end, he'd be paying for the night of 'romance'. He was good with that. At least Dack made the effort.

"We have you in one of our luxury suites." The man wrote the number of the room on the card sleeve holding a plastic key.

"Do you offer room service?" Mason asked.

He got a look as if he was either a moron or a snob. "No, sir, we don't. We have a continental breakfast in the morning, and there are some restaurants I can recommend within walking distance."

"Thank you." Mason tried not to take his frustration out on this poor man. He took the key and headed to the elevator. The lobby was spacious and had several people lingering near a lounge area. But no bar. No bar!

He rode the elevator up with a young couple and three children who pushed the buttons on the panel as if it were a video game, so they stopped at every floor. Mason stepped out at the seventh and hunted for his room, noticing the carpet was slightly worn and badly in need of a steam cleaning.

He slid his key into the slot of the door lock and peered in. The 'suite' consisted of one king-sized bed and an extended area where a sofa and coffee table acted as a living room. He put his bag on the dresser and picked up the mattress, inspecting it for bed bugs. There weren't any, thank Christ!

He took his phone out of his pocket and dialed Dack.

"Hi, babe!"

"When are you coming? There's no room service and I'm starving." Mason was not pleased.

"No room service? Damn! Make reservations someplace nice, Mason. You're good at that."

"Look, it's Valentine's Day and making reservations at anything exceptional will be a challenge. When are you coming? How long does it take to pack an overnight bag?"

"Babe, I've been gone ten minutes."

Mason checked his watch. "Forty. You've been gone forty."

"Don't be like that. I tried to do something nice."

Inhaling deeply to calm down, Mason asked, "Okay. When are you going to get here so we can walk around and hunt down some food...and booze."

"Five minutes."

"I'll be waiting in the lobby."

"No. Wait in the room. Naked."

Mason peered at the modest bed. "I'll be in the lobby."

"Okay. See you in a bit."

He disconnected the phone, stared at the small leather travel bag on the bed and ran his hand over his hair in exhaustion. He removed the wrapped gift—the wallet—and placed it on the dresser, then headed down to the lobby...to wait.

An hour had passed and Dack was not answering his phone nor text messages. To say Mason was furious was an understatement. He returned to the room, stuffed the gift into his belongings, left the room keys on the dresser, and shouldered his leather bag. He stormed out of the hotel lobby and stood on the sidewalk, starving, about to kill Dack, and wondering why he continued to put up with this type of behavior.

"I gotta get something to eat." He adjusted the shoulder strap and headed down the block, making his way through all the happy couples who were celebrating this day of 'love'.

*I don't love you. I hate you!*

## CHAPTER 5

Parker decided to leave the karaoke club, having had enough of the squawking voices. As the night grew later, the drunks decided to have their chance at a song, and even Parker knew when enough was enough. He figured he'd stayed an adequate amount of time to put in a good showing for the crew and stood, pushing in his chair.

"Have a hot date, Parker?" Dixie asked.

"Nope. Just me and movies on demand."

She pouted her lip sadly for him.

"Bye." Parker waved at each co-worker and left the building, standing on the sidewalk in the cool fall evening, wishing he did indeed have something special planned. The world around him was like Noah's ark, walking two by two, arm in arm, straight couples as far as the eye could see.

The nibbles of appetizers in the karaoke club didn't fill him enough to satisfy him and he tried to think of what food he had leftover at home. Weekends were the time for grocery shopping excursions so he knew the cupboard was getting bare.

But the idea of going into a restaurant on a night meant for romance and couples was intimidating. Hitting a drive-thru for a burger seemed about right.

Then he thought he remembered where a sub place was nearby and spun on his heels to reverse his direction. He came face to face with Mason, who appeared as stunned to see him as he was to see Mason.

"Mason? Are you headed back to the bar?"

"No. The parking garage. Did you just leave the karaoke club?" Mason pointed.

"Yeah. Where's Dack?" Parker glanced behind Mason.

"Where's Dack?" Mason repeated with venom. "Hmm. Where is he?"

Parker held up his hand. "Never mind. You left together and I thought—"

"You thought?" Mason held up his overnight bag. "I thought too!"

"I don't get it." Parker stepped out of the stream of pedestrians to stand near the brick wall of the Dive on Inn.

"He made reservations for us at a hotel, stopped home to get clothing and…" Mason blew out a breath in fury.

Parker checked his watch.

"Yes, an hour and a half ago." Mason shifted the shoulder bag like he was about to throw it like a shot-put down the street.

"Did you call him?" Parker could tell by Mason expression that was a stupid question. "Never mind. Well…good luck."

"I'll need it."

They passed each other as they walked in opposite directions. Then Parker heard Mason ask, "Hey. Did you eat anything yet?"

Parker spun around and shook his head. "I was going over to the sub shop. I figured every restaurant within a fifty mile radius of here will be booked for Valentine's Day."

"Mind if I join you?"

Parker lit up. "Nope. Not one bit."

Seeing Mason shifting the bag in irritation, Parker asked, "You want to drop that off at your car?"

"No. It's fine."

It didn't look fine. Parker walked down the busy street with Mason, wanting to be nosy and ask him questions about his relationship with Dack, but he thought better of it. "So are you from LA?"

"No. North Carolina. But I've lived here since I was twenty. So, I consider myself a native now."

"I'm from New York."

"I know. I can hear it in your accent."

"My accent?" Parker laughed and avoided couples coming their way that appeared about to steamroll over him if he didn't move, like a game of chicken.

"Yeah. Your accent." Mason laughed. "I got rid of mine twenty years ago."

"But I tried so hard to lose it, ya know? Not sound like I'm from da Bronx."

Mason cracked up with more enthusiasm and gave Parker a sweet smile. "I like it. Here in LA we don't even have an accent."

"No. I suppose you don't. Nothing regional. You could pretend to be a southern belle. North Carolina is close enough."

"Why, I do declare!" Mason batted his lashes and flipped his wrist.

"Nope. No way." Parker chuckled and loved Mason's playfulness. "Although those belles do have a 'coming out' party."

"Yeah. My parents would love to have given me one of those as a kid." They waited at a signal with a crowd of people, all hooked arm in arm.

"Bad time coming out?"

Mason shrugged. "They didn't lynch me but they wanted to. I don't speak to any of them. They don't give a shit and neither do I."

"Oh well."

"I don't care. I'm tired of worrying about everyone around me."

"I'll bet. It takes it out of a person." Parker assumed Mason meant Dack.

They made it to the sub shop and Mason held the door open for both of them. Parker entered first and got in line, reading the menu over the heads of the young people making the sandwiches. "Wonder if they have a Valentine's Day special?"

"Get the meatballs marinara," Mason said with a thick Brooklyn accent.

Parker couldn't stop laughing. "Da Godfathah…" he joined in the fun. "I'll make you an offah ya can't refuse."

"Don't tempt me." Mason's focus turned to the menu.

"Huh? Don't tempt you?" Parker's heart skipped a beat.

"Never mind."

When their turn came to order, Parker asked for one of the healthier choices, with sliced turkey and loads of vegetables. Mason chose a similar sandwich and they both grabbed a bag of oven-baked potato chips and a bottle of water.

Mason tossed his shoulder bag under a small table for two and sat on the metal chair. Parker brought napkins to the table and they unwrapped their food and ate hungrily.

"So?" Mason asked after he swallowed. "You like working at Judas?"

"Yeah. I do. So far so good." Parker pulled open the chips bag and munched a couple before brushing off his hands.

"Your columns are a hoot. I've been a fan of yours since I found your blog."

Parker widened his eyes in surprise. "Shut up."

"No. Really. You're the gay man's Carrie Bradshaw."

"That's very flattering. Thanks."

"Yeah. I read all your advice columns and then don't take any of it." Mason shook his chips onto his wrapper and ate them with his sandwich.

"Well, that's the hardest part." Parker knew what they were both referring to.

"Why aren't you seeing someone?"

"I just got to LA." Parker shrugged, looking around the area since this sub shop was a straight man's Mecca. "I'm not into hookups and I suppose finding someone who is decent and loyal isn't easy."

Mason made a noise in his throat of agreement, and maybe a little frustration.

Parker ate quietly for a while, cognizant of men coming and moving right beside their table. "How long have you been going out with Dack?"

"Six months, give or take." Mason ate the last bite of his sandwich and worked on the chips.

"And you met at work?"

"No. I met him ages ago, but we reconnected when I helped him get the job at the magazine."

Parker nodded and wanted to change the subject but didn't know what else they could talk about. "So…is it easy getting advertisers to buy—?"

Mason's mobile ringtone went off. He held his finger up to Parker. "Sorry. You mind?"

"No. Go ahead." Parker did mind but didn't want to say he did.

Mason turned in his chair, giving his profile to Parker and held the phone to his ear. "What do you mean where am I?" Mason said into the phone.

Parker kept eating, finishing, crushing up the wrapping and trying not to look interested.

"I waited nearly two hours for you! What the hell took you so long?"

Parker finished his water as well, figuring it was time to go home.

"Fine!" Mason disconnected the phone, nearly threw it, and pocketed it. "I have to go."

"Okay." Parker stood, tossing out the garbage as Mason shouldered his bag and threw out his scraps as well.

They walked back in the direction of the parking garage and Mason was so quiet, Parker didn't want to say a word. They had to split at one point, so Parker said, "Have a nice weekend."

Mason appeared on edge, and all he did was nod in Parker's direction in reply and walk off.

Parker had no idea how Mason put up with it. But the sex must be very good indeed.

~

Mason stormed back to the hotel. He didn't stop at the front desk and rode the elevator up, trying not to spontaneously combust since there were other people in the elevator with him. He exited at the seventh floor and stood in front of the door, pounding it since he left his key on the dresser inside.

After a minute it opened.

Dack, in a pair of black briefs and nothing else, held a glass of champagne out to Mason. "Happy Valentine's Day, baby."

Mason bit his lip on his lecture and walked passed him, dropping his bag on the dresser. The lights were low and a scent was in the room. Cinnamon?

Dack slunk towards him sensually, holding the glass to Mason's lips. Mason drank the champagne and took the fluted glass from Dack. As he chugged the contents, Dack began undressing Mason, kissing his chest and shoulders as they were revealed.

"Why does it smell like spices in here?" Mason slowly decompressed at the affection.

"Come and see." Dack took the empty glass and led Mason to the bathroom. A bathtub full of bubbles, surrounded in candles was waiting.

Mason smiled. "You romantic fool. Why were you so late?" He stepped out of his shoes, then his pants, briefs, and socks.

"Had to get ready for you." Dack pushed Mason against the doorframe, going for his lips.

Mason let go of his anger and upset and cupped Dack's handsome face. He moaned as Dack began kissing his way down his neck, then knelt in front of him.

Widening his stance, Mason watched Dack take his cock into his mouth to suck. "Oh, God, yes."

Dack chuckled with his mouth full and drew Mason's cock deeply until he was stiff. "Wanna come in my mouth or ass?"

"Decisions, decisions…" Mason put on a comically thinking face, tapping his chin.

"Mouth now? Ass later?" Dack cupped Mason's balls and resumed sucking.

"Fuck," he said as a comment on the pleasure, and not his decision on what sexual act to do. Mason closed his eyes and pressed back against the door frame as Dack sucked him hard and fast, holding the base of his cock. Opening his eyes, watching the act, and the determination in Dack's expression to make him come, Mason began to rise. He closed his eyes again and arched his back, holding Dack's head so he sucked deeply. "I'm there."

Mason felt his balls tighten up and the pleasure begin deep in his groin. Dack moaned and sucked stronger, milking him and intensifying the climax. As Mason recuperated he stared into Dack's gorgeous face in the flattering candlelight. *Christ, I love you.*

"Soak time?"

"Soak time." Mason was l[...]
Dack stripped off his briefs and [...]
filling two more glasses of champag[...]

"Happy Valentine's Day, Mr [...]
bubbles at him.

Mason raised his glass in a toast. "Hap[...]
you too, babe." They tapped glasses and dra[...]
then began playing under the soapy foam, gigg[...]
kids.

~

Parker tried not to think about Mason and Dack but [...]
he could do on his drive home. Since it was late and afte[...]
hour, he made it in fifteen minutes. He was in a lousy mood [...]
hated the holidays, since they were the cause. Or at least the[...]
reminded him of how alone he was in LA.

He headed up the stairs to his fourth floor unit and entered it,
feeling the small space like a vacuum from the lack of humanity.
He kicked off his shoes at the door and changed, washing up and
in no mood for anything physical. Since tomorrow was Saturday
he could catch up on his workout then.

He picked up his laptop after filling a glass with filtered
water, sank into the sectional sofa, feet on the hassock, computer
on his lap, and pointed the remote control at the TV. As Bill
Maher's *Real Time* played in the background, Parker opened up
his email box and caught up with his friends in New York.

It was nearing ten on the West Coast so Parker didn't expect
to see anyone online from back home.

Besides, everyone he knew was coupled up, and most likely
had plans for the night. He actually thought of calling his mom
just to say hi, but since it was nearing one in the morning on
their side of the country, he reconsidered.

ight after

*a hotel*

ie sofa,
on and

ttan if
:utely.

d to the bathtub and climbed in as
oined him at the other end and after
ie.
Bloomfield." Dack blew
y Valentine's Day to
k the champagne,
ling like school
was all
rush

ı a gotta a minute? I know how busy you are ogling naked men all day." Parker smiled. His cousin Claire Epstein owned a male modeling agency with her partner Jenine Spencer.

"Oh, I know. It's a tough job, but someone's gotta do it."

"Any new pretty boys to brag about?"

"Some here and there. So? When are you going to get one for yourself…to fuck?"

Parker loved her straight forward no-nonsense manner. Always did. Since Claire's brother Scott was out, and dating one of Claire's top models, Ian Sullivan, Parker knew he could tell her anything.

"No. And I'm not into the pretty boy scene."

"That's such shit. Everyone wants to fuck a model."

"Not everyone."

"Sure, whatever… How's the new job? I need to get a copy of your magazine."

"Well, my column will be in the March issue. So, yes, grab it and tell me what you think about it. They have me writing a *Judas' Rainbow* blog as well. So the advice doctor is always in."

"I love it. Your personal blogs were so awesome. Of course I'll pick up the magazine when it comes out."

"Cool."

"So, come on, Parker, why are you calling me? It's not just to bullshit about work."

"Why not? I can bullshit with the best of them." Parker hit record on the remote control for the show so he could watch it after he hung up.

"Fuck you. What's going on?"

"There's this guy at work."

"Well, I assume he's gay since he works for *Judas' Rainbow.* Correct?"

"Well, I doubt every male employee is—"

"Fast forward, Parker."

"Man! You are such a New Yorker!" he laughed as he spoke.

"Like you ain't? What? A month in Lala land and you're already eating avocados and shaving your balls?"

"Shut up." He cracked up.

"Okay. This guy. At work."

"Yeah, well, I go for older, more mature men, but not like old-old."

"I remember. Last guy you dated was forty-something."

"Yeah, Lee..."

"Right. Lee. He left you for that twenty-year old stud-muffin Damon."

"Ouch!" Parker flinched. "That isn't helping."

"Sorry. Go on."

"Well," Parker rubbed his eyes tiredly, "This guy is going with a twenty-something stud-muffin too. It's not fair."

63

"Acknowledge—move on. Look, babe, you have to find a guy who wants a thirty-something."

"I keep thinking I did, and then they leave me for a newer model."

"Got news for you, cookie."

"What?"

"I saw Lee last week walking his dog down the Avenue of the Americas."

"And?"

"We chatted. He's on his own."

"No! You knew that and didn't call me!" Parker sat up and shoved his laptop aside.

"Why? I thought he was old news. Why would you want to go back to him after he dumped you for that kid?"

Parker scrubbed his eyes in frustration. "What's wrong with me, Claire?"

"You're fabulous. They're too stupid to realize it. But I have to tell ya, Lee felt like a moron. Those young guys are fucked up. They are an ego boost for these older men, and that's it. Style but no substance. Take it from a gal in the biz. They think it's what they want, but then, look out. Reality sets in and other than a roll in the sack, the young ones aren't good for much."

"You're just saying that to make me feel better."

"Nope. Saying it from personal experience."

Parker cracked up. "Claire, what am I going to do with you? You're incorrigible."

"I know. Look, we're the only two cousins still single and not dating only one guy. Even Brian and Jordan have found men. I mean, how horrible are we?"

"Jordon cheated. He started out straight and came out late in life." Parker reached for his water to drink, looking at the television with the muted sound, seeing the panel on *Real Time* arguing.

"Came out late, avoided marrying a lesbian and fell in love with his wedding planner. Boo hoo."

Parker choked on the water as he laughed. "Damn!" He coughed and set the water down. "Woman, come out here and visit."

"No. You come here. I can't do my job from Smog-ville, and you can write your column from here, Carrie Bradshaw."

"Nah. Not sex in New York, sex in Smog-ville. Cough."

"How bad do you have it for this guy?"

"Not too bad yet. But getting there."

"Does he show any interest in you?"

"Not really. Tonight after work we hit a karaoke bar—" When Claire went hysterical with laughter, Parker waited. "Anyway. He's with this real pretty muscle-dude. The guy's name is Dack. Not Jack. Dack. Like *Dack*!" he yelled.

Claire laughed so hard she was wheezing over the line.

"Anyway, he gets on stage and sings Tom Jones, takes off his shirt, and well..."

"Aww... Hot?"

"Ridiculous. I can't compete with that."

"Of course you can! Parker!"

"No. I won't. I can't sit there and try to win this guy over and compete with some Adonis who probably fucks like a porn star."

"Babe."

"No, Claire, don't." Parker peeked at the television then the laptop.

"I'm thirty-*cough*-something too. I've dated young, pretty models. Yes, they're eye candy. Yes, they are fun to flaunt—yes, even nice to fuck. But..."

"Well, they sound nice to do everything with. Including spending overnight with on Valentine's Day."

"They're boring!"

"Sure, Claire."

"They are. Not only that, but they cheat. They see some skirt with legs up to here..."

Parker got it, even though Claire was using her straight analogy.

"And they stray. Those pretty boys want a tight, fit twenty-ish body to fuck too."

"Believe me, Claire, Mason is tight."

"Mason. Dack's older man?"

"Yes."

"How old?"

"Forty."

"And Dack?"

"I think twenty-five or six."

"It'll never last."

"Why?"

"You watch. How do they get along at work?"

Parker thought about it. "Kind of shitty sometimes."

"Uh huh."

A beep sounded. Claire said, "Got a call. Can you hang on?"

"Sure." Parker slouched low on the sofa and kept watching the muted debate on the panel of the HBO show. A minute later Claire came back to him. "Can I let you go, Parker? Jenine is crying in her wine. Her date stood her up and she's been drinking since nine. She's completely stewed now and a wreck."

"Fuck!"

"You think you have it bad?" Claire blew out a loud breath. "Jenine and I could write the book of crappy dates."

"Okay, Claire. Thanks for being a good listener."

"Anytime. You've been there for me."

"See ya."

"See ya." Parker hung up and turned up the volume on the television set and placed his laptop back on his lap. "Life sucks.

Then ya die." He shrugged and started brainstorming for more columns to write for his daily blog.

~

Mason lay in bed, relaxed after the blowjob, a bath, and half a bottle of champagne. Dack was in the bathroom, Mason assumed preparing for either their sex or bed, so he puffed up the pillow under his head and waited, watching for him. Hearing a hum of a text message, Mason thought he had shut his phone off to ensure they had the night distraction free. He climbed off the bed and checked the pockets of his slacks. His phone was off. Dack's was humming.

"Dack?" Mason walked near the bathroom door. "Babe?"

"Huh?"

"You okay?" Mason heard Dack make a noise as if he were in pain, then rustling or movement, and became concerned.

The door swung open after what felt like a long while and Dack looked guilty. But of what Mason had no clue.

"Just…" Mason said, and tilted his head. "What's wrong?"

"Nothing. All good." Dack walked near the bed and didn't get in it.

"Your phone hummed like it got a text. I was hoping we could give it a rest for the night." Mason climbed back in bed.

"Oh. Sure." Dack located his smartphone and before he shut it, he stood reading what he had missed.

"I bought you a gift." Mason tried not to get annoyed and waited—patiently—pointing to the wrapped wallet. When Dack began texting as he stood, naked, near the dresser mirror, Mason could see him both coming and going. "Are you really texting someone. Now?"

"Just this one. Yoseph." Dack peered at the gift and then finished his text and began to open it.

Mason peeled back the blankets, hoping his body would entice Dack to join him more quickly. His tactic failed. He looked down at his chest, the soft hair on it leading to his treasure trail, and then at Dack's hairless chest, tattoos, and shaven pubic area. Again Mason inspected his own body dreading the idea he had to shave every hair off himself to compete. He had no intention. He wasn't a bear. He knew his body hair was reasonable and not excessive. All he had was an inverted triangle of chest hair. Since he had been blond as a young boy, his arm and leg hair were quite light in color.

Crumbling up the wrapping paper and checking out the wallet, Dack didn't acknowledge the gift verbally, but seemed to like it. After he put it into his overnight bag, he grabbed his phone, chuckled as he read it, and kept texting.

"Dack!"

"Hang on! He's telling me about the taste of cherry flavored Valentine's Day condoms!"

Pulling the blanket back up to his chest, Dack rolled to his side and groaned in frustration. "Dack."

"Dude! Hang on." Dack kept texting, using his thumbs. "Put the TV on or something."

"The TV?" Mason tried not to get angry. "I don't want to watch TV. I want you here in bed with me."

"Aww." Dack made a sad face at Mason. "That is so sweet." He kept texting.

*I hate you.* Mason shut off the light on the nightstand and tried to go to sleep.

## CHAPTER 6

Mason began to stir as sunlight filtered into the hotel room. He stared at the sheer curtains and the thick drapes framing them, parted to allow light in. Mason rolled over to see an empty bed. The digital clock read nine-forty-five. Listening, trying to hear if Dack was in the bathroom, Mason climbed out of bed to search. Dack was gone and so were his belongings.

He found a note on the dresser near the empty bottle of champagne.

*Had a blast! You rock, big daddy! Personal trainer appt at the gym! Kisses!*

Mason hadn't even heard him get up and leave. '*Big Daddy*?' He didn't want to be anyone's daddy, let alone a twenty-six year old man's.

He entered the bathroom and turned on the shower, catching his reflection in the mirror. He touched the scruff on his face and sighed. "I never learn. I never fucking learn."

~

Parker had come back from a long street run and cooled down before his shower. When he was in his jeans and T-shirt, he made a pot of coffee and popped two slices of bread into the toaster. While they were toasting, he began writing up a shopping list for the week of food. Unlike the rest of the universe, he wasn't keen on weekends off. Since he hadn't established a good friend base in LA, he preferred the time at work and the routine rather than trying to kill a couple of days with errands and laundry.

The toast popped and the coffee brewed. He spread peanut butter on the crunchy slice of bread and poured almond milk in his coffee, then sat again to finish figuring out what he needed from the grocery store.

His cell phone rang. Parker checked the time on his watch. It was nearing noon. He figured it was his mom. Locating his phone on the counter in the kitchen he read a number he did not recognize but it had a New York City area code. "Hello?"

"Yez, iz dis Parker Douglaz?"

Parker blinked at the strong accent. "Yes. Who is this?"

"Iz Claudio Ernesto. Your cousin, Claire Epstein. She say you live in LA."

Parker smiled. "Yes. I do."

"I work for her. Yes? She say if I'm in town. I can call you? Perhaps dinner?"

Parker felt his cheeks heat up and he shifted his stocking feet on the kitchen tile floor nervously. "So, you work for Claire?"

"She is your cousin, right?"

"Yes." Parker sat down at the table, picked up his pen and tapped it on the pad nervously.

"She say you are single and maybe no mind if we make dinner appointment."

*Oh God. Claire!*

"Uh sure."

"I am in town only tonight. But I would love special night."

"*Oh.*" He nodded as if he got it. *Sympathy fuck. Thanks, Claire.* "Well, I'm not really into—"

"I stay at hotel. In WoHo?"

"WeHo. West Hollywood."

70

"Yes! WeHo. I knew mistake when I say. I have photo shoot she arrange and then…free."

Parker rubbed his face and could imagine this was probably one of the best looking fuckers on the planet. Those were the only type of men Claire signed. Greek gods. "Um…"

"No? Already plans? Iz okay."

The disappointment in his voice got to Parker. "No. It's fine. I can meet you at your hotel lobby and figure out a place to eat."

"Wonderful. Yes."

"Where are you staying, Claudio?" Parker aimed the pen at the pad, hoping he wasn't too average for one of his cousin's stunning stars. He wrote the information down as Claudio dictated it, even though he knew the hotel and had even explored its little bistro restaurant online after he had found it.

"Eight? Iz good?"

"Yes. Eight is fine."

"I will see you then. You have my number so…no can make it, call."

"I'll be there. I won't let you down."

"She say that about you."

Parker wondered what else she said.

"I will know you when I see."

"How?" Parker asked curiously.

"I see picture on your social site. Very handsome man."

Parker tried to remember when he took that picture. It was a year old. "Shit."

"*Perdao*? Sorry. What?"

"Nothing. Yes. I'll be there."

"Good. See you then."

Parker hung up and put the phone down, nervous as a school girl on her first date. "Claire!" he shouted in terror, then continued to eat his breakfast quickly.

Giving up on trying to keep sane, Parker threw the pen up in the air, grabbed the pad and got ready to get his errands done.

~

Mason packed his small shoulder bag and checked the hotel room, making sure it wasn't a sty. He threw out the wrapping paper from the wallet gift, as well as the empty bottle of champagne, and had a last look around. He picked up the card keys from the dresser and used the elevator to descend to the lobby.

He stood at the concierge desk and waited his turn. A young woman greeted him.

"I'm checking out." Mason put the keys on the counter.

"Yes. How was your stay, sir?"

"Fine."

She printed out a receipt and handed it to him. As he had assumed, the room expenses were on his tab. He nodded, took the receipt and left, walking in the cool, windy afternoon to the parking garage at his office building where he had left his car.

Could he keep doing this to himself? Sacrifice his personal feelings for a trophy? A trophy who treated him like shit? *Am I that shallow?*

Mason tossed his luggage into the trunk of his Audi, sat behind the wheel, and headed home. As he drove to his condo off Wilshire, he tried not to believe it was a total loss. He'd had a decent time while Dack was there. The bath, the blowjob, the... They didn't have sex. They both fell asleep.

He pulled slowly into the steep drive after the gate opened and knew he had errands to tend today—laundry, shopping, banking...the things you do when you work nine to five and can't do them all week.

That was another thing.

He wanted to take Dack with him on a cruise or to Hawaii. He needed a vacation and wondered if it was a way to get Dack to stop being distracted by everything else and just enjoy him. Enjoy each other.

He'd even gone so far as to get brochures from a travel agent, and show Dack the different choices. Dack had acted excited but wouldn't commit to time off.

It was probably for the best. Mason figured if he did book it, Dack would be a no show, leaving him at the airport and forcing him to spend a week on his own.

He parked his car, headed to his condo and once inside, dumped out his overnight bag on his bed, sorting through the laundry and toiletries. After he was organized, he wrote up a quick list of food to buy and left the house, checking his phone but knowing he'd not hear from Dack until he saw him on Monday at work, unless he initiated the contact.

It was an effort in futility and he tried to convince himself he'd be better off without Dack.

~

Parker was already starving by five and paced his small home. He'd done all his errands, tried to write a column for the blog but failed since he was so nervous. He had even changed his clothing five times, finally deciding on wearing a suit and tie.

He'd left several messages on Claire's voicemail, but either she was deliberately not answering his calls, being sly, or she was out doing her thing and deciding not to be social. Which wasn't too unusual for a woman as busy and crazy as his cousin.

Using every distraction method he could come up with to pass time, Parker finally gave up trying to entertain himself with TV, the newspaper, or novels, and was done preening by seven. He walked to Santa Monica Boulevard to begin, 'sort of' heading to the hotel, without actually going inside to wait the last hour. But if he stayed five more minutes in his apartment he'd go insane.

He strolled the busy main street, staring into the shops, seeing pretty young males strutting their stuff everywhere, some in couples, some in groups, none alone. Even the ones who were flying solo had dogs to partner up with.

Yes, he had more time to kill, but at least he was outside in the fresh air with people and not just his computer, his work, and his muddled head.

He walked to a few of the more popular restaurants, reading the menus, wanting to give Claudio a good selection of local cuisine. He felt his phone hum and dreaded getting stood up. His cousin Claire had sent him a text. '*GET LAID!*'

He stopped where he was and leaned against the wall of the restaurant he was near. He texted back, '*PIMP!*'

He got in return, '*Lol!*' and then she vanished from his contact. Parker pocketed his phone and didn't know if he wanted to 'get laid' by a guy he did not know—one who was going back to New York tomorrow. If all he wanted was sex...

He spun around to look at the men who came and went, as if they were the menu on the restaurant wall. Take your pick—twinks, bears, daddies, fetishes, geeks...

*Mason.*

"Get out of my head!"

Parker didn't realize he'd yelled that out loud until a pudgy bald man said, "I didn't do anything to you!"

"No. Sorry." Parker held up his hand in apology.

"But I can. Do you want to go for a drink?" The little man looked hopeful.

"Sorry. I can't. I would, ya know? But I have to meet someone." Parker tapped his watch in a clichéd gesture.

"Oh well." The man shrugged and walked off.

Parker decided since he was in West Hollywood he would take Claudio to an upscale restaurant. After all, if Claudio was a model for Spencer & Epstein...he made good money, Parker knew that much.

He was still a little early but he walked to the hotel, trying to prepare himself for the possibility that plain ole him would disappoint strikingly handsome Claudio Ernesto. Had he Googled him? Oh hell, yeah.

Brazilian, six foot-two, twenty-three, bronze and dark-complected, smoldering eyes, long-ish black hair, into soccer, sports cars and auto racing.

Parker was so intimidated and freaked out that the guy was so young, he wanted to either kill his cousin or kiss her. Kill her. Yes. Kill her.

He opened the lobby door and peered into the marble-clad interior, which had a modest sized waiting area, since WeHo wasn't exactly the open space capital of LA. He could see right through the room to the polished brass elevators, two side by side. A concierge was stationed behind a high marble and brass desk, wearing a black suit, and beyond him by the far wall was a small flight of stairs which led down to a bar and patio that served gourmet food. Though Parker had never stayed there, he knew the place by reputation and had looked it up on the 'net ages ago after he had walked passed it. It wasn't on the main drag, but one block off of it, and the neighborhood was mostly high-priced apartment houses and permit only parking.

"May I help you?"

"I'm meeting one of your guests here."

"Shall I call him to let you know you are here?"

"I'm a little early." Parker checked his watch.

"We have a lovely lounge if you would like a drink while you wait."

"Yes. I would." Parker could use something to calm his nerves. He was a wreck.

As he passed a small portico with a fancy Georgian style loveseat and mirrored wall, he paused to straighten his tie and jacket and kept walking down the short flight of stairs to the well-lit area. One side had a bar nearly the entire length of the room, ridiculously well stocked with dozens of bottles—a television was playing over the display, and opposite the bar was a single row of tables with glass windows behind them. At the far end was a small patio, with a tiny waterfall, all nestled between the hotel and an apartment building with balconies hanging overhead.

The young woman behind the bar immediately greeted him. The room was empty but for a few couples who were outside on the patio enjoying the pleasant evening.

He sat on a barstool and looked at the choices of colorful bottles behind her.

"What can I get you?" She was very attractive and Parker bet she cleaned up in tips.

"Any suggestions? I'm meeting a date here and I'm a nervous as hell."

"Blind date?" She smiled and placed a coaster in front of him.

"Yes." Because this was WeHo, Parker added, "I've seen his pictures on the 'net, but…"

"Oh." She nodded and put on her thinking face. "Hmm. How about something not too strong so you're still sharp, but something to take the edge off?"

"Perfect." Parker interlaced his hands in front of him on the bar. "What on earth could that be?"

"Cognac."

"Sounds good." He ran his hand through his hair and looked at his reflection in the mirror behind the bottles as she poured. She placed the glass in front of him.

He asked her, "How old do you think I am?"

She cocked her eyebrow and gave him a once over. "Twenty-seven?"

"You just got a big tip." He held the cognac up to swirl around the glass. "Now tell me the truth."

"No. Really. How old are you?"

"Eighty. Don't I look great for my age?"

She chuckled and leaned back on the edge of the counter behind her. "So is this like an internet dating site thing?"

"No. It's a nosy cousin from New York thing." He sniffed the drink and then shot it down, nearly choking as he did.

"I would have given you tequila if you were going to do that."

"Oh God." He shivered and began coughing. "Fuck..." He held up his hand. "Sorry."

"I've heard the word before. Don't worry."

When Parker noticed her glance towards the entrance of the bar, he turned to see. "Shit."

Claudio was standing on the landing, looking like he was right off the pages of a glossy glamour magazine.

"Wow. That him?" she whispered.

"Yes." He kept coughing and wiping his teary eyes. "Fuck."

"Parker?" Claudio asked, the name rolling off his tongue like velvet.

Parker stood and tried to be normal as he died of embarrassment, still clearing his throat. He thumbed over his shoulder and said, "She nearly killed me with cognac."

Claudio laughed softly and extended his hand.

Parker clasped it and melted down to his shoes at the raw sensuality of this gorgeous stud. The three inches between their heights made Parker feel like the little woman. And he'd be this god's bitch in a heartbeat. The man's dark suit was custom made, form fitted to his every curve and his cologne or aftershave scent made Parker's mouth water.

"Can I have a drink as well?" Claudio gestured to the bar.

"Of course." Parker felt like an idiot. He took his seat after Claudio did, on the stool beside his, and the woman appeared to swoon as she stared at Claudio.

"What can I get you?" she asked, placing a coaster in front of him.

"I do not know. I think not the cognac since you nearly kill my friend." Claudio shot Parker a dazing smile.

Parker almost came in his pants from the zing of sexual potency. Oh, he got why older men wanted young models. He did indeed. But they were flings. One night stands. Not partners.

"How about something sweet and very LA?" she asked.

"Yes. Perfect."

Parker stared enthralled at Claudio's perfect profile for a moment then asked the woman, "What are you making him?"

"Alvarado Street."

"And that is?"

"Silver Tequila, cinnamon-infused agave syrup, lemon juice, lime, cinnamon and tangelo."

As they waited for the woman to mix the cocktail, more couples began to enter the small restaurant/bar area. The woman told them, "Just have a seat anywhere you'd like," and continued mixing the cocktail.

Parker began asking himself if he would fuck Claudio tonight. It should have been an easy answer, but for him it never was. Nothing was easy for Parker.

The drink was served to Claudio and Parker watched as he took a sip, licking his full lips.

Parker had to stop becoming mesmerized by this man's beauty or he'd act like a moron all night.

"Mm. Iz very nice. Taste." He offered the glass to Parker.

Parker would have preferred tasting it off Claudio's mouth but took the drink and sipped it. "Wow. Nice one."

"Would you like one too?" the barmaid asked.

"Uh." He gave Claudio his drink. "Let me get back to you on that."

She nodded and moved on to help the new patrons who had sat down at one of the tables, offering them menus and taking drink orders.

Parker stared at Claudio as he sipped the cocktail. "I have a few ideas in mind for dinner, but of course I wanted to see what you have a preference for."

Claudio turned to face Parker full on and when they connected gazes, the intensity nearly blew Parker off the stool.

"I like it all. You decide."

"Have…have you been to LA before?"

"Once. Yes. But just for shoot like this. A weekend. And I had no one to spend with. So?" He shrugged.

"There's a great place a short walk from here."

"The night is beautiful. A walk sounds perfect."

"What time is your flight tomorrow?" Parker got lost in Claudio's brown eyes, the dark lashes that surrounded them.

"Early." Claudio put his hand on Parker's leg. "But you no worry."

Parker's body covered in chills. He peeked down at that hand on his thigh and his dick pulsated between his legs.

"Have you decided yet?" the barmaid asked.

"Huh?" Parker wanted to grab Claudio's hand and drag it to his cock.

"Did you want another drink?" she asked.

"No. Just the bill." Parker felt Claudio's fingers slip off and was able to function as the blood drained from his dick and made it to his brain cells. Claudio finished the drink quickly as Parker took his wallet out of his trouser pocket.

When he was handed the bill and saw it was for over thirty dollars for two drinks he nearly choked and fell over. He slipped his credit card into the slot and kept a straight face.

As they waited for her to return with his credit card slip, Parker had no idea what he and Claudio could discuss during dinner. They had nothing in common.

He noticed Claudio check himself out in the mirror behind the bar, running his hand through his hair. A little vanity was to be expected in these pretty models. But rumor had it they were insecure.

He signed his credit card slip, giving the young woman a decent tip, although fifteen bucks a drink was outrageous in his opinion. Parker tucked his wallet back into his trouser pocket and straightened his suit jacket as he followed Claudio up the stairs, watching this man's ass and legs as he moved.

They walked through the lobby and Parker caught a glimpse of them as a couple as they moved past the mirror—two men in suits, ready to enjoy the atmosphere of southern California's liberal pinpoint in a red state.

Parker opened the door for Claudio and they walked into the night air, cool, breezy and lit by streetlights. With a gesture towards Santa Monica Boulevard, Parker showed Claudio the way. "So, what did you come to LA to model for?"

"It was a fashion magazine catwalk." Claudio hesitated when they arrived at the Boulevard.

"Left." Parker again gestured the direction and the two of them walked side by side as the space allowed. Yes, everyone in the area was gawking at the luscious Brazilian but that was either a perk or a pitfall of being with a model. Parker was the ugly duckling by comparison and even though some men would have been proud to be seen with such perfection, Parker wasn't the type to become a model groupie.

Being the invisible-plain man beside someone so striking was tough to swallow. "Catwalk. Right. Well, with your height and grace I'm not surprised."

"That is very kind of you to say." Claudio gave Parker a sweet smile.

"You must get complimented all the time." They paused at a traffic signal and the breeze blew strongly down La Cienega Boulevard.

Instead of answering, Claudio just gave Parker a slight smile.

"It's right there. You see the green awning?"

"Good. Yes."

Parker again took the lead, opening the restaurant door, either because he was the older of the two of them, or the 'local', which was fine. He approached the hostess in the crowded room and said, "Two, for dinner."

"Did you have a reservation?"

"No." Parker checked his watch, it was after eight and he did notice one or two tables vacant.

"One moment." She did a deliberate once over of pretty Claudio and decided he was just fine for her pricy establishment. Or at least that's how Parker read it.

"This way." She didn't even hesitate. They were two handsome men in suits, how could she refuse? *Or at least one handsome man and his sidekick.*

"Will this table be all right?" She held two menus.

"Yes. Perfect." Claudio sat down at a table for four in the large, very noisy room and took one of the menus.

Parker had a choice to sit beside him, or across. He chose across since at this point he was more interested in conversation with this man than in groping his knee. He sat, unbuttoned his suit jacket and took the menu.

"Your waiter will be here shortly to discuss the specials and take your drink order."

"Thanks." Parker read over the selection after she left.

"What do you recommend?" Claudio looked up over his menu.

"I've never been here before." He took a glance at the prices and nearly passed out. It was going to be an expensive night and he assumed he was taking this man out all the way, in an effort to get him to go 'all the way'. Or that's what Parker assumed Claudio had in mind. It was sex for pay, just instead of cash, it was food and booze.

Why he had thought this was a good idea, Parker didn't know. But between his cousin Claire's pushy nature, and his own loneliness for a man's touch, he didn't think it through and now felt as if he were some dipshit who had hired a gigolo.

The last time he had gotten laid was with Lee. As Parker tried to determine just how many months ago that was, considering the bad breakup, the move, the settling into LA and the new job, the waiter approached their table.

"Hello, gentlemen. My name is Fabio and I will be your server tonight. We have some seasonal specials…"

Parker listened without interest as he had already decided on chicken breast and house salad.

"Can I start you off with a drink while you decide?" Fabio batted his lashes at Claudio, and Parker again felt like the ugly step-sister. He wasn't going to get booze but changed his mind at being ignored. "A tequila shooter, please."

Fabio went over a list of different tequilas until Parker had lost interest. "Whatever. Just anything is fine."

Claudio met Parker's gaze, as if he felt some strange vibe. "Yes. Same too for me."

The waiter left and Claudio leaned his elbows on the table to speak more confidentially to Parker in the bad acoustics. "I make you upset?"

"Huh? No!" Parker shook his head and mirrored Claudio's body position so they were nose to nose. "No. You are perfect. Why would you ask me that?"

"You seem angry at someone. The waiter? Yes?"

Parker had no idea he was exuding some weird vibe. "No. Not at all." He smiled and touched Claudio's hand to reassure him.

Claudio instantly picked it up and brought it to his lips to kiss.

Parker gulped audibly but in the noise only he could hear it.

"I will make nice night for you. You will be happy man."

"Oh, God..." Parker broke out in a sweat and his cock thickened.

As gently as his hand was held, it was released and Parker nearly fell off his chair from his nerves. The confidence of Claudio was going to give him performance anxiety. He loved to be the bottom boy and had a feeling Claudio would be yearning the same role. Two bottoms, no top, equals awkward sex.

"So...uh...you are from Brazil?" Parker knew this was going to be a long night.

## CHAPTER 7

The conversation was strained. Parker felt as if he were interviewing Claudio, since Claudio didn't offer much more than one or two word answers, and asked him nothing about himself.

They drank three shots of tequila and two microbrew beers each, ate appetizers, side salads and main entrées, finally saying no to dessert since they were both stuffed.

Parker excused himself to stop at the men's room and Claudio smiled politely as he did.

He stood at a urinal, slightly buzzed by all the alcohol, but the amount of food and bread had kept him from being wasted. After his did his business, he stood at the sink to wash his hands and check himself in the mirror. He looked okay. A man in a suit tends to appear handsome. He ran his hand over his hair but didn't fuss. He couldn't compete with a Brazilian model at least ten years his junior.

On his way back, walking passed the bar, he heard loud laughter and actually recognized it. He stopped short to see Dack, dressed in a skin-tight sleeveless white tank top and equally skin-tight black jeans, completely drunk, standing beside a man seated at the bar. The man had snow white hair and was wearing a business suit. Parker ducked behind a slight bend in the wall and watched Dack flirt overtly with the old man...yes *old*—this was not a man in his forties, but more like turning seventy, yet reeking of cash.

Dack Torington, a frilly mixed cocktail elevated in his hand, stood between the knees of this old codger and kept touching his white hair and grizzled jaw.

Parker hustled by, trying not to be seen, and met Claudio, who was still sitting at the table waiting. "Shall we go?"

Claudio glanced down at the bill the server had left in a black folder.

Paranoid Dack would see him, and not wanting Dack to know he had spied him with another man, Parker plopped down on the seat and opened the folder up. When he read the total had come to over two hundred dollars, he nearly died. He removed his wallet, hoping, waiting for Claudio to offer to pay half? The tip? Something?

Claudio made no move, perfectly comfortable being babied, 'kept' or pimped. Whichever he was doing.

The waiter approached and Parker, with a frown, handed off his credit card. He suddenly felt like the old man with the white hair, playing sugar daddy to a young stud for a fuck.

Claudio appeared bored, brushed his suit jacket sleeve, ran his hand through his hair, and checked his Cartier watch for the time.

The waiter returned, thanking them.

Parker added the tip and winced at the total but bit back his expression as best he could. He took his copy, pocketed his card and stood.

Claudio was right behind him. Parker could hear Dack's obnoxious laughter as he left, cringed and wondered why life was the way it was. It made no sense. It reminded him of an old J. Giles song. *Love Stinks*.

He walked Claudio back to the hotel, deep in thought, hands in pockets, neither speaking.

When they were standing in front of the main lobby's door, on a sidewalk with a steep grade and shady trees blowing in the

February night, Claudio moved closer to Parker, touching his arm. "Come up."

Parker met his eyes. "It's okay."

"No. You come. I insist."

"I thought you had to wake up early for your flight."

"I do. We no take much time." Claudio hooked Parker's elbow and Parker wondered if Claudio felt as if he had to repay the debt of the dinner somehow. A true hooker.

*Fine!*

Parker figured if Claudio was offering, he would accept. What the fuck? *Everyone else is screwing pretty models, why not me?*

They walked by the concierge without a glance. Claudio pushed the elevator call button and they stood in the quiet of the lobby waiting. The elevator door opened soundlessly and Claudio touched Parker's hand to lead him inside. Claudio pushed button number three and they rode to his floor quietly, deep in thought.

Parker's heart wasn't in it. He just wasn't sure if his body was either. Seeing Dack with that old man? Did Mason know? Was Dack and Mason's relationship open? Or had Parker just witnessed Dack cheating?

Why would Dack cheat on Mason? With an old guy? A *really* old guy?

*I never would!*

Claudio opened his hotel room and entered. Parker followed and had a look at the opulent style.

Immediately in view was a sunken living room, balcony, a flat screen TV on one wall and a loveseat and matching sofa opposite. A divider which was a nothing more than a wooden art deco stencil of a floral vine design on perforated wood separated the bedroom area. The room was large and so very LA chic.

Claudio immediately approached Parker and slid Parker's suit jacket down his arms. He tossed the jacket onto the sofa and worked on Parker's tie, staring at Parker's lips or his chin.

*Does this guy think I'm ugly and need a sympathy fuck?*

*Do I want a sympathy fuck?*

His tie was removed and his shirt buttons were opened one by one. Once Parker's top half was revealed, his shirt hanging open on his chest, Claudio ran his lips over his sternum and licked at his nipples.

Parker was certainly aroused now.

Claudio backed up, and slowly began undressing for Parker.

Feeling his heart accelerate under his ribs, Parker licked his lips as this spectacular specimen of manhood began to strip.

His suit jacket, tie, shirt, shoes, and socks—gone. Only wearing his trousers, Claudio walked to the bedroom side of the room and removed condoms and lubrication from a small leather bag.

Parker watched Claudio strip off his pants, to his briefs. Then he beckoned Parker with his index finger.

When Parker was standing near the foot of the bed, Claudio lowered his briefs down his legs, showing off a lovely dark, uncut, semi-erect cock and closely shaven black pubic hair.

He lay back on the bed, bent his knees and spread his thighs in invitation.

Two bottoms. Parker had had a feeling. He rubbed his face in exhaustion and had no idea how to vocalize the dilemma.

As if Claudio either sensed it, or wanted to entice, he crawled to the foot of the bed, and opened Parker's trousers. Parker's soft cock was exposed and he felt embarrassed he wasn't stiff as a board with such a beauty to light the fire in him.

Claudio took him into his mouth and hummed sensually, nudging Parker's pants and briefs down his thighs.

Parker held onto Claudio's shoulders and watched as Claudio sucked him hard. When Claudio had accomplished giving Parker a stiff cock, he again, lay back and spread his legs, reaching for the condoms.

Parker tried to jerk off to stay hard, not wanting to be the top, not interested at all.

"I no turn you on?" Claudio blinked as if it was the most impossible notion on the planet.

"No. I mean. Yes, you do. I just…" Parker couldn't spit it out. This wasn't his friend, his companion—it was a stranger he had nothing in common with.

"No? No want sex? You are gay?"

"Yes. I'm gay. I just prefer…"

"Prefer?"

As he began to tuck his cock back into his pants, Claudio again drew closer, taking him into his mouth. "This time I no stop."

"Okay." Parker felt his face burn with humiliation.

Claudio sucked hard, holding Parker's balls in his palm, making a great effort.

Parker wanted to come. He seriously did for so many reasons. He stared at the curve in Claudio's perfect ass, at his hair, his cheekbones, his mouth filled with Parker's cock. He closed his eyes. *Mason.*

Parker imagined Mason sucking his cock. It worked like a charm. He held onto Claudio's shoulders and fucked his mouth, going into a fantasy in his head about Mason and him together, fucking, getting topped, a good hammering by that man, and holding him in his arms all night after.

"Oh fuck. I'm coming." Parker arched his back and squeezed Claudio's shoulders tightly.

Claudio drew hard and allowed Parker to come in his mouth. Parker withdrew from the hard suction and recovered, trying to steady his balance.

"Iz good?"

"Yes. Wow." Parker noticed Claudio look back at the clock on the nightstand. "Do you want me to go?"

"If you no get angry. I have early flight."

"Yes. Of course." Parker pointed to the bathroom. "Can I just wash up?"

"Yes!" Claudio nodded enthusiastically and waved to the bathroom.

Parker closed himself in and stood at the sink to wash his cock. He caught his eyes in the mirror and sneered at himself. "Happy, slut?"

He finished up and exited the bathroom, pickup up his shirt and put it on quickly as Claudio checked his phone for text messages and arranged a wakeup call with the front desk, using the phone beside the bed.

Parker didn't wear his tie, stuffing it into his jacket pocket.

Claudio slipped on his briefs and met him at the door. "It was nice evening."

"Yes." Parker smiled but he was not happy.

"I will say thank you to Claire."

"Right. Have a good flight back." Parker kissed Claudio's cheek and left the room. When the door closed behind him, he felt like shit and headed home, pissed off, feeling cheated and stupid, and wishing he had said no to his cousin from the beginning.

~

Mason sat in his den with his laptop, working. He checked his phone, too often, for a text or voicemail reply from Dack but never got one. He hadn't heard from him since last night at the hotel and knew that Dack went nowhere without his phone and was attached to texting so much so he'd go through withdrawals without it. Mason had called twice, didn't leave a message either time, and texted him once asking him how he was, early that morning. He refused to continue reaching out to Dack, and got the hint.

He surfed the net looking at similar magazines to theirs and seeing which advertising accounts they had landed.

It was nearing ten and Mason had a busy day of errands, laundry, and catching up on paying bills. As he inspected his bank statements online, he spotted a few charges to his credit card account from Dack. The champagne, the expensive bubble bath and candles—everything for their Valentine's romance had been on his tab. Was he upset? He wasn't sure yet. The costs weren't obscene and they had all been for him.

It just seemed 'typical Dack' to plan the event, buy the accessories, and then bill him.

He grew weary of the internet and shut it down. Wearing his soft sweatpants and a T-shirt from J Crew, he lay lengthwise on the sofa in his living room and turned on the television. He was bored. It was Saturday night and he imagined since he had a 'boyfriend' these weekend nights would be spent together, be it out having fun or snuggling on the couch. But it seemed if he didn't make an 'appointment' with Dack in advance, and request…no, *beg*, him for his time, then Saturday nights he was on his own.

Mason pointed the remote at the television and surfed through the channels, knowing he had to do something to get out of the pit he had dug for himself. He just wasn't sure he was ready to do it.

## CHAPTER 8

Monday morning Parker entered the office feeling as if he had a sign on his forehead that read *loser*. He was so upset with himself for letting that model suck him off he sat home all day Sunday and wrote up blogs, both for his personal website and for the magazine's, trying to decide if any of his ranting was appropriate for publication or it was just him blowing off steam.

Henry was standing near Dack's desk, leaning on it as Dack reclined in his chair, playing with a rubber toy head that when you squeezed it its eyes, ears, and tongue popped out. Parker didn't even want to look Dack in the face after seeing him in the restaurant with another man. As he dragged his chair out from his desk to sit down, he overheard Henry telling Dack, "Just write him a love note. You know Mason can't stay mad at you."

Parker wondered if Mason had figured out the latest transgression. He wouldn't get involved in the mess between those men if someone paid him to. Parker booted up his computer and stuck his removable drive into the port to retrieve what he wrote over the weekend and see if in the light of a new day it was even slightly appropriate for the magazine.

"...or follow him into the men's room and give him a blowjob," Henry said.

Parker resisted rolling his eyes, but who was he to judge? He opened the button of his suit jacket and scooted closer to his computer to check on inter-department emails.

Henry shut up suddenly so Parker looked their way. Mason had just come into the office and walked right behind Henry and Dack without greeting either, entering his office and closing the door.

"Go in there!" Henry prodded Dack. "Apologize. You want me to write you a note on what to say?"

Parker had no idea why Henry was so invested in that doomed relationship. He kept his mouth shut and opened the files he had downloaded to re-read.

"Go. Go on!" Henry pushed at Dack's shoulder.

Dack tossed the toy on his desk and got up, walked to Mason's door and rapped his knuckles on it. "Babe?"

Parker cringed. *Babe?*

Dack entered the office, closed the door and all Parker could hear was muffled tones.

Henry walked by Parker. "Hi, Parker, how was your weekend?"

"Good." He nodded, looking at Henry and wondering why he did the things he did.

"Are you seeing anyone?"

"Not at the moment."

"Do you want me to fix you up with someone? I know lots of single guys."

"No. Thanks, though." *Oh, a Miss Match. Got it.*

A slightly raised tone of voice came from the closed office. Both he and Henry glanced at it.

Henry leaned down to whisper, "Lover's spat. I guess Dack didn't call Mason all weekend. He lost his phone."

Parker choked at the lie.

"Well, the poor guy. He can't help it," Henry said, wringing his hands. "He's so in love with Mason. I think those two make the cutest couple."

"Do they?" Parker tried not to puke. "Well, time to work."

"Do you need a cup of coffee? I'm headed that way." Henry pointed to the employee lounge.

"I'll get it. Thanks though."

"And if you need a man to take out to dinner. Let me know." Henry flipped his wrist. "I have some friends who would eat you up!"

"Thanks. No." Parker smiled tightly and opened up a file that read, '*Men and Fetishes...Can we become addicted to testosterone junkies and models too pretty for their own good?*'

~

Mason crossed his arms. "You lost your phone."

"Yeah. I swear." Dack held up his right hand in a vow. "I couldn't find it anywhere."

"And so you couldn't think of another way to contact me? Like use another phone or email me?"

"We didn't have plans, did we?" Dack crossed the room, moving close enough to touch Mason.

"Not formally."

"Ya miss me?" Dack straightened Mason's tie sensually.

"I always want you around. I thought you wanted me around too."

"Aww. You are so cute." Dack pressed his cock against Mason's, making Mason rush with chills. "I like how much you want me."

"So..." Mason backed up so he could think. "You found your phone now?"

Dack took it out of his pocket, as proof. "Here it is."

"Good."

"Love the new wallet." Dack headed to the door.

"Good. So, when—"

"Back to work." Dack left the office.

"When..." Mason stared at the door, which was left open. He could hear Dack's voice as he spoke to Dixie, laughing.

*I'm never going to tame you, am I?*

Dack's laughter, though it was not aimed at him, felt as if it was a painful jab. Mason dropped down on his chair and rubbed his face, trying to get into his work.

~

Parker helped Henry, who was the art director, when he asked him for his opinion. No, Parker hadn't been an art director before but he knew a good layout when he saw it. He scrolled through the mockup pages on the computer making notes.

Beside him Dack was on the phone, actually working, setting up shoots for the lifestyle section of the magazine.

After sending Henry his opinion, Parker typed up a new blog, seeing how cynical the ones he did over the weekend were. Yeah, he kept the title but wrote a softer column. *'Men and Fetishes...Can we become addicted to testosterone junkies and models too pretty for their own good?'*

*'...Fetish, (noun) an object, idea, or activity that somebody is irrationally obsessed with or attached to.*

*'...Aren't we all as a species irrational? And who sets those perimeters to begin with? Too much booze? Too much pot? Sex addicted? Hoarder? The stereotype for a fetish doesn't fit the dictionary definition. Isn't a fetish a quirk? Can you say you have a uniform fetish without overloading your home with police or Gestapo uniforms?*

*'...Fetish is such a harsh word for such a moderate sexual addiction. Men love what? Everything. You pick an idea, a type, or an article of clothing and someone will worship it to 'obsession'.*

*'...Is loving something or some 'thing' in particular, a fetish simply because it gives us an erection? What if it's a person? What if we love muscle men, models, bears or motorcycle mamas? Do we cross the line from adoration to fetish-obsession?*

'*When is enough enough? And who gets to decide?*

'*...must we go through an intervention? Or do we look into the mirror one day and say, Hey, buddy, time to quit that bad habit?*'

Hearing Mason's door open behind him, Parker had an impulse to hide his computer screen, as if the fetish he was writing about was between Mason and Dack. He resisted the impulse and pretended to reread his copy, when in reality he was keenly aware of every move Mason made.

The handsome forty-year-old looked at Dack as he walked behind him, an empty coffee cup in his hand, on his way to fill it in the lounge. Dack ignored him, laughing while he spoke on the phone, his fingers tapping at the keys of his computer, working. Yes, a miracle—Dack was still working!

Parker spotted Henry watching as well, as if he were the concerned mother hen worried about her hatchlings. Did Henry initially fix Dack and Mason up? *Hmm, the plot thickens.* Or...when Mason said that he had met Dack years ago, how was Henry involved? Did he arrange the reunion?

Parker continued writing while Mason vanished into the lounge.

'*...fetishes, the occult, religious fanatics, satanic worship? Can we really place an obsession for an 'irrational activity' in the same league as loving a man with muscles or a big cock?*

'*...When does a fetish turn into a sickness? And who gets to decide on initiating the intervention?*'

Mason exited the lounge with a steaming cup.

Parker got lost on him. Lost on his tall, fit frame, his angular jaw, his sleek designer suit and perfectly groomed brown hair...

As Mason walked behind Dack, who was still wheeling and dealing via the phone, Mason obviously couldn't resist him. He touched Dack's hair affectionately.

Dack ignored him, Henry appeared about to stand and applaud, and Parker...he went back to his work, fighting with himself to not be jealous.

*You only want what you can't have. Love stinks!*

~

Mason sat at his desk with his hot cup of coffee and sent a flirty email to Dack. '*Hey sexy, how about I take you out for dinner tonight and a hot fuck?*' He sent it and smiled, going over his list of calls and emails for advertising clients.

After an hour he checked for a reply. Nothing was sent by Dack. Curious, Mason stood and looked out of his door. Dack was working on his computer. He knew the emails popped up when they were sent. He felt confused and sat back down, resending it, waiting. Nothing came back.

Out of curiosity, Mason sent an email to Sigourney, seeing if the computer was working today or the internet decided to go wonky. He wrote, '*Got us two new advertisers for April.*'

She wrote back immediately, '*You rock!*'

The email was working.

Mason called Dack on his work phone. He could hear it ring. Dack picked up, "Dack Torington."

"Hey."

"Hi." Dack's voice sounded unenthused.

"Did you get my email?"

"Yeah, sorry. Busy tonight."

"Doing?"

"Ya know. Guy stuff."

"Guy stuff? And I can't be included? I'm a guy." Mason walked to his door and looked out. Dack's back was facing him and he could see Parker typing at his computer beside Dack.

"You hate that shit. You know, me and Yoseph out partying. Maybe another night."

Mason tried not to grow annoyed.

96

Dack spun around in his chair and they met gazes. Dack said to Mason directly, "Don't be mad."

Parker took notice and looked over his shoulder.

Mason disconnected the phone and returned to his desk. Was he mad? Yes. And weary of the game.

~

Parker watched Dack hang up the phone and frown. He couldn't resist. He asked Dack, "Was that Mason calling you?"

"Yeah. He's a possessive fucker."

"Are you two in a committed relationship?" Parker knew he should butt out.

"Yeah. I guess so. Why?" Dack gave Parker's crotch a deliberate glance. "You interested?"

"In you?" Parker tried not to choke at the absurdity.

"I'm flattered, Parker. You're hot." Dack winked at him and stood up from his desk, buttoning his suit jacket. "Gotta go. Maybe some other time."

"What?" Parker choked on his laugh.

Dack winked at him again and walked away.

*You egotistical jerk. I wouldn't touch you with a ten foot pole encased in a three inch thick condom.*

Parker shook his head at the thought and got back to his work.

By five he had written two columns, one for the magazine blog, one for his own, which was now connected to all the social networks promoting the magazine, and he shut down his computer.

One by one the employees waved goodbye, and Dack had never returned from his…whatever he was doing when he left. It certainly wasn't his job to keep tabs on the flounder.

Parker heard Mason's office door open. Henry seemed to sprint to his side and behind Parker he heard Henry say, "He really loves you, Mason, he's just so busy."

*Busy?* Parker was about to comment. *Busy what? Tricking with old men for cash?*

"It's okay, Henry. Don't feel like you have to be responsible for Dack." Mason met Parker's gaze when Parker looked over his shoulder.

"He's a good man, Mason. He's just young. He loves you very much." Henry seemed to be a one-man cheerleading section, all for Dack.

"Okay. Thanks, Henry." Mason appeared slightly embarrassed by Henry's gushing.

Parker stood and pushed his chair under his desk, buttoning his suit jacket. He didn't deliberately time his leaving with Mason, but it didn't bother him that he had.

He followed Mason out of the office, staring at his broad shoulders, the way the suit fit him, his legs, his conservatively cut brown hair...*gawd! Why are older men so infatuated with twenty year olds?*

Mason glanced over at him as they left the office at the same time, headed to the elevator.

"Hey," Mason said, sounding uncomfortable.

"Hey." Parker felt the same way. What did they have to talk about? How lousy it was fucking pretty young men?

"Liked the new blog post." Mason smiled wryly.

"Oh? Read it?"

"Sure. It's published through Judas now. Why not?"

Parker nodded, smirking.

"Where do you come up with your ideas? Fetishes?"

"Ya know. Everywhere." The elevator door opened and they entered it together.

Mason pushed the button to the parking garage. "What's your fetish?"

Parker looked him straight in the eye and said, "Men close to my age."

Mason seemed to gulp, or gasp silently, his hazel eyes widened.

Feeling clever at the little *zing!* Parker looked down at his feet and smiled to himself. The door opened to the parking lot level. "See ya."

"See ya." Mason waved, still appearing slightly off guard.

Parker chuckled as he walked to his car. *Yeah, I like ya. Deal with it.*

G. A. HAUSER

## CHAPTER 9

Mason looked back at Parker as Parker climbed into a sporty
Hyundai Veloster. Before he got into his own car, he watched
Parker drive off, out into the Monday evening rush hour. Two
thoughts occurred to him.

Was Parker writing about him in his blog? Model-musclemen
fetishes? And…was Parker attracted to him, or mocking him?

*Men close to my own age?*

Mason sat down behind the wheel and turned the ignition
key. *That was a direct slam. But how am I supposed to take it?
An insult or a compliment?*

"Both." Mason's lip curled in annoyance as he backed out of
the spot. He was wondering if perhaps this 'relationship' with
Dack was just a fetish and not reality—like an erotic fantasy
where he has a pretty partner on his elbow and feels good about
himself.

"Well?" Mason glanced at his eyes in the rearview mirror.
"Feel good about yourself, Mason?"

He grumbled and turned the news report on louder, trying to
drown out his thoughts.

He didn't want to go straight home, not to an empty condo,
boring television or more work. Instead he crawled through the
congested streets to find parking near some of his favorite bars in
West Hollywood. Old haunts. Ones he'd not been to in ages.

100

Managing to sneak into a parking space that was free after five p.m., Mason checked his phone and thought about calling some friends to see what they were up to, but discussing Dack and his bullshit would be top on his buddies' list of topics. And he wasn't up to it. Not tonight. Besides, who went out on a Monday?

Maybe he'd meet someone new. A man 'close to his own age'.

Mason pocketed his car keys and fastened the button on his suit jacket as the evening cooled down substantially. He tucked his tie into his suit to stop it flapping in the breeze and walked down Santa Monica Boulevard.

Who was he kidding?

This was a young boy's town. Gay men his age retired to San Francisco. Most of the little twinks didn't give him a glance. How old did he look? Wasn't forty the new thirty?

Here in WeHo it felt like the new eighty.

Were these boys even legal?

Mason hadn't strolled around West Hollywood for ages. And now he recalled why.

He peeked into a glass storefront at the reflection of his face. Did he look ancient? He hadn't been concerned with his own age before. Not really. He was doing well financially and had dated quite a lot of young men. Dack was just the latest conquest. He did lean towards younger men in their twenties but…

Mason waited at a traffic signal of a large intersection. Two slender men were standing nearby, both in slinky revealing outfits, jeans with so many holes in them they should be shorts, and jackets opened to midriff T-shirts. One bleach blond, the other an African American with long weaves. Both were short in stature and so damn adorable Mason tried not to stare.

The blond caught him peeking.

He elbowed his pal and they both gave Mason a gander, a good once over from head to toe, grinning.

Mason thought he would die of embarrassment. Did they think he was an old letch?

"Hey," the mocha skinned beauty said to him, very flirty.

Mason looked behind him to see if he was the one that was being addressed. They giggled at him, seeing his modesty.

"Hey?" Mason wished the traffic light would change.

"You like young men?" the blond asked, tongue in cheek.

"How old are you two?" Mason had to know.

"Eighteen." The blond laughed as if either he was lying or it was a joke.

The mocha prince elbowed his friend and said, "Sixteen, but we won't tell."

"Oh, God." Mason was about to die and looked around to see if vice police were preparing to descend on him in a sting operation netting old sex offenders. The light changed and he hurried across it, not looking back.

*Sixteen? Is that what this area has become? A haven for babies?*

*Oh no. No way.*

Mason scooted past the go-go clubs with twinks showing off their packages in G-strings, and looked for a bar that didn't cater to gay men. He couldn't deal with it right now. He stopped at a Mexican restaurant and peered inside. It had a bar area and seemed very upscale and conventional. Mason entered it and spoke to the hostess who was seating people. "Do you mind if I just sit at the bar?"

"No, go right ahead. It's the same menu as the restaurant." She smiled.

"Thanks." Mason approached the sparsely populated bar area, since it was only Monday and just after five. He sat down and loosened the knot in his tie.

"What can I get you, sir?" the young bartender asked.

"Old scotch!" Mason shook his head and didn't elaborate, picking up the menu from a holder on the bar.

*I am out of my mind.*

~

Parker changed into his running outfit for a quick evening sprint and lifting weights in the complex gym before dinner. He put his T-shirt on over his head and located his reflective jacket so he wouldn't be road kill in the darkness. Tucking his key into the pocket of the neon green windbreaker, Parker heard his phone signal a text or email. Before he left the apartment he glanced down at it to see if he needed to respond. To his astonishment he found a picture of Dack, taken of him stripping? Dancing? He had no clue but the guy was showing off his cock at a bar or club. The email had been sent to the entire staff of the magazine and Parker wondered if that had been intentional or...oops.

He hoped Mason was with the guy taking the picture, because if he wasn't, that was a pretty nasty thing to do to him.

Just as Parker put the phone down to prepare for his run, it buzzed again. He had to pick it up. Dixie had replied, *'You wild man! Say hi to Mason for me!'*

Several other co-workers also added their comments when Dack sent another one that read, *'Shit! delete this! I didn't mean to send it!'*

Parker laughed and then put the phone down and headed out for his run, chuckling at what a complete idiot Dack was.

~

Still seated at the bar, Mason held his phone in his hand and read the updates and exchanges in fury.

*'Thanks for sharing, Dack, but we already knew you had a great bod!'*

*'Do you want to do a nude spread for our next issue?'*

*'Oh honey, put that away or you'll poke someone's eye out!'*

One scotch down, and working on his second as his steak fajitas were being prepared, Mason began replying, not 'to all' but to one. *'Where the hell are you? And who are you flashing your dick to?'*

He hit send and his temper was flaring so hotly he began to feel flushed. He removed his jacket and lay it across his lap.

Dack didn't respond. Lord knew where he was. And if he was with Yoseph, what he was doing exposing himself in a public spot? Drunk again, out going wild with his peers, and showing no modesty or maturity whatsoever.

Dack responded to 'all' *'delete it! OMG, don't tell Mason!'*

*'Don't tell Mason?'* Henry sent, *'who took the pic?'*

Mason put the phone down on the bar and rubbed his face in agony. The bartender brought his plate of food out to him as well as a cloth napkin wrapped around silverware. "Can I get you anything else?"

"Refill this." Mason finished his drink. "Thank you."

"My pleasure."

~

Parker returned from his run, sweat dripping down his face and chest. He kicked off his shoes and stripped the day-glow jacket off, then headed to the kitchen for water, anxious to shower. He peered at his phone and checked what he had missed. When he read the stream of comments, including Dack asking for people to delete the photo and not tell Mason, Parker felt horrible for Mason.

"Oh well. You decided to date a douchebag, not me." He gulped the water, removing the rest of his sweaty clothing to take a shower.

As he stood under the water, scrubbing, he wondered how much a man could endure. It was inspiring a new blog about tolerance and thick skin—forgiveness vs humiliation and being a doormat.

He had to admit, he felt sorry for Mason. Yeah, the guy invited this kind of crap when he began dating someone like Dack, but…

*Do any of us know what we are in for when we first start to date a man?*

Parker finished up in the shower and slipped on a pair of jeans and an old NYU sweatshirt. He looked at the phone again and out of kinship for what he had just been through with Claudio, he emailed Mason directly.

'*Hey, I'm here if ya need a friend.*' He sent it and opened the refrigerator to prepare a salad for dinner.

His phone buzzed. Standing at the counter tearing lettuce into a bowl, Parker read Mason's response to him. '*Thanks. Good to know there's one person who isn't participating in the pigpile.*'

Parker took a moment to read all the preceding emails that had been sent between staff members, 'to all' and most had been ugly, tormenting, or prompting Dack to show more of his body.

Parker knew it was good natured teasing but when you are down and out, it came across as mean in spirit. He'd been there. With Lee. He knew.

"Oh fuck it." Parker called Mason's number after drying his hands on a dish towel.

"Hello?"

"Mason, it's Parker."

"Oh, hello, Parker. Enjoying the email debate about Dack's cock?"

*Uh oh.* Mason was drunk. "No. I'm not. I just thought you might need a small bastion of sanity in the insanity."

"Well, Parker Douglas, an ally in a sea of ignoramuses."

"Where you at, Mason?" Parker worried he would get behind the wheel.

"Stupid enough to go to WeHo and see little boys in skimpy outfits."

"Don't drive drunk." Parker leaned against the counter, his arm crossed over his chest.

"Glad someone gives a shit."

"Look. I live in WeHo. I can give you a lift home."

"I can take a fucking cab."

Parker rubbed his face tiredly. Silence passed between them.

"Did you hang up?" Mason asked.

"No. I'm here."

"Why do you care?"

"I'm just that kind of guy. I like you, Mason. Why shouldn't I be upset when I see that kind of shit from people we work with?"

"You like me? You don't even know me."

Parker blew out a breath in frustration. "Fine. I don't like you. See ya."

"Wait."

Parker looked at the bowl of lettuce and was hungry for dinner.

"Sorry. I'm just...you live in West Hollywood?"

"Yeah. I do. Beverly Boulevard."

"I'm just around the corner."

"Where?"

"The fancy Mexican place on Santa Monica."

"You...you want me to come there? Make sure you get home okay?"

"Yeah. Come here. Make sure I get home."

Parker tilted his head at the tone. "Are you mocking me?"

"No. I'm mocking myself. Look, don't worry. I'm a big boy and I can find my way home. Bye."

"Hello?" Parker looked at his cell phone. The line was disconnected. After groaning in frustration, Parker put the food back into the refrigerator and changed his clothing. All the while he was telling himself, *You idiot! Don't get involved! This guy's as big a douchebag as the man he's dating!*

But Parker was like that. He couldn't ignore people who were in need. Maybe he was the biggest douchebag of all.

He walked briskly, hands deep in his leather jacket pockets to the restaurant. It was four blocks from his apartment house. He entered the establishment and looked around the area.

"May I help you?" the hostess asked. "One for dinner?"

"No…I'm…" Right before he said he was meeting someone, he spotted Mason at the bar under dim lighting and on his own. "I found him." Parker nodded and walked into the bar area, which wasn't overly crowded since it was Monday evening.

He leaned against the barstool beside Mason and noticed him dazed off, staring at a half-eaten plate of food. "Mason?"

Mason looked up, startled as if he'd been deep in thought. "Parker? You didn't have to come. I was just going to hang out until I felt good enough to drive. I'm fine."

"Can I join you?"

"Sure." Mason gestured to the stool Parker was leaning against.

Parker thought Mason did indeed sound less intoxicated. He removed his jacket and hung it on the back of the bar stool, sitting down. Since he was beyond starving, he picked up the menu.

The bartender approached him. "Can I get you something to drink?"

"Just ice water. Thanks." Parker nodded and read the menu.

"Parker. You didn't have to come. I feel like an idiot asking you to."

"It's okay. I told you. I live right around the corner."

When the bartender brought Parker's water, Mason said, "I'll take some water too, and put whatever my friend is ordering on my tab."

"Of course." The bartender left to get another glass of water.

"The fajitas were good." Mason pointed to his plate.

"You sure? You barely ate any of it."

"It wasn't because it wasn't good. I just lost my appetite."

Parker noticed Mason's phone on the counter near him, as if he'd been hovering over it all night.

The bartender brought Mason's water. Parker said, "I'll take the chicken burritos, side of rice." He handed the man the menu, and it was tucked back into a stand on the counter.

"Coming right up." The bartender gestured to Mason's plate. "You want me to wrap this up for you?"

"No. Just take it." Mason appeared miserable.

The plate was removed.

Parker sipped the water and leaned his elbows on the bar, staring at Mason's reflection in the mirrored wall behind the bottles on the counter.

"Ya ever feel like the biggest schmuck on the planet?" Mason sipped the water.

"Yup. I think at one time or another, we all do."

"I feel like I can't show my face at work tomorrow."

"You?" Parker choked at the absurdity.

Mason rubbed his eyes and Parker could tell this was wearing on him heavily.

"Parker?"

"Hm?"

"You ever date younger men?"

Immediately Parker thought of Claudio. "Yes."

"Any luck with them?"

"They're good for one thing." Parker thanked the bartender as he placed tortilla chips and salsa in front of him.

Mason laughed sadly. "Yeah. One thing."

Parker ate the chips, wondering since Mason was not too drunk to drive whether he'd overstepped his bounds and made a bad decision on coming here.

"Are you seeing anyone?"

Parker finished chewing and glanced at Mason. "No."

Mason nodded, as if digesting the information.

Parker wanted to ask Mason if he thought Dack and him were 'exclusive'. What he wanted to do was tell him about spying Dack with the old man at the bar Saturday night. But really, was it his job or his business? He and Mason weren't even friends. They were work colleagues and only that for a week.

"Fetish." Mason sipped the water, staring into space. "Yeah. You know what the deal is, Parker. You know."

"Need an intervention?"

"Yeah. Maybe I do. I keep making the same mistakes over and over."

Parker sat up as a plate of food was set before him. The aroma was tantalizing. "That looks great, thanks."

"Good. Enjoy," the bartender said. "Can I get you dessert, sir?"

Mason shook his head. "I'm good."

Parker unrolled the cloth napkin and put it on his lap, cutting the food and seeing steam billow out. "I eat out too much. I can't really afford it."

"I hear ya. My fucking condo dues and mortgage is killing me as well."

"Then why are we both here?" Parker chuckled. "I went food shopping yesterday to avoid this."

"I'm paying."

"No. You're not." Parker blew on the food.

"Tough. I am."

"I'm not one of your kept boys." The minute Parker said it he regretted it. It was formed from his jealousy, and not from Mason's generosity. "Sorry. Mason, I'm sorry."

"I deserved it." Mason's phone hummed. He looked pained to have to read it.

"Are they still at it?" Parker ate the food.

Mason picked up the phone, holding it out as if he may need reading glasses if he held it too close. "It's Dack, begging my forgiveness." Mason put the phone down, not responding.

"Is he a good guy, Mason? Or just a good fuck?"

"Lately he's neither." Mason continued drinking the water, eyes facing forward, into the reflection behind the row of bottles.

"He's not even fucking you?"

"No. I mean. We are still having sex. At least oral."

Parker wondered if he continued prying if he was only torturing himself, or maybe gong over the line with Mason. What the hell. "You giving him or him giving you?"

"Him giving me. He…"

"He?"

"Lately…" Mason looked uncomfortable.

"Look, Mason, don't talk about it if it's not my business."

"Who else do I have to talk to about it? Henry? Dixie?" He made a noise of frustration in his throat and looked at the empty water glass as if he wished it were vodka.

"Okay." Parker kept eating. "Lately?"

Mason frowned and said, "He doesn't want me to give him oral and we aren't having sex."

"But you did in the beginning?"

"Yes."

Was Parker going to tell Mason about the other guy? "Do you think he's seeing other men?"

"Oh fuck yes." Mason laughed in anger, shaking his head and setting the glass of ice down.

"Oh." Parker used a tortilla chip to push the food onto his fork. "At least you know."

"I don't know. I mean, he's not telling me what he's doing, but I'm not that much of a moron to think he's not…"

"Cheating."

Mason rubbed his head through his hair.

The bartender filled Mason's water glass. "Still doing okay?"

"Fine." Mason forced a smile and Parker knew how hard that must be.

After the young man walked away, Parker said, "I wasn't going to tell you."

"Tell me what?" Mason peered at him suspiciously.

"I was out to dinner Saturday night and I spotted Dack."

Mason said nothing but was very interested.

"He was laughing with some old guy at the bar. Looking cozy."

"Old guy? Like me?"

"No!" Parker lowered his voice. "Christ, Mason. You're not old. Are you fucking kidding me? No. This guy, he was like near seventy or eighty."

"Shut up." Mason laughed and shook his head in disbelief, picking up the water to drink. He muttered, "Eighty," as if it were absurd. "If anything I expect Dack to be with a nineteen year old."

"Nope." Parker shrugged. "Just telling ya." He finished his food and put the silverware on the plate, wiping his mouth and hands with the napkin. The bartender took the empty plate and refilled Parker's water as well. "Can I get you dessert?"

"No. I'm stuffed."

After the bartender left, Mason asked, "What was he doing with this eighty-year-old?"

"He was standing between the guy's knees, touching his hair, his cheek, wearing skintight clothing and drunk on his ass."

"Eighty?"

"The fucker dripped of cash. Solid gold Rolly, expensive suit, the works."

"No. No way."

Parker took out his wallet and removed twenty dollars from the billfold.

"I said I'd pay." Mason held back his hand.

"Then that's the tip." Parker tossed it on the counter.

"Hang on." Mason touched Parker's arm.

Parker did, waiting as Mason put enough cash with the twenty to cover the bill and tip. They walked out together, Parker putting on his leather jacket, Mason, his suit jacket.

"Are you okay to drive?" Parker asked.

"Fine. Perfectly fine." Mason asked, "Which way to your apartment?"

Parker wondered if Mason thought he was going to get an invitation. He wasn't. "I live that way. Why?"

"We're headed in the same direction. I parked that way also."

Parker nodded. They began walking down the nearly vacant street. The wind was cold and blowing hard from the west.

"You're a decent guy, Parker. Thanks for coming down here."

"There was no way I was going to let you drive drunk." Parker stopped when the block for his apartment came up. "I live up that way."

Mason nodded.

They stood together in awkward silence. Did Parker want him? Yes. Did he want him with an appendage named Dack attached to him? No!

Mason held out his hand. "Thanks."

Parker received that hand. When they touched Parker felt instant heat and attraction for Mason. Out of his mind attraction. The grip grew tighter, hotter.

112

Parker looked down at the contact then up into Mason's light eyes that were glowing in the streetlamp's halo. Mason tugged Parker towards him. Their bodies brushed but they did nothing other than stare at each other, in a dare? How far would this go? Who would flinch and back up first?

~

Mason knew his life was a mess. There was no doubt he'd made many bad decisions along the way. In his not too distant past, men like Parker were nearly invisible to him—Parker was not a strikingly gorgeous-ego-reeking-pretty boy. Or a man with a bulging ripped chest and attitude...

But now, seeing Parker as a friend *and* a man, Mason was smitten. Parker was absolutely gorgeous, inside and out. And what a difference the 'inside' beauty made. It was as if Mason had an epiphany. Beauty was indeed, skin deep.

In the chilly breeze he felt the heat of Parker's legs and hand like an invitation into a cabin with a roaring fire on a winter's night.

He drew Parker even closer, waiting for Parker to be insulted and push him away. Their crotches touched in the dark shadows of the buildings and swaying trees. He could hear Parker's breathing now, when he couldn't before.

With his free hand he ran up Parker's leather sleeve to his shoulder, with his right, he drew Parker's clasped hand to his own chest. Parker's lips parted and he appeared either excited or anxious.

When he felt pulsating from Parker's cock against his thigh, Mason shivered with a chill down his spine. Mason drew closer still, towards Parker's lips.

The throbbing of Parker's cock became more pronounced as their bodies tightened. Before their lips made contact, Parker lowered his eyes and looked away.

Mason got his answer. He released their grasp and stepped back.

"I..." Parker pointed to some area down the street. "I have to..." He backed up.

Mason watched him leave, staring at him as he escaped.

He didn't stop staring until he discovered which building Parker had vanished into. Only then did he exhale and recuperate from the lust, walking to his car.

~

Parker stood inside his lobby door, leaning against it and closing his eyes as he struggled to get his body under control. Shaking, craving that man, but not the baggage that went with him, Parker jogged up the stairs to his unit and struggled with the key his hands were trembling so badly. He managed to get inside, then covered his face and moaned in agony.

I Love You I Hate You

## CHAPTER 10

Tuesday morning, Parker stopped at the employee lounge for coffee before sitting at his desk. He was slightly nervous about last night, but had slept all right, not stewing over it.

"Hey, Parker." Sigourney entered the lounge, carrying an enormous white ceramic mug with the magazine's logo on it. "Loved your new blog! Did you see how many hits we got overnight on it?"

"No. Good?" He set a cup under the espresso machine and put a little sealed plastic pot of French vanilla flavored grounds into the compartment.

"Oh my God! Never got such a huge overnight head count before. How many can you do a week?"

"I can do one a day, and still write a column for the monthly edition."

She pumped her fist and stood beside him, picking out hazelnut flavored espresso to brew next for herself. "The blogs can be small, but I want the magazine columns to be big. Not just a skimpy half page. Get down and dirty with it. Full page text with great shots from Dack's portfolio to keep it sexy."

He laughed as he waited for the last of his coffee to drip into his cup. "Really? No. I can't do that."

"Yeah. You can. I don't mean anything gross. Just talk about sex. Talk about relationships. Do your Carrie Bradshaw on steroids."

115

"And the blogs?" He stepped back, pouring soy milk into his mug as Sigourney made her coffee.

"How about four hundred words tops. Post them every night before you go home." She turned the machine on. "Look at the stats, babe. Look at the stats!"

"Will do." He smiled and carried his coffee out of the lounge. The minute he did he spotted Dack and Mason, standing in front of Mason's office, which was right near his desk. As Parker approached, blowing on his hot coffee to sip, he could tell Dack was apologizing, looking 'so sad' or at least putting on a great act.

Trying not to stare, Parker set his cup down and slowly pulled his chair out, he couldn't help but overhear.

"...Mason, it was just a prank. I was drunk. Yoseph—"

"I don't want to hear it."

"Baby...let me make it up to you..." Dack purred.

Behind his back Parker envisioned Dack nestling up, maybe adjusting the knot in Mason's necktie. He turned on the computer and removed his stick drive from his pocket to plug into the port transferring what he had done at home onto the work computer.

"Mason, baby...tonight. I'll make it up to you tonight. Okay?"

"I'm busy tonight."

"Tomorrow...all weekend. You know that trip you want to take me on? To Hawaii?"

Parker cringed and then cursed himself for reacting. He hoped Mason wasn't looking.

"Dack, let me get back to my work."

Parker heard the door to Mason's office close. He peeked.

Dack was standing still, appearing slightly stunned. Perhaps his tactics worked up until now. He met Parker's eyes and Parker almost spun around to avoid it, but it was too late.

I Love You I Hate You

At first Dack's expression appeared annoyed. But soon it morphed to something else. "You free tonight, Parker?"

"Huh?" Parker was shocked silent. *Are you kidding me, ya slut?*

Dack gave a paranoid glance at Mason's door, as if Mason may open it and find him flirting. "Some other time, Parker. I have an appointment right now." Dack put his hand to his ear in a clichéd gesture and said, "Call me," quietly.

Parker's mouth was gaping as he watched Dack leave, a smug grin on his face and a cocky strut. The urge Parker had to yell after him, "Are you kidding me, ya jerk? In your dreams!" was huge, but he just grumbled and turned to his typing for release.

*'Ego- the great equalizer between the pretty and the plain...So? You're attracted to beautiful boys who you want to fuck? You are not alone. Many men and women are smitten by looks and sex appeal. Just watch celebrities pose on red carpets, flaunt their looks and fashions at posh parties. Who wouldn't want one of those living dolls on their arms or in their beds? Who wouldn't? Me for one. When your date is more concerned with his reflection and looks for it everywhere from the mirrors on the walls to the back of silver spoons, you know you may just have a problem.*

*'...the question is...are airheads worth the high maintenance? And why can't an average guy or gal get a break?'*

Parker glanced behind him at the closed office door and shook his head at the absurdity.

~

By lunchtime, Mason had made a number of email contacts to get ads lined up for the next month's issue, even hitting High Street retailers across the pond in the UK for a big spread on their glossy pages. He left his office to head to the local deli to buy a sandwich. Parker was not at his desk, and most of the staff

117

was taking a break for lunch, either eating in the employee lounge or out. He buttoned his suit jacket, and as he made his way to the lobby, he was able to see inside the lounge. Parker was there, eating, laughing with Dixie and Morris. When the handsome man laughed his light eyes sparkled and dimples appeared near his mouth. Mason slowed his pace to admire him.

When Parker's gaze slowly met his and they connected, Mason instantly recalled last night and how close they came to a kiss. He began to smile to convey his affection for the lovely man, when Parker's attention was drawn back to Dixie. Mason could see Dixie touch Parker's forearm to bring him back to their conversation.

Mason felt his own expression drop and he continued out to the elevator, standing in front of it, checking on the time. Even if he didn't have Dack lingering around him, Mason didn't think beginning another office relationship was smart.

As he stepped into the elevator, which had several people inside headed to the street level, Mason thought to himself, *When have I ever done anything smart?*

He stepped out of the elevator at the ground floor and walked down the block to a café, crowded with office workers rushing to eat on their hour break.

It was a gorgeous day with bright blue skies and a brisk breeze. But the beauty of the weather didn't make a difference to Mason. He had to do something about his life and do it soon.

~

"I don't know how he stands it," Dixie said, sipping a healthy carrot high-potency vitamin drink and eating a vegetarian sandwich. "If my girlfriend was out without me? Flashing her tits into a camera phone?" Dixie blew out a breath in anger. "I'd clock her one."

Morris nodded. "Mason does take a lot of crap from Dack. I mean, I know Dack really loves the guy, but, come on."

Parker didn't think Dack loved anyone but Dack.

"I don't know, Morris," Dixie said, chewing her food. "Dack's like...all over the place. Mason seems like a 'settle down' kind of guy."

"It's the age difference," Morris said, then looked at Parker. "Right?"

"No comment." Parker met their gazes and noticed them both giving him curious looks. To cover his faux pas, he said, "I haven't been working here long enough to know about them on a personal level."

"Yeah, but come on," Dixie said, "Mason is forty and Dack is only twenty-six."

"Going on fifteen," Parker muttered under his breath and ate his last bite of the turkey sandwich he had made that morning at home.

"Huh?" Morris leaned closer. "Going where?"

"Nothing." Parker shook his head, knowing his jealousy was to blame. He could have kissed Mason last night. But then? If Mason and Dack got lovey-dovey here at the office? He'd go ballistic and be furious with himself.

"But you write blogs about relationships, Parker," Dixie said, capping her carrot juice bottle. "You're the expert. You're the one who we will go to for all our advice from now on."

Her smile made him realize she was teasing, or at least he hoped so.

"You're our Ann Landers," Morris added, laughing.

"Who?" Dixie tilted her head.

Morris rolled his eyes. "You see, Parker. Age. The great divide." He looked at Dixie and said, "Carrie Bradshaw circa 1955!"

"Gawd, Morris! I wasn't even born then!" Dixie stood and rinsed her plate.

"Well," Morris said, throwing out his trash from his lunch, "There were tons 'Ann's' after she was gone. Never mind."

"Huh?" Dixie again looked perplexed.

Parker didn't even try to explain it. "Google her." He stood and tossed out his napkin, pouring himself a fresh cup of coffee.

Leaving Dixie and Morris to debate gossip columnists, fact and fiction, Parker carried his mug to his desk and noticed Henry hide something he was doing, under cover of his own desk.

Parker couldn't imagine what he was up to.

As if realizing he'd been caught, Henry put a small package he was gift wrapping back on his desk, and continued to tape the paper neatly.

Ignoring it, Parker sat in his chair and brought up the work he was doing before he stopped for his lunch break. He sipped his hot coffee and reread the text. Henry tried to tiptoe behind him, which was absurd since the office simply wasn't that large, and went inside Mason's office.

Parker swiveled on his chair to watch. Henry placed the wrapped package on Mason's desk and tried to sneak out, meeting Parker's gaze and appearing guilty.

"Is it Mason's birthday?" Parker asked.

"Um, no." Henry closed Mason's office door quietly. "I…well, it's just a little something from Dack."

"From Dack." Parker knew that was a lie, but had no doubt Henry was going to tell Dack to say exactly that.

"Yes. Well, Dack's not good at wrapping gifts, so I offered."

"Uh huh." Parker spun back to face his computer, not wanting to know.

"You see, Dack and Mason, well, their relationship is…complicated. And Dack, being so young, needs a little help from time to time to keep things running smoothly."

120

"Uh huh." Parker was running a dialogue in his head about how absurd that was and how Henry needed a new pastime. He began typing, splitting his attention.

"And...I adore them both, you know? Well, I just think with a little mentoring, Dack will be a fine husband for Mason one day. He's just slightly wild and needs a little taming."

"Uh huh." *Oh my God, can you say 'delusional?'*

"And...well, Mason is such a good influence on Dack. Dack is so young and impressionable. He loves a father figure—"

*Grandfather figure more like.*

"He really wants to be a star. He's trying to get on Celebrity Get Off My Island Fitness Stars..."

Parker swallowed his snarky comment, biting his tongue.

"And he will be a star of some reality show. I mean, he's just what the producers of those shows want—big, brawny, handsome..."

*Stupid.* "Uh huh."

"But you know, if Dack does get a dose of Hollywood, well, he'll need a good man like Mason to keep him grounded and away from drugs and wild parties."

"Uh huh." Parker stopped typing and looked at Henry. "Like he's not doing now."

Henry appeared sheepish. "Well, he's not doing drugs. At least I don't think he is."

"Uh huh." Parker went back to typing and sniffed loudly, indicating Dack probably did cocaine, but it went right over Henry's head.

Henry finally shut up and Parker heard someone come into the office, talking. He glanced up to see Dack on his cell phone, yes, he looked the part of a gorgeous young celebrity, but Parker knew Dack's head was filled with celebrity dust.

Henry rushed him, grabbed Dack's arm and began whispering into the ear free of the phone.

Parker knew he was filling Dack in on the gift 'he' had bought to pacify Mason's anger. Dack told his telephone contact to hang on and listened to Henry eagerly.

Parker returned to his blog and wrote, '*Enablers...are the people who supply us with our dose of poison and fixes for our habits, just as bad as the addicts? Me thinks so!*'

Dack nodded, smiling and then met gazes with Parker to give him a sexy wink.

*As if!* Parker sneered and kept his focus on his work.

~

Mason ate his lunch in the café, needing some down time from the office crew. Bringing back a large double espresso, he returned to his office, seeing everyone at their desks working, even Dack. Dack smiled slyly at him, giving his groin a good leer, which even though Mason thought it was over the top, it made his cock tingle. He ignored him, tried to catch Parker's eye, couldn't, and opened his office door. On entry he noticed a small wrapped package on his desk. Mason set his cup down, took off his suit jacket and closed his door. He sat at his desk and eyed the dark blue shiny paper, perfectly folded and taped. Which immediately made Mason suspect Dack had not wrapped it and either Henry had, or a store employee had.

He succumbed to the curiosity and opened it. The box was marked Tiffany. That surprised him. Mason opened it and inside was a tie pin with an Audi symbol on it. Now he was stunned.

A second later a light knock came to his door and it opened before he could call out, come in. Dack, appearing right off the pages of their own hot sticky magazine, slipped in, closing the door behind him.

His chiseled square jaw was dark with his shadow, his teeth were perfect, like snow white caps, and the sexy leer made Mason stiff in his trousers.

"From you?" Mason asked, simply because Dack's beauty was too much for him.

"Mm hmm." Dack ran his hand down his own chest to his balls.

Mason stood and walked over to him, feeling not only a blast of heat from Dack's unbelievable sex appeal, but his own realization that he was nothing but a pushover.

"Thank you." Mason stared at Dack's full lips.

Dack looped a finger into a belt loop on either side of Mason's trousers and tugged him close. Mason connected to Dack's hips and was kissed. The scent and raw sensuality of Dack overwhelmed Mason instantly.

Dack left Mason's lips and sunk to his knees, opening Mason's fly. When Dack had Mason's cock inside his mouth, Mason cupped Dack's handsome face and moaned.

*I love you. Oh God I love you.*

~

Parker knew exactly what was going on. Henry gave Parker a 'thumbs-up' as if the plan had worked. Parker shot him a smile, which was pure sarcasm, but Henry didn't know.

Parker glanced at the closed door and had a bad feeling. A feeling sex was going on inside that office. He rubbed his face and sipped the rest of his coffee which was going cold. The last gulp left a bitter taste in his mouth, and he hoped so did Dack's cum in Mason's.

He shook off the sense of jealousy and annoyance and tapped keys.

'...*Mythology...not only the stuff of legends. Every culture has stories to tell about life's hard lessons. Narcissus stared into his reflection and fell in love...and fell in—Atlas was doomed to hold the weight of the world on his back—Pan lusts after nymphs but is always rejected because he is ugly...*

'...There are stories from Aesop about tortoises and hares, slow and steady wins the race...Hans Christian Andersen reminds children not to eat houses made of candy...

'But as adults, do we ever learn? We are still children, reaching for candy, kissing our own faces in mirrors, and carrying the weight of the world on our backs...

'The one lesson I want to know is...does slow and steady win the race? Or do nice guys finish last?'

The door opened behind him. Parker heard low masculine laughter, love croons. He tried not to wince. Like he was a rubbernecker at a traffic wreck, dreading the beheading and craving it, he peeked.

Dack closed the door behind him, gave an exaggerated wipe of his mouth with the back of his hand, indicating in no uncertain terms he had just swallowed a mouthful...and whispered to Parker, "Wish it was you?"

Parker was so unprepared for the egotistical comment he didn't have that snappy answer.

Dack chuckled as if he already knew the answer, and returned to his desk, picking up the phone, appearing very self-satisfied. He gave Henry the 'thumbs-up' then did an obscene gesture for him. Dack pretended to hold a cock in his hand at his mouth, and used his tongue to push his cheek out, as if that cock were inside his mouth. It made Henry laugh and Parker cringe.

He typed, '*Answer...Nice guys finish last, but tops finish first.*'

~

Mason pinned his necktie with his new white gold tie tack. He brushed his tie flat and tucked in his shirt, sitting at his desk, feeling sexually satisfied and happy. Getting back to his emails, he was about to continue asking his clients for money for the next issue when his phone hummed. He peeked at it and noticed it was from his bank. Slightly concerned, he read the text message, which was automated.

'*Alert- a suspected unauthorized transaction has occurred. Below is the listed transaction. If you have authorized this transaction, please follow the link and accept the payment, if not, notify us immediately.*'

Suspecting a scam, or phishing expedition, Mason went to his online bank account directly to check his recent purchases. When he spotted the one in question was from Tiffany and for over a thousand dollars, Mason gasped and stared down at his tie tack in amazement. "Are you kidding me?" He removed it and put it back in the box, intending on returning it. *I hate you, you fucked up asshole!*

He was about to go to the office door, open it and yell his head off in front of the staff. But since he was duped again, Mason called his bank first. "Yes, hello. I am having unauthorized charges made to my account. Can you cancel that card and send me a new one?"

Mason waited as the banking employee verified his information.

"Did you not make that last purchase in question, sir?"

"No. I did." He certainly wasn't going to blame the bank or Tiffany for Dack's behavior. "I just want it canceled from today on."

"Done. A new one will be sent to your home address. Let me verify that address…"

Mason was so angry he was about to scream. "Yes. Thank you so much for your help."

"My pleasure. Anything else I can do for you today, Mr Bloomfield?"

*Yes! Kill my boyfriend!*

"No. Thank you." He hung up and typed a nasty text to Dack, but erased it. He was so angry at the moment, he just slammed his phone on the desk and stewed, staring at the Tiffany box and wondering how he could be so stupid.

~

After Parker saved his work in progress he felt the coffee begin making its way through him. He picked up his mug and walked passed Dack's desk, which was vacant. After dropping off his mug in the lounge, placing it into the dishwasher, Parker headed out of their office to the men's room just down the hall. He opened the door and couldn't see anyone at the urinals, but did see feet under one door of a stall.

Parker stood to do his business and heard whoever was inside the closed stall, hiss as if he may be uncomfortable. He tried not to eavesdrop because it was not only rude, it was nasty to listen to someone having 'issues'.

He finished, and right before he flushed the urinal he heard someone say, "Fuck!" then a stream hit the water in the toilet.

Parker flushed the urinal and headed to the sink to wash his hands, trying not to even think about what was going on behind him inside that stall.

He dried his hands on paper towels, checked his face and hair quickly and prepared to leave the room. Just as he did the stall door opened and he caught Dack, appearing flushed and quite 'pained', not to mention embarrassed.

Parker had too many thoughts in his head to even consider the implications of a man, hiding in a stall, struggling to pee, let alone it being Dack!

Dack, trying to cover up what may or may not have been going on with his urinary tract, pretended to be just fine and dandy, and headed to the sink to wash his hands and preen.

"Anyone ever tell you you have a great ass?" Dack grabbed his own groin. "Wouldn't mind bending you over the bed."

Parker rolled his eyes and left the restroom, headed back to his desk. *Okay. What do ya got, kid? A kidney infection, or the clap?*

"Ew." Parker made a face to himself in disgust. As he returned to his desk and the last half hour of work, he recalled Mason telling him, *"He doesn't want me to give him oral and we aren't having sex."*

*Aha! Dude! He's got an STD and at least he's not sharing it with you! Oh, fuck.*

"You pathetic asshole!" Parker looked at the door Mason was behind. "You too." He shook his head and reread the latest blog before he posted it.

## CHAPTER 11

Mason closed down his computer and left his office, the box with the tie tack in his hand. Dack and Parker were still at their desks. Without a glance at either, Mason stormed passed them both to the exit and waited outside the office entrance at the elevator. He was still fuming. Now he couldn't use his credit card until he was issued a new one. Though he should throttle Dack, he was still deciding how to handle it. He had to break it off. Had to.

"Come on!" He poked the call button again and again but the elevator wasn't coming to his floor any faster. When someone stood behind him, Mason glanced over his shoulder. Parker was there, looking down, maybe at his own feet.

Mason blew out a loud breath in frustration and stepped aside so they were not in a line but side by side.

"You okay?" Parker asked.

Mason gripped the box tightly and decided whether blowing up and telling Parker what had happened was wise.

"Uh oh." Parker looked concerned. "Did you find out?"

Mason spun to face him head on. "Yes! How did you know?"

"Some things aren't easy to hide." Parker shook his head.

The elevator finally opened and they both stepped into the empty space. Parker hit the lobby button and they were closed into privacy.

"I swear, Parker, I'm such a fool. I keep putting up with it."

128

"Did you get anything for it?"

Mason tilted his head curiously. "What?"

"You know. Like penicillin or something? Those new strains can't be messed with."

Before Mason could ask what the hell Parker was talking about, more people heading home stepped onto the elevator, pushing them to the rear. "What?" Mason asked him again, softly.

Parker's mouth parted like he was about to say something, then he shut up.

In silence they rode down to the ground floor parking area and Mason waited until he and Parker could speak privately. He touched Parker's arm and asked, "What are you talking about? Penicillin?"

"Uh…" Parker bit his bottom lip. "Never mind."

"Oh no you don't." Mason grabbed Parker's jacket sleeve and brought him over to where their assigned spots where in the parking garage. He nudged Parker to lean back on his Audi and asked, "What the hell did you find out about Dack?"

"Shit. Mason." Parker threw up his hands.

"What the fuck? He has some fucking STD?" Mason felt sick.

"I think so."

"He told you that? He said, 'hey, Parker, I got gonorrhea'?"

"No. Nothing like that." Parker rubbed his forehead and appeared upset.

"Parker!"

"Fine! I was in the men's room about a half hour ago. Someone was in the stall, in agony trying to piss. Okay? Guess who!"

"Oh fuck!" Mason threw up his hands, still clenched to the box and about to explode.

"Get checked out, dude."

"Fuck!" Mason slapped the box onto the trunk of his car and rubbed his face with both hands in anguish.

"I could be wrong." Parker picked up the little box and opened it. "Is this what he got you?"

"Fuck!" Mason had never even gotten the crabs. Never. He was safe, always, and just the thought that Dack had picked up something, and didn't mention it...

"Nice. Henry has great taste."

"Henry?" Mason stopped short. "Henry got that?"

"Um..." Parker covered the lid on the box. "I think I better shut up and go home."

"Dack gave Henry my credit card details?"

"What?" Parker choked on his laugh of disbelief. "Oh, man. You've got a live one, Mason. Detach and run away."

Mason fell back against his car and slid down it to crouch low. He hung his head and tried to think, but he was going out of his mind.

Parker looked around the parking garage but they were in between cars so Mason knew they couldn't be seen easily. Parker lowered to be at eye level with Mason, leaning on the car beside him. "Mason, first things first. Go to your doctor."

Mason nodded, rubbing his jaw. He couldn't concentrate.

"You told me he doesn't let you suck or fuck him."

Though he heard Parker's words, Mason wasn't really listening. He felt so betrayed and used, he was beside himself in misery.

"Mason?"

"Huh?"

"Ya need someone to take you to the doctor?"

"What? No. Huh?" Mason tried to get to his feet. Parker helped him. "No. I can make an appointment and take myself. I'm not that pathetic." He made eye contact with Parker. "Am I?"

130

"No. But I know how shaken up I'd be right now if I thought someone gave me the fucking clap."

"Fuck!" Mason checked his watch. "I wonder how late my doctor's office is open." Mason scrolled through his phone apps trying to find the listing for the doctor so he could call and make an appointment. He looked up when Parker made a noise, clearing his throat.

Dack was headed to his car, whistling spinning his keys around his index finger, looking as if he hadn't a care in the world.

Mason went crazy, rushing at him.

~

Parker jumped in surprise as Mason gripped Dack by his shoulders and threw him against a car fender. "What did you do to me?" Mason yelled, his voice breaking with nearly a sob.

"What?" Dack was stunned and stared at Parker. "Did he say we fucked? He's been gasping for it, Mason, but he's lying!"

"Oh, you gotta be kidding." Parker shook his head in disgust.

"You gave me an STD, you slut?" Mason shook Dack roughly.

Parker took one step to intervene but stopped.

"No! I didn't! Did that fucker tell you that?" Dack again shot an accusing glare at Parker.

Parker held up his hands and shook his head. "Don't involve me, dude."

"Dack!" Mason appeared homicidal and Parker didn't blame him.

"He wants me! He's been coming on to me since he started working here! He's just jealous, Mason. Don't believe him!"

Mason threw Dack away from himself and huffed for air. He pointed his finger at Dack and warned, "I'm getting tested. If I got anything, I'll fuckin' beat you down."

"Ya didn't get anything from me, dude. Chill." Dack held up his hands.

Mason stormed to his car, grabbed the tiny box off the trunk and held up it up to Dack. "And you're cut off! Ya got that? No more spending on my account!"

Parker choked on his cough of shock. Henry bought that with Mason's credit card? The gall was overwhelming Parker. He'd never seen anything like this.

Mason climbed into his car, slammed the door, and peeled out, leaving a cloud of burning rubber in his wake.

Parker couldn't catch his breath from all the drama. He heard a shoe scuff and was brought back into focus by Dack's sneer. "If ya wanted me to suck you off, I would have. You didn't have to fuck it up for me and Mason."

"What?" Parker laughed at the joke.

"Dude, all ya had to do was ask." Dack climbed into his red Charger and backed out of his space, and then he too vanished.

Parker's mouth hung open as he tried to think. "You're blaming me? Are you out of your mind?" It took him a minute to recuperate. Parker headed to his own car and sat behind the wheel, trying to make sense of things that seriously had no basis in reality. "And I think my life is crappy?" He started his car and headed home.

~

Mason was so angry he couldn't think straight. He drove to Rodeo Drive and gripped the box in his hand after finding parking. Lost in his head, worried about having something nasty and not knowing it, Mason was so preoccupied he nearly walked into someone coming out of the jewelry store.

"Sorry." Mason shifted his stance to let the two men pass.

"No problem." The young man with long hair smiled at him.

Mason thought he looked vaguely familiar but was distracted by a handsome older man who was holding the door open for his young companion. He met the older man's blue eyes, then glanced down to see a gold police badge and holstered gun on his belt.

Mason tried to think where he had seen the two men before as they walked down the sidewalk and disappeared from his sight. He entered the jewelry store and stood still for a moment, gathering his thoughts.

"May I help you, sir?"

Mason shook off the odd sensation that he knew those two men somehow and approached a salesman behind the glass counter. He handed him the box. "This was a gift and I wondered if I can return it." Mason reached into his suit pocket and unfolded the bank statement he'd printed, showing the purchase.

"Do you have the receipt?"

"No. Like I said. It was a gift. Look. You see it was purchased on my credit card?" He showed the man the paper.

"This shows 'a' purchase on your credit card from our store, but it doesn't show that this item in particular was purchased."

Mason was in no mood to argue. "The guy used my credit card without my permission."

"Have you reported it to the police?"

"No. But I told the bank to cancel the credit card."

"One moment." The young man walked over to another man in a suit to confer.

Mason took his phone out of his pocket and called Dack. Amazingly, he answered. "Dack."

"Hi, Mason. I'm sorry. Don't be mad at me."

"Whatever. Do you have the receipt for the tie tack?"

"Huh? No. Why?"

"Does Henry?"

"You're returning it? Mason! You love your Audi."

"Dack!" Mason lowered his voice and noticed the two men who were discussing his predicament glance over. "Dack, I don't want to spend over a grand on an item I can't afford right now."

"Can't afford? Mason, you're rich."

"No. I'm not rich." Mason rubbed his eyes tiredly.

"I can ask Henry. He probably has the receipt."

"Okay. Please, Dack. I don't want the tie tack and I can't deal with it right now."

"Mason..."

"What?"

"Let me make it up to you."

Mason looked up when the clerk returned to him. "I'll call you back." He hung up and gave the man his attention.

"I'll credit your account, sir. Thanks for being patient."

"I was just calling someone to see if I could get the receipt."

"It's fine. The manager remembers the man buying it here yesterday. No problem. The purchase plus tax is the exact amount on your credit card paperwork."

"Thank you." Mason nodded in appreciation and waited as the man returned to a cash register and reversed the charges.

Mason looked at his phone again to see if he could find his doctor's office number and he did.

Tapping his shoe impatiently, Mason waited as he was given a new receipt with the charges credited. He thanked the man and left, passing an armed security guard at the door.

Once Mason was seated behind the wheel of his car he dialed his doctor's number and stared out of the windshield as the traffic drove slowly by and the evening was already dark by five-thirty.

"Dr Hudson's office, may I help you?"

"Yes, this is Mason Bloomfield. I'm a patient of Dr Hudson. I was wondering...I..." Mason was so humiliated he couldn't believe he had to ask this question. "A...my....I may have been exposed to an STD and I need a test." He felt his face go hot and his stomach churn.

"Okay, Mr Bloomfield. I can give you the address of where we have a lab that can take your blood and you can come in to see the doctor for an examination."

"What's the soonest I can come in?" Mason tried to think if he had any symptoms.

"Let me check. Can I put you on hold?"

"Yes." Mason's call waiting beeped. He looked at the phone, saw it was Dack and didn't answer. The woman returned to his call.

"Mr Bloomfield?"

"Yes."

"We can fit you in very early tomorrow morning. Can you come around eight?"

"Yes."

"Good. Why don't you do that first, and then the doctor can give you information on where to go to give a sample of your blood. There's a lab in the building he works out of tomorrow, and that will make it easier."

"Okay."

"Do you want me to email you his information? Or have you been to the LA Medical Center to see him previously?"

"No. I've just seen him at his private office on Sunset Boulevard."

"Okay. Let me send you the information and a confirmation of your appointment."

"Thanks. You have my email info?"

"I do. I just sent it to you now."

"Thank you." Mason hung up and checked his email in box. The information was there. He listened to Dack's voicemail.

'*...baby! the minute I found out I had something wrong I stopped fucking you and didn't let you suck me. But it's not an*

*STD! If you got something like that, it wasn't me! I'm sorry. I should have told you I was sick. Forgive me. Oh, baby, forgive me.'*

Mason hung up and started the car, driving home, angry, frustrated, and heartbroken. *I hate you, you fucking liar.*

He parked in the underground lot of his complex and, with his head down, feeling like shit, he walked to the elevator. Once he was inside his condo, he tossed his keys and phone on the kitchen counter and headed to the bedroom to undress. Naked, he stared at his dick and wondered. He entered the bathroom and turned on the light, inspecting his cock. Nothing appeared wrong. He urinated and felt no burning, trying to decide if perhaps some of the symptoms had not surfaced yet. If Dack had burning in his urinary track, surely Mason would too, eventually.

He moaned unhappily and showered, simply because after thinking and talking about being infected made him feel filthy. He rinsed himself under hot water, soaping up, checking every inch of his crotch for a sore spot, something. Maybe he was okay. Dack did stop having sex with him, and he didn't let Mason suck him.

He shut off the water and stood a moment trying to think, and maybe not think.

After he was dry and in a soft pair of sweatpants and an old UCLA sweatshirt, he poured a glass of whiskey for himself and sipped it. He heard his phone buzz with a text. With the glass in his hand he leaned his elbow on the counter and read the text.

Dack. Begging.

Dack only begged when he was in the doghouse.

Mason picked up the phone and dialed, sitting on the soft velour sectional sofa, sipping the drink, trying to decompress.

"Hey."

"Hey," Mason repeated. "Am I bugging you?"

"No. I just finished my frozen pizza. Ready to either zone in front of the crap box or computer."

Mason liked his voice. It's deep mature tone. "I just wanted to thank you for earlier."

"Why? What did I do? I was the bearer of bad news."

"News I needed to hear. I appreciate it." Mason heard Parker sigh deeply.

"Did you go to the doctor yet?"

"No. I made an appointment for eight tomorrow. I just returned the tie tack and came home." He sipped more of the whiskey.

"Well, look, at least you'll know."

"It's been a while since I've had a complete physical and been tested for everything. Maybe I'm due."

"Do you fuck around a lot?"

"No. I don't fuck around at all. But…"

"But…Dack does."

Mason closed his eyes and slouched low in the soft cushions of the couch. "Yeah. Dack does."

"I assume you and he always use protection."

"Yes. Always. If I give him a blowjob I make him wear a condom."

"Jesus. If you think he's that bad, why—"

"Because I'm a schmuck." Mason finished the drink and set the glass on a side table. "I'm a shallow asshole who gets off on the youth and looks of young men. Okay? There. I said it."

"You're not the only one. A lot of guys fall into that trap."

"They have a sexy lure, but they're a bunch of fucking narcissistic bastards."

"Yup."

Mason rubbed his eyes with his thumb and index finger. "You…you ever do it? Ya know. Fuck someone just because they're young and hot?"

Parker let out a low laugh.

"No?" Mason had no idea how to interpret it.

"Yes. I do succumb now and then to the temptation."

Mason exhaled loudly. "Then it's not just me."

"Oh hell no. But when I do it? I have instant regrets and there's no follow up. It's like it was good for the moment, and then it's gone. And I feel like crap and beat myself up."

Mason chuckled. "Man, we are alike."

"I don't want that kind of man. Mason, I am so tired of that stupid shit."

Mason leaned his elbow on the arm of the sofa, pressing the phone close to his ear. "What kind of man do you want, Parker?"

A pause followed where Mason could hear Parker breathing, maybe thinking things through. Parker then said, "Mature, not into games, loyal, smart, funny…"

Mason chuckled again. "Mr Impossible?"

"Mission Impossible." Parker laughed with him. "No. He's out there. I still have hope."

"How will you find this perfect man? Do you hunt on the web?"

"Oh, hell no. You think that's the way to find a decent guy?"

"No. I don't. Not by a long shot."

"I'm just leaving it up to fate."

Mason heard his call waiting again. He peeked. It was Dack. He ignored it. "Fate."

"Yeah. I mean, I'm not actively on the hunt. I was through my twenties and it didn't do me any good."

Mason rubbed his inner thigh near his cock. He wasn't turning himself on, he was worried. "You ever catch anything, Parker?"

"My boyfriend in college gave me crabs. I nearly kicked the shit out of him."

"I guess it's about trust."

138

"Yeah. Trust and maturity. Those are top on my list, Mason. Top on my list."

"Top?" Mason tried to smile. Take this conversation out of the rut it was in. He heard Parker chuckle and was glad.

"Yeah," Parker replied, "A top is high on my list."

"Really? I took you for a real dominant male." Mason's cock did tingle now.

"I can be. I guess. It's about preference. Maybe that's why I like my men slightly older."

"Is forty a good number for you?"

"A perfect number."

Mason heard his call waiting beep again and reality hit. "I suppose dating a jerk that may have an STD from a self-absorbed dipshit isn't 'top' on your list."

"Well...not normally."

"I don't blame you. I feel as if I'm coated in something nasty. And I wouldn't touch me either."

"Mason. We all make bad decisions."

"I keep making them. Why, Parker? Is my self-esteem so fucked up I need a trophy on my arm to gain confidence?"

"You tell me."

Mason figured the answer was obvious. "Am I keeping you from anything?"

"Just a night of work or the nightmare of TV."

That brought a smile to Mason's face. "You haven't been in LA long."

"No. Not long enough to make any real connections with people."

"It's hard relocating and making friends..."

"At our age?"

"I wasn't going to say it." Mason picked up his glass and tipped the last drop on his tongue, wanting more.

"I'm good with myself. I'm not one of those guys who needs to be out every night to feel as if I'm normal."

Mason stood and carried the glass to the counter, pouring more whiskey into it, enjoying this conversation with Parker immensely. Man to man. Not man to immature, conceited boy.

"I admire you." Mason capped the bottle and returned to his spot on the sofa. "You're grounded and seem to have your act together."

"Somewhat. I'm not immune to the occasional bad date. And I broke up with a guy because he cheated on me."

"Back in New York."

"Yeah. Fucker. I thought I had found my Mr Impossible."

"How could he cheat on a guy like you?" Mason sipped the whiskey then rested it on his leg.

"How? Because he found a hot young model to fuck."

"Parker, you're really hot yourself. Christ, the body on you."

Silence came from the other end. Mason listened carefully and asked, "Are you there?"

"Yeah. I'm here."

"Don't you think you're attractive?"

"For an older guy?"

"No!" Mason shook his head and put the glass down on the side table, sitting up. "Parker, you're really fucking sexy."

More dead air followed.

"Why do you keep shutting down when I tell you that?" Mason was confused.

"I just don't know what to say back. Are you fishing for a compliment?"

"Huh? No." He thought about it. "Why? Do I look old and nasty to you?"

"Uh. No." Parker sounded amused.

"Do…" Mason rubbed his forehead. "Do you think I'm attractive?"

"Yes."

"The other night…" Mason thought about how close they came to a kiss. "If I didn't have Dack in my life, would you have kissed me?"

"Yes."

"If…if I get rid of Dack?" Mason straddled his legs and sank into the sofa cushions, head on the back, staring at the ceiling. "Would you go out on a date with me?"

"Uh…"

Mason flinched and closed his eyes. "Never mind."

"No. Hang on."

"What am I thinking?" Mason scrubbed his hand over his hair. "I may have a fucking nasty bug and I'm asking you out?"

"Mason! Shut up for a second."

Mason did, biting his lip, not used to the potency of a powerful smart man debating with him. He liked it. It was an amazing turn on.

"Ya calm?" Parker asked.

"No. I'm a raging inferno, but I'm listening."

"Christ, you're a fucking live one, Mr Bloomfield."

"Answer the question. But first let me put in a disclaimer."

"Go for it."

"If I'm clean. Ya know? Not infected with anything nasty. Okay? I mean, I wouldn't want to go with a guy—"

"Mason?"

"Yes?"

"Shut up?"

He did.

After a moment, Parker said, "Though I hate the idea of being sought after by a guy on the rebound—"

Mason was about to protest but Parker anticipated it and kept talking.

"Hang on, Mason…let me finish." Mason could hear Parker take a deep breath. "Yes. Yes, I would date you. But I'm thinking about the office, and the nightmare of Dack on my back. And yes, I meant to make that rhyme."

Mason replied, "Oh, God. I don't know what to think now. I hate to admit how much I want to see you socially."

"Why do you hate to admit it? Because I'm not a twenty year old fashion model?"

"No. Because I don't want to scare you off. I don't want you thinking I'm rebounding or desperately need a man to cling to."

"Do you?"

Mason gave it serious thought. "I admit. I like a man in my life. But not a man who is unreliable, can't show up when I make plans with him, and pretends to show affection when he just doesn't have it in him."

"You just described Dack."

"I did."

"Was he good in the sack?"

"Not exceptional, no. But he was pretty to look at."

"He wasn't even a good fuck?"

"Wow. Am I going to share that with you?" Mason picked up the whiskey and gulped some, liking the burn and the slight headiness he was getting from having an empty stomach.

"You don't have to."

"It'll end up in one of your blogs."

Parker laughed loudly and Mason enjoyed the sound of it. "How about tonight I'll spare you the gory details. Let's leave that intimate talk for another time."

"Our first date?"

Mason smiled in delight. "Yeah. Is it too early to ask you out?"

"Did you break up with Dack?"

"You were there when I did."

"Really? In the parking garage. That's the end?"

"It was for me. I'll make sure Dack knows it was for him too."

"Rebounding. You are rebounding, Mason, don't deny it."

"Can't we call it 'moving on'?"

"A rose by any other name."

Mason chuckled. "Damn. I'm not used to being with someone smarter than I am."

Parker laughed. "Yeah. Sucks, huh?"

"No. It's having the opposite effect."

"Well, that's interesting, to say the least. Okay, Mr Bloomfield. How about we see how the week progresses, and decide on Friday if we should actually make a date-date."

"Fair enough."

"Goodnight, Mason."

"'Night, Parker." Mason disconnected the call and checked his text messages. Dack had written four—*'Baby! I'm sorry. Call me. Please.' 'Mason, I'm begging you, forgive me.' 'I'll never lie to you again! I swear!'*

And the last one read—*'U R a fuckin' hottie. Meet U in ten!'*

When Mason read the last one again he realized Dack had mistakenly sent it to him!

"Are you kidding me?" He deleted all the text messages and the voicemails from Dack and dropped his phone on the sofa, finishing his drink and staring into space.

## CHAPTER 12

The next morning, Parker straightened his tie in the mirror of his dresser of his bedroom. The conversation last night with Mason gave him a lot of food for thought for both his life and his blogs and columns. His phone buzzed with a text and he picked it up off the dresser and read one from his cousin Claire. *'You never thanked me. Lousy in bed?'*

That reminder of his own night of youth and model idolizing felt like a slap in the kisser. He dialed his cousin's number, checking the clock and knowing New York was three hours ahead and most like Claire was busy at her desk.

"Well?" She answered her phone, obviously seeing his name on her caller ID.

"Don't do that to me again."

"Are you kidding me?" She coughed on her laugh. "I thought you'd be begging me for his home address or another hot dude."

"It sucked. It was like being with a cardboard cutout." Parker headed to the kitchen and removed the sandwich he'd made last night for his lunch, putting it into a plastic bag while he cupped the phone between his ear and shoulder.

"Honey, you're not supposed to exchange intellectual conversation with those boys. They're just good for a romp."

"Claire." Parker grew annoyed. "I thought you knew me better than that."

144

"Know you?" She laughed. "You went out with him, didn't you? Did you at least get a goodnight kiss?"

Parker thought about the blowjob and groaned. "I have to go to work."

"Okay, cuz, later!"

He disconnected the call and now had to rush. Who was he to criticize Mason? He was just as bad!

~

Mason sat in the waiting room of a busy medical center. He usually made appointments to see his doctor at his small office practice, but obviously this was urgent to Mason and he didn't want to put it off.

The staff behind the administration counter had already given him a 'wallet biopsy' and even taken payment before he was actually seen by the doctor. When did visits to the doctor and having to pay up front get this bad? He couldn't recall. He rarely visited the doctor except when he needed antibiotics for the flu. After what felt like an eternal wait, he was called into the back area and led to an examination room.

The nurse asked him to step on a scale and then took Mason's blood pressure after he removed his suit jacket.

She documented the results and said, "He'll be right in. Meanwhile, take off all your clothing and put that robe on."

He looked at the blue cotton material with white strings that was folded on a chair.

"Opening in front." She left the room.

Mason was trying to bite back his fury and unknotted his tie, laying his clothing on a chair as it was removed. When he was naked he slipped the robe on and felt cold in the sterile room. He sat on the crackling paper-covered examination table in just his black socks and leaned his palms on the edge, hunched over and feeling like a fool.

After the mistaken text message Dack had sent last night, Mason had no further contact from him. Thinking about seeing him at the office made Mason irritated, but at least he could tell Dack in person to *get lost*! Of course, the old adage of you don't shit where you eat began to run through Mason's head. But he had, and intended to again, with Parker.

There was a light tap at the door and his doctor peeked in. Seeing Mason ready, he entered and closed it behind him. As Dr Hudson washed his hands at the sink, he asked, "So, Mason, you've come in for some tests?"

"Yeah. My partner picked something up, I have no clue what, and just told me last night." Mason sat upright and folded his hands on his lap.

Dr Hudson dried his hands on paper towels and put on a pair of rubber gloves. "Any symptoms?"

"No."

"What do you want to be tested for?"

"Everything. Including AIDS."

The doctor made eye contact with him. "Have you been using protection?"

"Yes. No exceptions."

"So you just want to rule everything out."

"That's the idea."

"Okay. Go ahead and stand up for me."

Mason got off the table as the doctor waited.

"Let me examine you first."

Mason nodded and the robe parted, since it wasn't tied. As his doctor touched his genitals, Mason stared at the ceiling trying not to be humiliated he was even being checked for a sexually transmitted disease. Was he a college punk? *Fer cryin out loud.*

"Any burning while urinating?"

"No."

"Pain ejaculating?"

146

"No." Mason felt his cheeks go red and couldn't watch the exam.

"I'll need a urine sample and a swap from inside your penis. then I'll send you down to the lab for them to take a sample of your blood."

Mason cringed and nodded, wishing he could strangle Dack.

~

Parker filled his coffee cup from the employee's lounge coffee machine. Considering it was just homemade espresso, it was excellent. Henry entered the room carrying a mug with the magazine's logo.

"Hi, Parker."

"Hi, Henry."

Henry placed a tea bag into his cup and used hot water which was from a spigot on the coffee machine. As the men stood side by side, Henry said, "Thanks for your input on the design layout. I'm so glad Sigourney hired you. You can do it all."

Parker chuckled. "I love being creative. In my last job they let me do a lot of the behind the scenes work."

"But? You like writing your columns best."

"Yup." Parker moved away from the machine and poured soy milk into the coffee cup.

"I read your last blog. Was that about Dack and Mason?"

"Not specifically." Parker blew on the coffee and sipped it, liking the vanilla flavor and scent.

"I guess you heard the latest."

"About?"

"Well, Dack called me frantic last night and asked me for the receipt for that tie tack."

"Why do you want those guys to be together so badly?"

"I don't know. I'm a sucker for romance."

"Do you have your own partner?" Parker studied Henry's thinning hair, his pudgy cheeks and round figure.

"Yes. Oh, I've been with Charles for decades." He waved his hand dismissively.

"Oh." Parker nodded and started leaving the room. Henry was behind him, holding his tea.

"I just thought they'd make a good pair, Dack and Mason. They seemed right for each other."

"Oh well. You tried." Parker shrugged.

"You think I should nudge Mason to keep working on it?"

"I think you should let the two men decide what to do from now on."

"Yes. I know you're right. I just want them to be happy."

Parker kept his comments to himself. He had no idea if Henry knew just how many men Dack was seeing behind Mason's back. And involving himself in office gossip and politics were a no-no in Parker's book. He brought his coffee to his desk and noticed Mason's office door was closed, but he had a doctor's appointment. Dack's desk was vacant.

It was still early, and a few employees were just arriving, getting their coffee and beginning work at their desks.

Parker put his cup down and sat in his chair, opening the button of his suit jacket. He booted up his computer and began working on his new column.

'*The Gift That Keeps Giving...Bad Love. The New STD...*'

~

It was nearing ten when Mason made it to the office. He felt flustered and irritated by the morning appointment with his doctor. All the tests the doctor could perform immediately proved negative. Everything else had to wait for lab results.

Mason was not happy.

As he entered the office he could see Dack was not at his desk. Parker was, typing away, and the rest of the staff was busy doing their work. Mason didn't want to disturb Parker so he walked behind him, leaving him alone and opening his office.

Once inside, he removed his jacket, loosened his tie and sat down, getting caught up on his calls and emails.

Henry poked his head in and knocked on the open door. "Mason?"

"Yes, Henry."

"Here's the receipt." He appeared sheepish as he entered the room, holding out a slip of paper and dropping it to Mason's desk. "I'm sorry. I need to stay out of it."

"You do. I can't figure out why you keep covering up for Dack." Mason didn't regard the receipt and kept reading emails, splitting his attention. "I mean, he's a fuck-up, and I keep thinking everything *you* are doing, *he* is doing. When all this time it's not him being kind and considerate, it's you!"

"I know! I know!" Henry nodded, head down, hands clasped in front of him.

Mason stopped looking at his computer and swiveled his chair to face Henry. "Man, you could have saved me a lot of aggravation if you'd just butted out and let Dack be Dack."

"I know. I just thought Dack could benefit from someone of your maturity and experience."

"He could. But he isn't going to and doesn't want to."

"Mason. I am so sorry."

Mason held up his hand and said, "Fine. It's okay. Just no more interfering."

"Will you break it off with him?"

"Yes."

"Poor Dack."

"Poor Dack?" Mason blinked but didn't vent his anger. "Let me get back to work."

Henry nodded and walked to the door. "Do you want this open or closed?"

Mason looked up, able to see Parker from the open door. "Open."

149

Henry nodded again and left.

When Parker turned to look over his shoulder, he and Mason caught eyes. Mason smiled. *You are a good looking man, ya know that?*

Parker smiled back.

Mason craned his finger at him. He liked the fact it made Parker laugh and blush. It appeared Parker waited for Henry to move away before he stood. He leaned against Mason's door frame and gave him a wonderful smile. "You survive?"

Mason beckoned him in. "Close the door."

"Uh oh." Parker chuckled and did, walking closer to the desk.

"Yes, I survived. But now I have to wait for the results."

"It'll be quick. Not like the old days."

"Old days." Mason rolled his eyes to be funny.

"You know what I mean."

"I do." Mason and Parker stared at each other. "I suppose it's still too early for you to consider a date?"

Parker blushed brightly. "Yeah, here's a good pickup line for you. 'I just got back from the doc getting tested for syphilis, wanna fuck?'"

"Ouch!" Mason flinched but laughed. "I'm asking you to dinner, not a fuck."

"I know. I can be a real sarcastic butthead when I wanna be."

"New Yorker." Mason smiled, rocking in his chair gently, his hands clasped over his lap.

"LA snob." Parker grinned mischievously.

"Dinner?"

"Let me think about it. It's only Wednesday."

"Oooh. You are cruel." Mason narrowed his eyes at him.

"And you haven't ended it completely with Dack yet. Am I right?"

"I *have* ended it."

"Where is the…err…"

150

"Fucker?" Mason offered.

"I wasn't going to say."

"No clue. Don't care."

"Really? So if I piss you off, you're apathetic in a day?"

"No. If you give me an STD I am."

Parker cracked up and nodded. "Duly noted."

A knock at Mason's office drew both men's attention.

~

"Baby?" was said through the door.

Parker turned around and then said to Mason. "Want me to let patient zero into your office?"

Mason reacted with a wince and made Parker laugh. Mason nodded.

Parker opened it up and Dack straightened his back and appeared insanely jealous. "What are you doing in there?"

Parker wanted to needle Dack, so badly it hurt. Quick retorts were rebounding in his head—everything from, '*Giving your man clean, hot sex*' to '*discussing just how many sugar daddies you swap germs with.*' But instead, Parker said, "We're work colleagues. We can talk."

"Baby?" Dack put on his best little boy pout for Mason.

"I'm not your baby. Get out of my office."

Parker loved Mason's reaction. *Touché!*

"What did this guy say to you?" Dack indicated Parker.

Before Parker even opened his mouth to defend himself, Mason was on his feet, looking like he was ready to kill. He stood nose to nose with Dack and sneered.

"Uh, okay. I think I'll just—" Parker took a step to the door.

"No. Hang on, Parker." Mason poked his finger into Dack's chest. "You and I are through. Got it?"

"Huh? No!" Dack whipped around to Parker. "He's just jealous, babe! Don't listen to him."

151

Parker knew Dack was thinking he was jealous of Mason, which couldn't be further from the truth. *You pathetic jerk.*

Mason poked Dack harder, making Dack flinch and pay attention to what he was saying, which appeared harder than it seemed. "He's not jealous. You think he wants to be involved with an ass like you? You think this intelligent, kind man is stupid enough to fall for a man whose only attribute is his appearance?"

"Yes!" Dack pointed at Parker. "He's gasping for it!"

"Oh brother." Parker rolled his eyes and crossed his arms.

Mason appeared stunned. He shook his head at Dack. "You are so incredibly self-centered you can't even get what's going on."

"Huh?" Dack looked from Parker to Mason. "I get it. You listened to his shit and now you're dumping me."

"No!" Mason showed his teeth. "You made me have to get tested for STDs and you fucking cheat on me constantly!"

"I don't have an STD! Did he tell you that?" Dack pointed at Parker again.

Parker couldn't believe how thick Dack was. "Man. I have to get back to my work. This is unbelievable, Mason."

"Dack!" Mason tried to keep his tone down but Parker could tell a scream was welling in his throat. "We're done. Do not text me, call me, or even look at me unless it's work related."

"Whatever!" Dack threw up his hands and swaggered out, giving Parker a look that could kill.

Parker watched Mason gather himself together after the blow out, exhaling loudly and running his hand over his hair. He gave Parker a quiet round of applause. "Step one—cut off the offending appendage."

"I would have done it weeks ago if Henry didn't keep meddling. All the while I thought it was Dack who was making those grand gestures."

"Oh? You can be bought off?"

"No. But I tend to try to give the other guy the benefit of the doubt." Mason looked out of the office door.

Parker did as well. Dack was already on his cell phone and typing on the computer with one hand. "Look. He's over you."

Mason snorted in agreement. "Believe me. He is."

"Later." Parker smiled at Mason and returned to his desk. He sat down to continue working.

Dack cupped the phone and said to him, "I told you I'd suck you off if you wanted. You didn't need to get Mason involved."

"Oh, Christ, get a clue." Parker shook his head and wrote more on his column, '*The Gift That Keeps Giving...Bad Love-The New STD...*

'*The Bad Boy...everyone loves them, right? From James Dean to Sean Penn, women swoon over tough guys, and gay men wish they could tame them and ride them like a wild stallion.*

'*Our anti-heroes of films and the novels, men like Clyde Barrow from Bonnie and Clyde, Brad Pitt in Fight Club, Heath Ledger in 10 Things I Hate About You... I don't need to list them. You know you love them all.*

'*Ahh, but the reality of the bad boy? Let me tell you something, my dear column readers...not so glamorous. Those dirty cheats not only treat you like a doormat, which of course you may be, and (subs aside) don't like it, but they are indeed the gift that keeps giving...*

'*...from heartaches, to sleepless nights, to cheap dime-store candy...*' Parker glanced at Dack who was laughing into the phone, surfing the net. '*...to herpes and Chlamydia, bad boys should be avoided, like poison ivy, or indeed, you will need to get that rash taken care of. Bad Boys equals Bad Love. Think you can change a man? Good luck. He'll change you. Into a sniveling coward who thinks he's getting all there is out of life.*

*But in reality? All you'll get with a bad boy is herpes, the gift that keeps giving...'*

He glanced at Dack and then sent the copy to Del to edit, checking his in box for anything he needed to do before he started his daily blog. Overhearing the conversation beside him, Dack said into the phone, "Okay, babe...tonight." He laughed seductively, then said in baby-talk, "You know I do...oh, yes. You know I do..."

Parker stifled a gag. To avoid listening, he picked up his empty cup and headed to the lounge to refill it. As he walked behind Dack's chair Dack gave him a sexy smile, which revolted Parker. He tried not to sneer and then felt a light pat on his bottom as he continued by. Parker spun around in shock and said, "Don't touch me."

Dack ignored it and laughed into the phone. "Yes. I know where to meet you, sugar daddy. And I can't wait for you to spoil me."

Parker clenched his jaw and kept going, pouring himself a cup of regular coffee and trying not to come up with blogs that were so dark and cynical, everyone would think he had gone crazy.

~

"Great," Mason said over the phone. "Yes, a full page ad in the new April Rainbow issue, and you'll have a black car against a lavender backdrop. Right?"

"We will. Our sexy new model has created a huge hike in the gay male market share."

"Yes. Mark Richfield has a way of doing that. Everything he touches turns to gold." Mason used the information he had on file for this luxury car client to charge for the expensive ad, sending the invoice for this contract via email.

"Or in his case, turns to rainbows."

"True. The man is attractive."

"In person as well."

"Oh? You've met him?" Mason made a paper copy of the contract for the ad for his own files.

"Yes. Christ, I attended a shoot for the latest sports car. I can't believe the fucker's over forty."

Mason stopped short and blinked. "Huh? That model is over forty?"

"And not airbrushed. He's got one hell of a good plastic surgeon or great genes."

"No. Mark Richfield is over forty?" Mason looked up the man's information on the search engine.

"He is. He's forty-one. Why? All the celebs look good now."

"Damn." Mason stared at the latest ad Mark had done for the car company. "You guys have hit all the right markets. Gay, older, younger, male, female...he has it all."

"He does. And he cost a lot! Believe me. Okay, Mason. I'll send the ad to you the minute our guys finish it up."

"Okay. Thanks." Mason hung up and stared at Mark's photo. He looked out of his door and couldn't see Parker at his desk. He closed down the screen with Mark's image on it, and picked up his coffee cup. He just recalled now why the young man and the older police officer had looked familiar to him when he was at the jewelry store on Rodeo Drive. It had been Alexander, Mark's son, and the man twenty years his senior who was marrying him—the police lieutenant, Billy Sharpe. He had read scads of gossip in the celebrity magazines about them.

So? Some of these older/younger relationships work? Maybe.

But it was something else he was thinking at the moment; just because a man was forty didn't mean he was unattractive and needed to boost his ego with shallow young partners.

Dack wasn't at his desk. Mason glanced briefly at the mess of paperwork on it and didn't regard it much. He kept walking and noticed Parker and Dixie laughing together in the lounge, both holding coffee cups. When Mason approached they looked up at him and smiled.

"Hello, Mason." Dixie was a charming young woman, with plump cheeks and a big warm smile. Mason liked all of the staff at Judas quite a lot.

"Hello, 'Pixie'." He teased and winked at her.

"Back to the grind." She waved over her shoulder as she left the room.

Mason stood by the coffee pot and poured, feeling Parker close by, watching him. "Is lunch considered a date?"

Parker chuckled. "Don't give up easy, do ya?"

"Nope." Mason didn't make eye contact with him yet, putting the pot back and sniffing the dairy cream to make sure it was still good. Once he'd poured and stirred, he glanced up.

Parker was studying his every move.

"Want to wait until I get my results back?" Mason said it as a joke, but maybe that was a consideration of Parker's.

"You're fucking hilarious. You know that?" Parker's blue eyes shone as he sipped the hot coffee.

"Lunch?"

"I brought mine."

"Did you?" Mason stood right in front of him, well within his personal space.

"Turkey and swiss on whole wheat, side of carrots and vanilla yogurt."

"Hm. Can't tempt you away for something?"

"Trying to budget." Parker's smile was such a tease and Mason knew he knew it.

"How about I get myself a sandwich and we eat it together?"

"That's doable. I don't need your test results to manage that."

Mason grinned shyly. Shy. When was the last time a man made Mason feel shy? "Good."

"Here?" Parker tilted his head towards the round tables inside the lounge.

"We can play footsie. No one will notice."

Parker laughed so hard he coughed on his coffee, covering his mouth and trying to stop.

Mason was very proud of himself for making him laugh. He sipped his own cup, feeling excited.

~

Parker cleared his throat and set his cup down so he could cough into a napkin for a minute. He kept cracking up and gave Mason a wry smile. "You dog."

"Sometimes."

Parker glanced behind him, knew they were not being spied, and closed in on Mason. He held Mason's tie right below the knot and drew close to his lips. "You know now much I'm attracted to you. And you're driving me crazy on purpose."

"Am I?" Mason's smile was devilish and Parker couldn't imagine him not being amazing in bed.

Parker straightened Mason's tie, smoothing it down his chest, feeling Mason's solid body.

"Now look who's driving who insane." Mason placed his mug beside Parker's and grabbed Parker's shirt collar.

Parker suspected a kiss was imminent. His breathing escalated and he felt the puff of Mason's exhale on his chin. The icemaker made a loud crackling noise and both men jumped apart in reflex, then laughed when they realized what it was.

"Lunch?" Mason asked again.

"It's a non-date." Still being playful, Parker tried to recuperate from the attraction they felt between them, and picked up his cup.

"Okay. Non-date. Noon?"

"Ish." Parker winked and walked back to his desk, feeling Mason's gaze on his ass.

## CHAPTER 13

At noon Parker felt a light touch on his hair. He glanced up and spotted Mason brushing past.

"Back in five." Mason smiled warmly at him.

Tingles washed over Parker as he caught that luscious grin and ogled those tight glutes.

Mason vanished from his sight. "Damn." Parker grabbed his crotch as it swelled and wondered if he too had a taste for bad boys. After all he knew nothing about Mason other than he made lousy choices in partners.

But Parker hadn't done much better. Though Dack Torington was an all-time low for any man.

And speaking of the kept boy…

Parker hadn't seen him at his desk since early in the morning. But Dack was one of the staff photographers and style coordinators. If he was going to take pictures, he couldn't do it from his desk.

Continuing to work until Mason returned, Parker looked up current trends on Twitter to see what was going on beyond the four walls of their magazine publishing office. This was a 'hip-chic' LGBT organization and he needed to keep up with the current affairs—even if that meant the distasteful hatred and discrimination same sex couples were enduring. Though they catered to the upside of gay and lesbian culture, keeping their pages colorful and filled with passion, occasionally Sigourney's editorial commentary was brutally frank. Ms Edina pulled no punches when it came to her opinion of the far right, its infringement of human rights and their war on women and gays.

So, for a moment, Parker got immersed in the depressing topic of battling ignorance with intelligence.

~

Mason stood in line at the café he usually ordered his lunch at and checked his phone when it buzzed with a text. Dack wrote, *'Dinner tonight?'*

*Are you oblivious or thick as shit?* Mason shook his head in wonder at how impossible it was for him to get it through Dack's head. *It's over!* He deleted Dack's message and stood at the counter as he got the attention of the employee.

"Can I help you?"

"Yes. I'll take the smoked turkey on marble rye and this juice." He held up one of the premium fruit smoothie blends that were loaded in vitamins.

She removed the wrapped sandwich from the refrigerator section of the display case. "Anything else?"

Mason noticed a few heart-shaped cookies. "Are those left over from Valentine's Day?"

"No. We don't keep the cookies more than a day. They were made this morning."

"I'll take one."

The woman bagged his sandwich and cookie and he handed her cash, thanking her. He carried his food out into the cool breezy afternoon as the downtown core filled with business people who had their brief mid-day break from work.

When his phone hummed in his pants pocket again he groaned in annoyance and wondered just how hard it was going to be to 'detach' from this rotting appendage called Dack.

Jogging through the lobby to catch an elevator filled with people, Mason stood with his hands full, his back to the crowd as

159

they rose to various floors. He stepped out at his and made his way into the office, seeing Parker busy at his desk. He looked up as Mason drew closer.

"Noon-ish?" Mason smiled. "Non-date?"

"Aye, aye, captain."

Mason tilted his head to the lounge and smiled as he heard Parker behind him. Once he'd placed his food and drink on the table, Mason washed his hands and tugged a few paper towels from the dispenser. Opening the button of his suit jacket, Mason watched Parker remove his food from the refrigerator, staring at the man's ass and legs.

Just before Mason sat at the round table, with five chairs surrounding it, his phone hummed again. He was about to scream, thinking it was Dack, and removed it to text him to *Fuck Off*! He realized it was an email in his in box from his doctor.

"Oh. Uh. Hang on." Mason held up his finger and Parker acknowledged him, sitting at the table.

Mason stepped right outside the lunchroom and called the doctor's office. "Yes, hi. My name is Mason Bloomfield and I just got an email asking me to call your office for my test results."

"Oh. Okay. Hang on a moment, Mr Bloomfield and I'll transfer you to the nurse."

Mason peeked into the lunchroom and Parker had already begun eating his sandwich, looking up at him. Even though he was nervous, Mason smiled at him.

"Mr Bloomfield?"

"Yes."

"This is Cherie Blank. I'm Dr Hudson's nurse. You are calling about your test results?"

"Yes. I'm shocked they came back so quickly. I hope…"

"The lab tries to have a twenty-four hour turnaround with this type of testing. I have your results right here."

Hearing computer keys tapping over the line, Mason closed his eyes and held his breath. "Okay."

"Negative. All your tests came back clean. You have nothing to worry about."

He blew out a loud exhale and felt so much relief he could cry. "Can you send me the lab results on an email?"

"I can."

"Thank you."

"No problem."

Mason hung up and stood at the doorway, as Parker looked up at him expectantly. "Clean."

Parker smiled. "That was quick."

"I guess if you've got something like that, they want to get you treated quickly." Mason sat down with Parker and began peeling back the plastic of the sandwich.

"So, clean and green...that's great news."

"Fuck. You have no idea." Mason bit into the sandwich and opened the twist top of the smoothie.

"What did Dack have, exactly?"

"He never told me."

Parker shrugged.

Mason chewed his sandwich and moved his foot to contact Parker's under the table, nudging it.

Parker cracked up, covering his mouth as he ate.

"Friday night?" Mason asked, leaning closer. "Dinner? That's it. And I'll even print out my results to show you."

"I believe you. You don't have to do that."

Mason glanced at the doorway. Very few employees remained to eat lunch in the office. Most used it as a break to get out into the fresh air. "You're evading my question."

"No. I'm just playing hard to get." Parker crunched on a baby carrot.

"That only makes me want you more."

161

"That's the idea."

Mason peeked once more at the doorway, then slid his hand along Parker's thigh.

"Now that's just playing dirty." Parker raised his eyebrow.

"You have no idea how badly I want to play dirty with you."

"Damn." Parker laughed, looking shy. "I'm not a model. I have chest hair." Parker teased. "And I don't shave my balls."

"Good. I'm sick of being with a Ken doll. I could use a little pubic hair to nuzzle into."

"Oh, boy." Parker chuckled and shifted in his chair.

Mason was on fire. He removed his suit jacket and loosened his tie. He sipped his juice and said, "I'd lay you on the bed, spread your legs and eat you from your cock to your ass."

Parker stopped chewing and lowered his dark lashes, crossing his legs under the table.

"I could eat you for an hour."

"Oh, Christ." Parker put his sandwich down and rubbed his hand over his hair.

Mason pressed his mouth close to Parker's ear and whispered, "You like to get fucked?" He heard Parker swallow in a gulp. "Fucked hard?" Mason was stiff in his pants and knew making love to Parker would be amazing.

"You're killing me."

"Is that a yes?" Mason sat back and took another bite of his sandwich.

Parker sat up straighter and asked, "Where would you take a first date?"

"Well," Mason leaned his elbow on the table and his chin in his palm, close to Parker. "I'd find out what his favorite food is first."

"I like it all." Parker gave him a nice smile.

"Then, I'd find out if he liked walks on the beach, or a night at the theater."

"Beach."

Mason ran his fingers along Parker's inseam slowly. "Maybe I could suggest a seafood dinner in Santa Monica, and a stroll on the sand."

"And?"

"Oh? More than just dinner?" Mason shifted his hand closer to Parker's crotch but didn't touch it. "I thought it was just...dinner."

"You suck."

"I do. Hard and deep."

Parker dropped against the chair back and looked down. Mason's hand was just about brushing the mound in Parker's slacks. "Fuck!"

Dixie stepped into the room with her coffee mug. The two men sat up and continued eating.

"Hello! Mason? Eating lunch in? How cool is that?"

"Yes. Brought my lunch back. I suppose if the conversation is good, I can eat anywhere." He winked at Parker.

"You guys are so cute." She filled her mug with coffee and left.

Parker met Mason's eyes. "Yes. Dinner."

"If we meet on Friday we can miss karaoke night."

"Please!" Parker made a face of begging. "I would rather shoot myself in the foot."

Mason placed his hand on Parker's inner thigh again. "Can I pick you up?"

"At...seven?"

"Six?"

Parker laughed shyly. "Six."

Mason slid over the small brown bag towards Parker.

Parker eyed it suspiciously.

"Open it."

He picked it up and looked in, taking out a heart-shaped cookie. "Left over from Valentine's Day?"

"Nope. I asked the same thing. Made fresh this morning."

Parker held it up to Mason's mouth.

Mason took a bite, wanting to devour Parker.

Parker broke piece off and ate it, smiling. "You're a real smooth character, aren't you?"

"I hope that's a compliment."

"Oh yeah. It is." Parker fed him another piece of the cookie. "Oops!"

Mason spun around to see Henry had spied their cozy posture and stopped short. Mason shifted backwards and finished his sandwich, crumbling the wrapper as Parker looked casual.

"Am I interrupting something?" The gleam in Henry's eye was so obvious Mason figured the gossip would hit the minute Henry's fingers were back on his keyboard.

"Nope." Mason stood, tossed out his trash and left the room, grinning.

~

"You and Mason?" Henry stood beside the table as Parker opened the top of his yogurt and licked the lid.

"Don't get crazy, Henry." Parker used a plastic spoon to eat the yogurt.

"Really? Does Dack know?" Henry sat at the table, rubbing his hands in glee, like he was savoring the gory details before he heard them.

"Can't you just play at home with your partner?" Parker laughed, but hated being part of office gossip.

"That's boring. You and Mason? That's hot!"

"Hot? No. Come on, Henry. It wouldn't seem hot to you unless I was twenty-one."

Henry laughed and looked modest or embarrassed. "No. You two make a better couple. Dack's a bit…"

164

"A bit...?" Parker finished the yogurt and stood, cleaning up the table and eating the last bite of cookie.

"He's slightly self-absorbed."

"Slightly?" Parker choked as he rinsed his hands.

"Want me to tell you how to woo Mason?"

"No!" Parker dried his hands and left the room, laughing under his breath about how silly Henry was.

As he returned to his desk he could see Dack standing at Mason's open office door, the two of them were talking. Parker's grin dropped and he kept advancing towards his desk, leery but trying to feel confident in Mason's word.

He sat down at his computer and before he began working, he listened to their conversation, which was right behind his back.

"...baby, give me one more chance."

"No."

"I don't have an STD. I got a fucking bladder infection."

"I don't care."

"Who told you I gave you the clap?"

"Dack, it's over. Get it? Like in go away?"

Parker tried to look busy but what was going on behind his back was too distracting to do anything but listen.

"You cheat on me. You don't think I get text messages from you that were meant for other guys?"

"I don't cheat."

"Bullshit!"

"I didn't want to say anything..."

Parker typed nonsense on the keyboard in case Dack was checking to see if he was listening.

"Can we close the door to your office?"

"No!" Mason blew out a loud exhale of air.

"Look, Mason, I make a little cash on the side as an escort."

Parker was so stunned he choked and coughed, covering his mouth, blowing the fact he was not listening.

165

"You disgust me." Mason sounded pissed.

"No. Not like that. I mean, kind of. Old guys. Old guys hire me and I hang out with them for dinner and shit."

*Oh my fucking God, Dack's a hooker.* Parker erased all the '*bahahahahahahaha*' he had just typed in reaction.

"Go. Away. Which part of it's over don't you get?"

"But, Mason. I love you."

Parker flinched. That was a powerful word. One he had only said once. To Lee.

"You love me? You don't love me. You hate me."

Parker stopped typing since it was just for the sake of looking busy and leaned his elbow on the arm of his chair, listening intently.

"Baby...I can't live without you."

Parker could imagine Dack's pout. With a guy that good looking, that was pretty powerful stuff to resist.

"Then why aren't you dead yet? Leave me alone. I have work to do."

Parker heard the office door shut and began typing again, looking busy. He peeked at Dack who walked slowly to his desk.

When they caught eyes, accidentally, since Parker didn't want to meet them, Dack said, "You busy tonight?"

Parker nearly died where he sat and made a noise in his throat of disbelief. "No fucking way!"

"Sheesh. Why is everyone so uptight around here?" Dack slouched in his chair and stared into his phone, texting.

Parker wrote up a new blog. '*Are Models Really That Dumb? Or does playing stupid get them into your trousers?*'

After helping the interns with their projects and completing another blog, Parker shut down his computer. Dack had done some work, but spent most of the time on the phone setting up models and working with fashion designers to get photos taken for their next issue.

He heard Mason's office door open and looked over his shoulder. When they connected gazes, Mason mouthed quietly behind Dack's back, "*You done?*"

Without answering, Parker shut off his computer, stood, and pushed his chair under the desk. He buttoned his suit jacket and walked quickly behind Dack, who was still on the phone but had sniffed out something was going on behind his back.

Mason didn't even glance at Dack as he met Parker at the exit of the office and they walked to the elevator together.

They stood quietly, but Parker could feel Mason's body was close, close enough to catch his scent of cologne and feel a slight heat from his aura.

The elevator opened and several people were inside it, heading home. As Parker stepped in, Mason touched his elbow discreetly and drew him in front of where he stood, all of the occupants were looking at the door and the numbered floor lights above it.

Parker was tugged backwards so he was contacting Mason's body. A hot cock pulsated against Parker's ass. He melted down to his leather Cole Haan shoes.

Mason began moving, ever so slightly, first side to side, allowing his stiff cock to roll over Parker's ass crack, then pushing forward and back, as if fucking.

By the time they stopped at the parking lot level, Parker was a pent up mass of carnal lust. The elevator empted out quickly and Parker felt Mason run both his palms down his low back to cup his ass. In his ear Mason whispered, "Tight."

"Holy Christ." Parker managed to get out of the elevator and put one foot in front of the other to walk towards his car.

Mason's footfalls followed. Parker stopped at his car and looked at him. Mason was giving him one of the most seductive leers Parker could recall getting. "You want me that bad?"

Mason's expression changed to confusion. He crossed his arms and leaned against the car that was parked beside Parker's. "Want you? You mean as in a conquest? Or?"

"I don't know. This sexual teasing is..."

"Is...?" Mason appeared upset. "No good? I'll stop."

"No. I mean." Parker stuffed his hands into his pockets for his keys and ran into his stiff cock.

"I'll lay off." Mason held up his hand and lowered his head, starting to walk away.

"Hang on." Parker grabbed after him, pulling him back to where he was. "Let me catch my breath." He tried to calm down from the elevator seduction but his cock kept throbbing, dampening his briefs.

Mason glanced around the parking lot. "I don't mean to push you. I just really like you."

"Yeah. The feeling is mutual. I just feel like suddenly I'm on some kind of treadmill."

"I was just teasing. I know you don't want to rush into anything."

"I don't. I do. I don't. I do."

Mason appeared surprised then broke out into laughter.

Parker joined him, dabbing his eyes. "All right. Look. You're my ideal guy. Okay?"

Controlling his laughter, Mason asked, "How am I your ideal?"

"Well." Parker took a step closer to him, running his hands over the broad shoulders of Mason's dark designer suit. "You're smart, have a great sense of humor." He ran his fingers up and down Mason's sleeves. "Strong sense of self, low on the egomaniac scale..." Parker finally met Mason's hazel eyes. Yes, hazel. Not blue, not green, but golden brown with a lovely emerald ring. "You're..." His heart began to beat strongly in his chest. "...you're fucking gorgeous, mature, and...a top."

Mason shifted his stance but didn't react, as if absorbing the words.

"And you make me laugh." Parker smiled at him. "A lot."

"Do you have any idea how much I want to kiss you right now?" Mason stared at Parker's mouth.

"If it's half as much as I want to kiss you, it's a hell of a lot."

"Let me come to your place."

Parker hesitated. Dack's presence was still strong. They had barely broken up.

"Or come to mine." Mason reached up slowly, touching Parker's face.

His cock trying to make a decision for him, Parker fought the battle of passion. "Friday. Let's do the dinner Friday."

"Is it the fucking STD thing?"

"No. No, it's not. And I..." Parker met his gaze again. "I overheard Dack say it wasn't an STD it was a bladder infection."

"I don't believe a word that moron says."

"The way he was suffering over pissing? I think he's telling the truth."

"Fine. If it's not that, then why are you making us wait?"

"Because this means something to me."

The sound of someone walking near made both of them look up. Two women were heading to their cars, chatting, not giving them more than a quick glance.

Mason took a step back, appearing slightly defeated.

Parker touched his jaw, feeling the sand papery grit of his five o'clock shadow. Instantly Mason met his gaze.

Closing his eyes, Parker went for that kiss. When their lips met, the fire that flashed through Parker nearly made him swoon. You could tell everything about a lover by their kiss.

Mason whimpered and cupped Parker's jaw. As the passion grew, Parker opened his teeth to Mason's tongue. How he loved men who were assertive. Aggressive!

Mason moved Parker backwards until Parker hit his car, then Mason nailed him to it, pushing their stiff cocks together.

Parker touched Mason's wrists, loving how strong Mason felt against him, his twirling of the tongue and deep growls of pleasure.

They kissed for a long moment, then Mason rolled his forehead on Parkers. "Damn."

Parker chuckled. "Right?" He heard a car drive by and peered over at the occupant to see if they were getting the glare or being ignored. Ignored.

He exhaled deeply and stared into Mason's eyes. "You make me want to break all my rules."

"Rules? What rules?" Mason smiled, pecking Parker on the chin playfully.

"My rules of common sense."

"Look, I get it. I do. I'm coming off the heels of a nightmare. And you don't want to get the fall out. I understand."

"I'm glad you said that."

"But."

Parker laughed. "Yes?"

"But that doesn't mean I don't want to fuck your brains out." Mason ground his cock against Parker's.

"Oh, fuck. Man, you're killing me." All of Parker's focus went to their groins making hot friction.

Mason backed off, as if finding the strength. "Right." He inhaled, straightened his jacket and said, "Friday."

"F...Friday." Parker wanted Mason to come home with him.

"Okay." Mason appeared disappointed but gave Parker a small wave. "See you in the office tomorrow."

"Yes." Parker watched Mason walk to his car. Mason turned back again and gave him another smile and wave.

Parker climbed behind the wheel of his car and caught his breath. "Wow. He is going to be amazing in bed. Damn." A horn honking startled Parker. He turned in the seat to look behind him.

The Audi had started backing out, and a red Charger honked at it as it raced behind it, slightly too quickly for a parking garage. When it passed Parker could see Dack behind the wheel. He wondered if the man has spied their kiss and embrace.

He started his car and knew he would find out at the office in the morning, whether he wanted to or not.

~

Mason pulled into his reserved space at his condo complex, thinking about Parker. Parker was right. There was nothing wrong with slowing down the speed of this promising relationship. And having Dack's shadow hanging so heavily on them, really put a damper on the fun. Mason hadn't dated men in their thirties and fucking liked Parker's maturity. He felt like the biggest ass on the planet for hunting young men when all the while men near his own age were so...

Normal!

Everything about Parker excited him. And he could not say the same for Dack. Only Dack's looks and body turned him on. The man was shallow and could not carry on a decent conversation about anything other than celebrity gossip or his potential to be on a reality series.

He headed to his unit, smiling to himself as he relived the kisses, and the feel of Parker's cock against his. Once inside his condo, he changed clothing and washed up, seeing his face had a slight redness to it from Parker's coarse beard growth. Mason touched it gently, smiling at his own reflection. "Like a top? Oh, am I going to fuck you good." The thought got Mason crazy. He reached into his jeans and touched his cock.

The relief of not having contracted anything from Dack, even if Dack was telling the truth and it was just an infection, was great. Add to that the potential of a great new man in his life, one he could connect with on so many levels, Mason was horny as hell.

He yanked his jeans down to his ankles and took off his shirt, then put lubrication into his palm. Standing at the sink, he closed his eyes and pictured kissing Parker, jamming his cock into Parker's tight ass.

"Oh fuck!" It took nothing. Mason came and pointed his dick at the sink basin, milking his cock as the waves receded. "Motherfucker. I am so fucking hot for you."

He stared into his own eyes and laughed at himself at the realization that he may be on the cusp of dating an amazing man. One who satisfied not only his carnal cravings, but his mind as well.

~

Parker was dealing with an erection that would not quit. He drove home in the traffic, touching it through his slacks, needing release. The contact with Mason was so damn erotic he was going out of his mind.

*Fuck you? You think I don't want to fuck you? Oh man!*

Parker managed to make it home, get out of his car and jog up the four flights of stairs to his apartment. Once he made it through the door, he stripped, leapt onto the bed face up, grabbed his dick and jacked off. Reaching between his legs to his ass, the moment he touched the base of his dick and balls, visions of Mason pushing Parker's face into the pillows and grinding in deep, Parker came, spraying his chest and splashing under his jaw. He slowed down his hand and squeezed the last few drops of cum out of his cock, catching his breath. *Shoulda asked you to come over.*

*Shoulda, coulda, woulda.*

"Ohh, damn." Parker closed his eyes and held his cock as he imagined Mason in his bed.

~

Mason stuck a frozen dinner into the microwave. He poured a glass of wine for himself and sipped it, thinking about Parker. Friday. It was Wednesday night, so he could manage to hold out 'til then. Right?

He leaned against the counter by the kitchen sink, waiting for the microwave to ding, the glass of wine to his lips. As he daydreamed he tried to come up with a fabulous first date. Santa Monica, gourmet seafood, walking on the beach...

He grew hard again. "Jesus." Mason squeezed his crotch and set the wine glass down when the microwave stopped. He opened the door and poked the fork into the frozen center, putting it back for another few minutes.

His phone buzzed with a text. Mason at first frowned, thinking *Dack*. He leaned over it and peered down at it as it sat on the counter near him.

*'that kiss. fuck you!'*

"Huh?" Mason picked it up and could see it was not from Dack. He felt confused and wondered if this was from Parker. He hadn't programmed Parker's cell phone number into his phone. He thought hard, trying to figure it out. Then he realized the area code was 212. New York. He laughed and texted back. *'Jacked off to it. fuck you back.'*

Immediately he got a response. *'ditto. damn you.'*

Mason cracked up and wrote, *'would've been better in my mouth.'*

*'ur killin me. u know that.'*

*'same here, mister. I wanted you to come over.'*

173

*'I did! all over myself!'*

The microwave stopped again and Mason glanced at it and then took the hot food out and burned his fingers as he set it on the stove top to cool.

*'bet you taste good,'* he wrote as he sucked on his burned finger.

*'y is Friday so far away?'*

Mason smiled and dialed.

"Hey." Parker sounded so sexy.

"I'm not the one with all the rules." Mason picked up the wine to sip.

"I know. I feel like a dumb schmuck. I could have had your dick up my ass instead of just fantasizing about it."

"Oh come on!" Mason moaned in agony. "You really know how to cock tease a guy."

Parker laughed.

"In some ways, I think it's kind of cool waiting." Mason smiled.

"Yeah?"

"Yeah. I mean, it's too easy to just be attracted and fuck. It's better this way. I like you as a person first."

"True. I suppose that's why there are all those first date fuck rules."

"Those are women's rules, not for us." Mason glanced at his steaming meal with little interest.

"Maybe, but, sometimes if…and I mean, I've only done this once…cough…maybe twice…"

Mason started laughing.

"…when I have fucked on the first date, first…meeting at the bar, choke, cough."

"God, you're hilarious." Mason set the glass down and dabbed his eyes. "Yes, once or twice…go on."

"Well, it sucked. I mean, yeah, maybe the fuck was good. But there was nothing after. Just a feeling of regret."

Mason sighed and said, "Yeah. I know."

"It's that instant of 'I love you! I hate you!'"

"Oh God. Been there. Just did that." Mason's smile faded.

"Right?" Parker exhaled loudly. "Aren't you sick and tired of the fucking games? The bullshit?"

"More than you know."

"But not the chase. Heh heh."

Mason grinned. "I will get you in my sites, you big dog."

"You already have me in your sites. I'm just waiting for you to pull that trigger."

"Ohhh," Mason moaned and closed his eyes.

"Inside my ass."

"Damn. You are the worst. You realize I know where you live."

"Ha. Yup. I know. I still have to buzz you into the building. And you don't know my apartment number."

"So? If I came over, you'd refuse me entry?" Mason smiled.

"Yup. Ya gotta wait 'til Friday."

"Will I get lucky Friday?" Mason picked up the plate of food which had cooled off a little, and carried it to his kitchen table, setting it down.

"Maybe."

"Parker."

"Yeah?"

"I really do like you."

"I really like you too, Mason. A whole hell of a lot."

"Can I come by tonight?"

"Nope. See ya in the office tomorrow."

"See ya." Mason smiled and disconnected the phone, making sure Parker's name was now associated with the phone number. He set the phone down and gathered a knife and fork to eat his dinner with. When the phone hummed again, he chuckled and picked it up to look. A photo of Dack in a compromising position with a very young pretty boy was sent to him from Dack's phone. The caption read, '*C what Ur missing? LOL!*'

Mason's smile vanished. He deleted it and growled. *Fucking hate you, you asshole.*

He dropped down in front of his food and ate, staring into space.

## CHAPTER 14

Thursday morning, Parker carried an armload of back issue's of their magazine. He'd picked them up from Sigourney's office and brought them to his desk to look over the past two years of the spring and summer issues. It was an effort to not repeat their themes, and to see what he had missed since he didn't work for the team back then. Parker sat at his desk and leafed through them, registering the look and feel of the magazine's niche market, keeping in mind fresh ideas.

There was a slight commotion at the entrance of their office—laughter and noise of loud voices, as if a celebration were occurring. He glanced up at the entrance of the office and could see a small group of employees, Dixie, Henry, Saul and Dack, coming in together, obviously excited about some event.

It was so loud that Sigourney stepped out of her office, hands on hips, appearing as curious as Parker felt. "Hello?" she called to their group. "Care to share?"

"Dack got accepted onto that reality show he was dying to get on!" Henry clapped his hands together in glee.

Parker stifled his choke of sarcasm. He was not a fan of reality TV and any show that would want a pretty-but dim-witted man like Dack was looking for conflict or...nudity.

Sigourney met the group to shake Dack's hand. "Am I losing you?"

Hearing what sounded like a promise of peace, Parker sat up. *Leave! Leave!*

"Yeah, Sig. It's a six month contract. I can't say no. I mean, I'll probably be signed to some big movie contract after they see me." Dack shot a dazzling grin at Parker as if Parker either could be jealous or hate to see him leave.

"Well!" Sigourney smiled. "We need an extra special karaoke night this Friday and a replacement for you, ASAP!"

"You knew this was coming." Dixie hopped up and down, as if she was overjoyed for Dack's success. "He told us he was auditioning."

"Yup. I remember."

Parker checked the time, wondering when Mason was due in or if he even knew already. Odds were Dack texted him the news.

Dack continued to engage his groupies, smiling and laughing as if he were already a red-carpet celebrity.

Mason stepped into the office and the chatter stopped instantly. Parker held a magazine on his lap but was riveted to the action. Appearing slightly confused by what was going on in the corner by Sigourney's office, Mason stood still, looking at them.

Dack swaggered over, as if they were still hot lovers. The others smiled or giggled, and Parker wondered if they were even clued in that Mason had indeed broken up with Dack. Parker knew Henry was aware, but did Henry mention it?

Mason quickly looked Parker's way as Dack approached.

"Baby?" Dack hung his arms around Mason's neck, pressing his crotch against Mason's.

Parker bristled and felt his jaw twitch.

Mason removed Dack's arms from his hold and stepped back. "What?" Mason asked flatly.

"I know you'll be so hurt." Dack pouted and made for full body contact with Mason again.

Parker put the magazine he was holding onto the desk and felt like screaming.

Mason pushed Dack away again, looking at the other employees who were witnessing the display as if it were already a bad reality television show.

"Can we talk in private? In your office?" Dack ran his finger over Mason's cheek, looking coy and trying to seduce.

"Jesus!" Parker began to wonder if things had not ended and Mason was still connected to Dack via texts, emails, or phone calls.

"No." Mason stepped away from Dack and began heading to his office, Dack in hot pursuit.

"But, baby! I have some news to share with you."

"I'm not interested." Mason caught gazes with Parker, and Parker could see the rage in Mason's expression.

Being either stubborn or dumb as dirt, Dack didn't let up until they were at Mason's office door, directly behind Parker's chair. Parker tried not to fume and could see the group across the room watching, whispering. The office intrigue was growing grotesque. Parker wasn't keen on being a party to it and was thinking of getting a refill of his cup of coffee or heading to the men's room. But he sat still, seeing how this would play out.

"Dack! I am not interested. I am not 'your baby' and I don't care what you have to say."

The look of upset on the other employee's faces was tough to endure.

Parker took a quick peek. Dack appeared crushed—Mason, a wreck, rubbing his hands over his hair. Parker wished he could get the hell out of the office without it looking like he was storming out in jealousy.

"But…Mason…it was something I wanted so badly. You were so supportive when…when…"

Parker whipped his head around when he heard a sob. Dack was crying? *Are you kidding me?*

~

Mason's anger deflated. He peeked at the rest of the crew, watching, waiting to see what he would do. He knew Parker was right there. Not more than two feet away from them.

"What did you want to tell me?" Mason asked softly, seeing the tears in Dack's eyes, threatening to spill.

"I…" Dack choked up and wiped his eyes.

Mason touched Dack's shoulder and tried to resist the urge he had to hold Dack and offer his strength or sympathy, something Mason had done too many times when Dack's life became too much for the young man.

He was keenly aware of Parker witnessing every move, every shift of their postures. But Mason didn't want to be unreasonably cruel either. "Come in." He gestured to his office. "Sit down and compose yourself." As Dack entered his office, Mason stood at the door and made eye contact with Parker. He knew Parker was not happy, but Mason had no idea how Dack would react. Mason knew Parker was a strong, smart individual while Dack…the opposite. Mason closed the door, seeing Parker's expression turn slightly hostile.

Mason stood near Dack and waited as Dack got a grip on his emotions. "What do you need to tell me?"

"I…I got the part. The celebrity reality show." Dack wiped his nose and still looked like he may fall to pieces.

"That's good, right? You've been going crazy wanting it."

"Mason." Dack jumped to his feet and approached him. "It means nothing without you to celebrate with." Dack fell into his arms and whimpered as he rested his head on Mason's shoulder.

# I Love You I Hate You

Mason sighed deeply and rubbed Dack's back in comfort. "You have to let go. I'll still be your friend, but that's it."

"Mason…" Dack pressed his lips against Mason's neck, holding Mason around his waist. "Squeeze me tighter. Please."

Fighting the conflict in his head, one that told him Parker would be furious if he knew, Mason held Dack, embracing him warmly. "It's okay."

"Love you, Mason. Only you."

Mason closed his eyes and suffered at those words. More than he thought he would at this stage in the break up.

~

The group by Sigourney's office had dissipated to their desks and began working. Henry had a smug smile on his face, as if the two lovers had reconciled and it was irritating Parker to no end. There was no conversation coming from the closed office behind him. What the hell? A make up blowjob?

Parker tried to function, picking up the magazine he had been thumbing through and forgetting why he was. Deep inside him was mistrust and an urge to knock on that office door. But did he have the right?

Was he going to act like a jealous boyfriend in the middle of the office? He and Mason hadn't even had one date.

Shades of Lee's treatment began to rush over Parker. Lee's constant mixed signals—*I love you. I hate you. I don't give a shit either way.* Lee had been emotionally abusive at times, and Parker struggled not to let that past baggage have any influence on his future relationships. But, didn't all past relationships do that?

He set the stack of magazines on the floor beside him and started a new column.

'*Spring may be in the air, but are we still suffering from the ghosts of relationships past? Whether we're carving pumpkins for Halloween, or watching* A Christmas Carol *on TV, is it*

181

*possible we are haunted by our own demons every month of the year?'*

He glanced over his shoulder. Why couldn't he hear talking? Parker was beginning to go crazy. How long would they be in there alone? Behind closed doors?

The temptation to email Mason and ask how he was enjoying the makeup sex was great, but Parker kept typing on his column instead.

*'...Nature and Nurture. Day one of our contact with our mother, and if he's around, our father, we begin to develop ghosts. Ghosts of how we deal with life, love and contact with other human beings.*

*'How we trust, how we communicate, and how we ultimately treat our partners. Ghosts bring back pain and pleasure to our new lovers whether we want them to or not.*

*'Even dogs react to past abuse. They cringe when you go to pet them if their last owners slapped them.*

*'Is it true? Are we all just beaten mongrels when it comes to love? And everything that happens after the past is just reliving the same chapter again and again?*

*'Or does that ghost sometimes bring out what we need? Does it warn us in advance to keep away from another bad deal?*

*'Ghosts of relationships past. Do we need a cleansing and exorcists to rid them? Or can we just turn the other cheek and learn from them?'*

Parker couldn't take it any longer. He grabbed his mug, headed to the lounge and avoided eye contact with anyone.

*I'm going to scream!*

~

Mason shifted away from Dack when he started kissing his neck and going for his earlobe. "No."

Dack appeared miserable.

"Dack, we're through. I'm sorry."

182

"No. Don't say that. You're the best thing that's ever happened to me."

"I can't." Mason moved behind his desk so there was a barrier between them. "Just go enjoy the experience on the show. I know how much you wanted it."

"But, I want you too."

"I can't. No. Dack. I just can't." Mason sat down at his desk and rubbed his face.

"Take me out one last time? Please?"

"No."

"Baby." Dack knelt beside Mason, swiveling Mason's chair, turning Mason's knees to face him. "Please."

Mason looked at Dack. Yeah, he knew what a complete ass Dack was, but...he was so fucking gorgeous. Jesus Christ! Too pretty. Too well built. Too everything.

Dack ran his hands over Mason's thighs, moving towards his crotch.

"No." Mason held his hands back. "Dack. No."

"But I love you. I never loved anyone like I love you."

"Stop saying that." Mason kept nudging Dack's hands off his legs. "You say that shit and then all the while you've been tricking with old fuckers for cash."

"I have expensive tastes. I like nice things. I won't do that again."

"Stop touching me." Mason was about to get up and leap over his desk if he had to.

"I promise. No more." Dack held up his hand in an oath, still on his knees beside Mason's chair. "I'll be yours. Your boy toy. Exclusive. Cross my heart."

Mason moaned and scrubbed his face in agony. "No."

"The infection cleared up," Dack whispered. "You can fuck me, suck me..."

"No!" Mason lowered his voice when Dack winced at his volume. "Dack. Why can't you just hear me? I don't want to pursue this. Please. You're making this exceptionally hard."

"Making it hard?" Dack didn't smile. "You once said just looking at me made you hard."

"Fuck." Mason stared at his desk. Not only did he have a ton of work to do, he knew Parker would be wondering what was going on.

Dack went for Mason's thighs again, rubbing them, squeezing them. "I'll rip up my black book. I'll move in with you so you can keep an eye on me."

"No." Mason nudged his hands off again.

"But I'll be living in that reality TV house for months. And I was going to get rid of my apartment and live with you when it was over."

"No!" Mason nearly cried he was so fed up. "Dack, how many times can I say no before you actually hear it?"

"I know you don't mean it."

"I do!" Mason heard a rap at the door. Before he could react, Dack yelled, "Come in!"

Parker opened it and immediately saw Dack on his knees behind the desk.

"I knew it." Parker closed the door abruptly.

Mason jumped out of his chair and hurdled over Dack to run after Parker.

Dack asked as he did, "Are you and Parker dating?"

~

Parker held up his hand as he tried to keep his coffee mug steady in his hand. "Get away from me, Mason."

"It's not what you think." Mason could see the office employees listening, some overtly, others not.

"Get. Away. From. Me." Parker was about to lose it. He placed his full coffee mug down on the desk to avoid spilling it.

Dack walked right behind them and smirked. He wiped his mouth just as he had the first time Parker had suspected he and Mason had oral sex together.

"Mmm," Dack hummed. "So good, Mason." He at his desk and picked up his phone at the same time as he tapped keys on his computer keyboard.

"No," Mason said, shaking his head. "We didn't."

"If you don't get the hell away from me, Mason, I'm going to get violent." Parker was about to push Mason away physically.

Mason reacted as if he had taken a blow, headed to his office and slammed the door.

Dack chuckled wickedly.

Parker tried to function. He forced himself to sit down at his desk and couldn't stand the laughter and cockiness from Dack beside him. He glanced back at Mason's office and sneered. *I hate you.*

~

Mason leaned his elbows on his desk, his head in his hands. Did he just blow it?

*No. I God no.*

Mason's phone rang. He grabbed it, hoping it was Parker. "Mason Bloomfield, can I help you?"

"Mason! It's Jon from Rolls. Just sent you the ad for your magazine and I wanted to know if it came through your email."

"Hi, Jon. Let me check." Mason scooted closer to his computer and tapped keys. "Yes. It came through and looks fine."

"Great. Let me know the deadline for the June issue and we'll have something for you then as well."

"Great. Thanks, Jon. I appreciate it."

"My pleasure. Can't wait to get my copy."

"Thanks. Bye." Mason hung up and opened the attachment. A full two page ad downloaded. "You have to be kidding me."

The top model was lying lengthwise on the front seat of the new car, wearing nothing but tight white spandex pants with a huge semi-erection showing under them. Not a question in his mind, Mason was looking at the Nation's Top Male Model's cock right through those clingy workout pants. "Jesus! I don't even know what kind of car it is." He gaped at the gorgeous man's long hair and chiseled jaw, his green eyes and full lips. "Why are we all such suckers for looks?"

Mason glanced at his closed office door and sighed loudly.

~

Parker kept trying to focus but Dack's obnoxious laughter beside him was driving him crazy.

Over the phone Dack gushed, "I know! I'm a celebrity TV star, Yoseph. Soon I'll be so rich and famous and maybe I'll get the Hollywood elite to invite me to their parties."

*Shut up. Just shut up.*

Parker tried to focus on work, but imagining Mason had just gotten a blowjob from this ass was infuriating him. He couldn't take it any longer. He picked up the stack of magazines and carried them to the conference room to work inside a private space. As he passed behind Dack, Dack had the gall to reach out for his ass.

"Don't you fucking touch me!" Parker yelled, realized everyone in the room had looked up at him and then he continued on his way, fuming.

He dropped the magazines on the table, sat down, and tried to compose himself for a moment.

Dixie poked her head in. "You okay?"

"Yes. Sorry." Parker sat up in his chair and began flipping the pages of the old back issues.

"Wanna talk?"

"Nope. Thanks."

"Can I get you a coffee?"

"Just had one." He smiled at her. "But thanks."

She gave him a slightly sad smile and left.

The last thing Parker wanted was for his new colleagues to think he couldn't handle working here. But the sense of keeping well clear of Dack and Mason was growing in him.

Just as he immersed himself in the back issues, coming up with ideas and jotting them on a pad, someone entered the conference room and closed the door behind him.

Parker frowned. "I'm busy."

"He was not sucking me off. He was begging."

"I said I was busy." Parker did not look at Mason.

"I repeatedly told him no, to get out, to leave me alone."

"Fine." Parker flipped the pages of another issue angrily. He glared at Mason. "Anything else?"

"You don't believe a word I'm saying."

Parker threw up his hands. "He was on his knees behind your desk! Didn't you hear him tell me how good you taste when he returned to his? Do you think I'm an idiot?"

Mason approached the head of the conference table adjacent to where Parker was sitting. He leaned both his palms on the surface to speak quietly. "No. I think Dack is the idiot. He's manipulating us. Can't you see it?"

Parker's head started to hurt. He rubbed his eyes and didn't know whom to believe. "I can't do this at work. I can't have a relationship with someone I have to see every day."

"Fine. If that's the reason, I respect it. But don't change your mind because you think that egotistical bastard has touched me sexually."

Parker didn't look up but heard the door shut and felt the gust of wind from it. He banged his forehead on the table repeatedly, moaning, "Shoot me now…shoot me now…"

~

187

By five, Mason was exhausted and fed up. He shut down his computer and left his office, seeing Parker and Dack were already gone.

"Morning meeting tomorrow!" Milly said cheerfully.

"Yes. Goodnight, Milly." Mason left the office standing alone at the elevator. He knew allowing Dack into his office had blown it with Parker. Though they hadn't even begun their journey together, Mason was crushed.

He entered the elevator and leaned back heavily on the far wall of the small space as it descended to the parking garage level.

"I'm the idiot." Mason checked his phone but no one was contacting him. No one at all.

## CHAPTER 15

Friday morning, Parker went through his normal routines to get ready for work but felt anything but normal. All night he had the desire to talk to Mason to communicate his doubts. Or maybe just getting reassured that he could trust Mason, and that Dack was indeed…a douchebag.

Preoccupied and trying not to get frustrated with the traffic, Parker pulled into his reserved spot, climbed out of his car, and noticed the silver Audi driving towards him. Out of courtesy he waited. He was no longer angry at Mason, and after a night to digest the information, was tending to believe Mason over Dack. It was common sense. Dack begging? On his knees? Maybe attempting a blowjob to reconcile? And Mason saying, 'No.' All within the realm of possibilities.

Mason exited his car, looking upset, possibly having the same kind of preoccupied evening Parker had.

"I'm surprised you waited for me." Mason walked with Parker to the elevator. "I thought I was going to be on your permanent shit list."

Parker pushed the call button and fastened his suit jacket. "I'm a reasonable man, Mason."

"I know. And if I were you? And came into my office to see Dack on his knees? I would think the same thing. Only I wouldn't talk to you for months."

They entered the elevator and faced forward, Parker pushing their floor number.

"I should never have let him into my office," Mason said, "That was a mistake I regret. But I felt as if I was a heartless bastard when he started crying."

"He got over it. Right after he left your office he was laughing with his buddies on the phone."

Mason exhaled loudly.

The door opened to their floor and they walked together to the lobby. Parker headed directly to his desk and dropped a memory stick on it, then noticed the other employees gathering near the conference room, some holding coffee cups.

"Meeting in five!" Morris called out to everyone.

Parker glanced behind him into Mason's office. He was looking through paperwork on his desk, appearing very unhappy. Parker looked at Dack's desk. It was disturbingly neat.

As Mason exited his office to head towards the conference room, Parker followed, staring at his ass and broad shoulders.

When he entered the room, everyone was taking the seats they had previously and Sigourney was already pouring coffee and checking her notes as the scent of fresh brew and sugary danishes filled the air.

Parker and Mason sat side by side and the urge Parker had to touch him was overwhelming.

Mason leaned both elbows on the table, looking at Sigourney, obviously the consummate professional, waiting for the meeting to begin.

"Okay, troops. As you can see we are minus one." She pointed to the chair Dack had occupied. "My guess is, though he is calling this a 'leave of absence', it's his ticket into the reality TV world. Anyone know a good photographer slash lifestyle editor?"

"I can ask around." Parker got a glance from Mason but nothing more.

"Not from New York, Mr Douglas." Sigourney smiled sweetly.

"Ya never know. So many of us East Coasters are relocating." Parker smiled back at her.

"Mason?" Sigourney asked.

"Huh?" Mason looked up, as if he'd been daydreaming.

"Did Dack say if he's coming tonight?"

"Tonight?"

"To karaoke? You know, as a goodbye?"

"I haven't heard from him since yesterday."

"Aww," Henry said, his bottom lip pouting.

Parker fidgeted, feeling nervous.

"Look, guys," Mason said, looking around the table, "I'm not with Dack anymore. I haven't been since Valentine's Day. So I have no idea what he's doing, where he's going or if he's coming tonight." Mason interlaced his fingers on the table and stared at them. "I'm probably not going tonight either."

"No," Dixie said, sadly, "You have to go. Did Dack break your heart?"

Parker knew Mason had broken Dack's, if he had one.

"Just not up to it. I'm…I'm fine." He straightened his back. "So, let's get on with the meeting, okay?"

"Good idea." Sigourney shifted some notes. "Our advertising manager has been so successful this week, our April issue will be huge!" She nudged Mason. "Love you!"

He gave her an apprehensive smile and Parker wondered why that phrase had been tossed around so much lately. Parker shifted his position and his leg brushed Mason's.

"Sorry," Parker whispered and moved his leg away.

Mason reached under the table, held onto Parker's thigh and drew it back to where it was, touching his.

191

At the masculine handling and assertive gesture, Parker became aroused. When Mason went to remove his hand, Parker snatched it undercover, and set it right back down where it was.

Mason turned to look at him and gave him a big relieved smile.

Henry asked from his seat on the opposite side of Parker, "A little hanky-panky going on?"

"No. Mind your own business, Miss Match." Parker smiled at him.

They continued the meeting, but this time, Parker kept his hand on top of Mason's, which was on his leg.

~

Once Sigourney sent them on their way, back to work with fresh ideas spinning in their brains, Mason tilted his head to his office as he and Parker made their way to that side of the room. Parker set his mug on his desk, tossed down his pad and pen, and entered Mason's office.

"I'm afraid to ask." Mason moved behind his desk and Parker kept the door open.

"Ask away." Parker stood in front of Mason's desk.

"Are...are we still on for our date tonight? Or is that all blown?"

A sly smile washed over Parker's lips as he stared at Mason's desk top. "Dunno. I mean, I don't even know what you decided to do...on our date. Tonight." He put his tongue into his cheek.

Mason loved the teasing and was glad it was back. He moved around the desk to stand beside Parker. "Dinner for two at The Lobster, and then a stroll on the sandy beach."

"Nice." Parker peeked out of the open office door.

Mason nudged it and it swung closed. He touched Parker's sleeve and it made Parker glance down at it, then into his eyes.

Raising his arms slowly, Mason cupped Parker's face and admired his gorgeous blue eyes. "I'm sorry. Forgive me."

Parker lowered his lashes shyly. "I should be telling you that. I overreacted yesterday and let Dack come between us."

"Between us?" Mason liked the way that sounded. He shifted so their bodies met at the hip. "Nothing between us now."

"Except two Perry Ellis suits." Parker's eyes lit up devilishly.

"Will you go out with me?" Mason felt his cock throb against Parker's inner thigh.

"Yes."

A rush of pleasure made its way over Mason. He drew closer to Parker's lips as he spoke. "Do you have to stop home...or?"

"Let me stop home. I don't want to go out in this suit. Is that okay?"

"Okay." Mason brushed their lips together.

"And...I want to clean up for you." Parker reached for Mason's hips and Mason felt their thick cocks press together.

"If I tell you you have a fabulous body tonight, will you hold it against me?" Mason grinned, using his lips to caress Parker's mouth and chin.

"Man, that's an old joke. And by the way, aren't I already?" Parker closed his eyes and went for Mason's mouth.

The phone on Mason's desk rang. Mason rested his forehead against Parker's. "Six."

"Six." Parker slipped out of his embrace and left, giving Mason a leer that set him on fire.

Mason reached for the phone, flustered as hell and tried to think. "Mason Bloomfield, can I help you?"

~

Parker smiled at his happy thoughts and sat down at his desk. He scooted his chair closer to his computer and typed his next column—'*Err human? Forgive divine? I don't know about divinity, but make up sex is always a viable option. But what if it's the first err? Do we consider the first time a couple copulates forgiveness? Or will it just be divine?*

193

'*Sexual compatibility, boys and gals. It's either there or it ain't. Can you tell if a man will be good in bed just by the way he moves? Flirts? Or touches you with that loving caress?*

'*And if you were holding out...waiting until you knew your man before you enjoy the horizontal bop and it's a flop. Does that mean we've erred again? Or could it just be divine intervention?*

Parker tapped his fingers on the keys without typing as he reread his own thoughts on the screen.

'*Do we really ever know a man until we have him between the sheets?*'

He glanced over his shoulder at Mason's office and smiled.

~

Mason called the restaurant for reservations and worked until five p.m. on getting them as many big two-page ads for their upcoming issues as he could. He hung up from his last call and knocked a few quick emails out to prospective clients before he left for the night. A light tap on his door made him smile. "Come in."

Expecting Parker, to his surprise Sigourney poked her head in. "Dude. You are rocking the advertising this month. We made so much moolah, I don't know what to do with it all."

Mason laughed and began shutting his computer. "When they see how gorgeous the magazine is, they all want in. Easy fucking work. Love my job." He stood and picked up his jacket from the back of his chair, putting it on.

"What are you singing tonight at karaoke?"

"Oh. Uh. I made other plans." He closed the gap between them.

Sigourney was barely five foot four inches in height, so he towered over her.

"Is it because Dack won't be there?"

"No. It's not."

"Then you have to go. We've hit that place every Friday night for three years."

"I can't get a free pass for one night?" Mason peeked up. Parker was standing at his desk, also shutting down his computer.

"You can't come for five minutes?"

"I...I have a date." He smiled.

"Oh?" She brightened up. "Bring him. We'd love to meet him."

"Ready?" Parker asked over Sigourney's shoulder.

She spun around, a look of pure surprise on her face. "Hang on. Are you asking me if I'm ready to go to the karaoke bar, Parker, or Mason if he's ready for your date?"

Parker met Mason's eyes and didn't answer, as if he didn't know what to say.

"He's asking me." Mason moved past Sigourney to Parker.

"Oh! Wow. That was quick. Was Dack's spot on the bed even cold yet?" she laughed as she spoke.

"Yes. Cold as ice and filled with bullshit." Mason tilted his head to indicate to Parker to head out.

"Come on, Mason. Dack is just young. He's a great guy." Sigourney walked with them to the elevator, which had the door open by Morris who was waiting for them.

Inside the small space was nearly the whole staff that had been waiting to walk to the karaoke bar together. Mason didn't have a chance to discuss with Parker how he felt about their attraction becoming office news.

The door closed and Sigourney didn't let up. "Does Dack know you and Parker are dating?"

"What?" Morris reacted as did the rest of the group.

"I knew," Henry said with a high-pitched lilt. "Saw them playing under the table at the meeting this morning."

"Oh, boy," Parker said under his breath, looking down as if he were embarrassed.

"We are not 'dating' yet. We're just going to have dinner tonight, that's all." Mason tried to downplay it.

"*Wooo!*" was replied in harmony from the gang.

"So, we can't go to the karaoke. I made reservations."

Another '*wooooo*' came from the chorus.

When the elevator door opened, they filed into the parking garage, walking out of the building to the street level.

"We'll still be there when you're done with dinner, so stop by," Sigourney said, waving. "Enjoy dinner!"

Parker stood by his car as the small group headed out, laughing, their footfalls echoing in the cement interior.

Mason walked closer to Parker. "Sorry. Should I have shut my mouth?"

"If you didn't say something, Henry would have."

"You okay with it?"

Parker shrugged. "Sure. I'm a big boy."

"I know." Mason smiled and glanced down at Parker's crotch.

Parker pushed Mason playfully on his shoulder and looked shy.

"Okay. So. At your place in..." Mason checked his watch. "Fifty-three minutes."

"And twenty seconds." Parker mimicked his action.

Mason waved to him and headed to his car, grinning happily. He couldn't wait to have Parker to himself.

~

Once home, Parker showered, shaved his jaw even though he had that morning, and made sure he was ready, inside and out, for whatever the evening entailed. Would he fuck Mason? Hell yeah.

196

He dressed in a pair of black slacks and a long sleeved black cotton shirt, made sure his shoes were polished and put on a soft Italian made black leather jacket. A last check in the mirror at his hair and Parker was ready. He pocketed his keys, wallet and cell phone, looked around the apartment in case they came back here afterwards, and then headed down the stairs to wait in front of the building.

When he stepped out into the dark evening air, the Audi was idling close by. Surprised, Parker approached it and tried the passenger's handle. It opened and he looked in. "Were you waiting long?"

"Got here a little early so I figured I'd wait in case you were still getting ready."

"Wow. You clean up quick." Parker sat beside him and took a look at Mason in his smart casual clothing—black jeans, a crew neck white shirt and a supple brown leather jacket.

The scent of his aftershave made Parker's mouth water. As Mason began heading to Santa Monica, Parker went for a sniff.

Mason chuckled. "*Dangereux* cologne. Like it?"

"It's making my dick hard."

"They probably used Richfield's pheromones."

Parker laughed and fastened his seatbelt. He noticed Mason glance at his legs or crotch.

"So. Where are you taking me for our first date?"

"I told you. Did you forget already?" Mason gave Parker another once over. "How am I going to keep my hands off of you?" Mason slowed for a traffic signal as they headed to the on ramp for west Interstate 10.

Parker reached to Mason's right hand and placed it on his leg.

When he did, Mason made an exaggerated face of pain and said, "You're cruel."

"You love it."

"I do." Mason winked.

197

~

Mason found parking in a public lot and walked beside Parker on the crowded boulevards of Santa Monica through the Third Street Promenade.

"I've never been here before."

Mason checked Parker's expression. "That's right. This whole California thing is a new experience for you."

"Well, I've been to downtown LA previous to living here when I interviewed for several jobs, and I checked out West Hollywood, but...not here."

"It's got a lot going for it, but the pier is pretty tacky."

"Like the Jersey Shore?" Parker smiled.

"Never been." Mason brushed his arm against Parker's affectionately as they scooted around other pedestrians.

"Never been to the Jersey Shore? Oh, Mason, you haven't lived until you've walked the boardwalk and eaten greasy pizza."

"Take me there."

"I will."

Mason directed Parker to the restaurant which was right on the waterfront. Parker unzipped his jacket once inside and Mason told the hostess he had made a reservation. "I hope we have a table at the window."

"You do." She smiled.

Mason gestured for Parker to follow the young woman and then he stared at Parker's tight slacks and the globes of his ass as he walked, licking his chops for a chance at him.

They were shown to a table with a grand view of the rest of the pier and the ocean, cast in darkness, behind it. The Ferris wheel had a lightshow on its spokes, distracting Mason from everything else at the moment. He sat down after putting his jacket on the seat back and relaxed as he was handed a menu.

"Someone will be right with you to take your drink order."

"Thanks." Parker looked over the menu.

Mason got lost on him. Was Parker a twenty-year old pretty boy? No. But the more Mason got to know Parker, the more attractive he became. Mason reached over the table and brushed a lock of hair back from Parker's forehead.

He looked up and the sexy smile was worth everything to Mason.

"You think you're going to get me into bed just because this place is so expensive?" Parker teased.

Mason moved his foot so they were in contact under the table. "Nope."

"You could have taken me to a fish and chips place. This is very pricy, Mason."

"First date. I had to impress you."

Parker's smile vanished and he touched Mason's hand. "No, actually, you didn't. You already impressed me with your friendship."

Mason was taken aback. His mouth parted to reply but he was so unaccustomed to someone as intelligent and classy as Parker he was at a loss. If it were Dack? He would have heard, "Mason, order me a bottle of champagne and get me the most expensive thing on the menu, okay, *baby*?"

A waiter approached, introduced himself and set two glasses of water down for them, and a basket of bread. "Would you gentlemen like a drink?"

"Mason?" Parker asked, as if he wanted to see what he would order.

"Just the winter ale on tap." Mason pointed to it on the menu.

"Same." Parker nodded.

The waiter smiled and left.

Mason was distracted as he stared at Parker, his brown hair, his cleanly shaven jaw and his full lips.

He hadn't even looked at the menu when the waiter brought their beers.

Parker looked up and seemed to just notice Mason was staring at him. At first Parker seemed confused then the waiter asked, "Have you decided?"

"The clam chowder and a Caesar salad." Parker grinned, like he was playing with Mason.

Mason whispered, "You don't have to order cheaply."

"It's what I want."

Mason certainly had never met a man who was watching his wallet, to save rather than spend. He scanned the same area of the menu and requested, "How about the chowder and the beet salad."

"Will that be all?"

"Yup." Both Mason and Parker handed their menus off.

Raising his beer glass, Mason made a toast, "To the bizarro Dack."

Parker laughed so hard he had to put his beer down to not spill it. "Oh, Christ, that is too damn funny." After controlling his hilarity, he tapped Mason's glass and sipped the beer. "Yes, I am the bizarro Dack, it's true."

"But you're better. In every way."

"Except his body and looks." Parker sipped the beer.

"Bullshit."

Changing the subject, Parker stared out of the window. Since it was dark, only what was lit by spotlights was visible. "Love the look of that beach."

"Have you dipped your toes into the Pacific yet?"

"I have. But I'm still game on taking off my shoes and walking in the sand."

"In the dark?"

"Why not? Will we get mugged?"

"No." Mason chuckled.

"You just want to take me home and have your way with me."

"I do, but I'll let you get sand between your toes if you want to."

Parker put his glass down and stared at Mason for a moment.

"What? Did I say something stupid? Again?"

"No. I just love the color of your eyes."

Mason put his beer glass down and tried to fathom what he had been missing all this time. *Why was I too blind to see?*

Their soup was brought out and the waiter asked, "Do you want your salads now too?"

"Yes, please." Parker smiled.

Mason nodded in agreement. "This will be a quick meal."

"We can always hit the karaoke bar." Parker tore a roll in half and began eating his soup.

Reacting to his suggestion, Mason cringed. "I'll pass."

"I think we'll be the topic of conversation."

"No doubt." Mason ate the soup. "Mm. Excellent."

"It is." Parker reached across the table and used his thumb to wipe something off Mason's chin.

"Am I being a pig?" Mason picked up his cloth napkin and wiped his mouth.

"No. There was nothing there. I just wanted to touch you."

The spark of desire inside Mason and his attachment to Parker grew. "Man. I had no idea what I was missing."

"Life's too short for regrets, Mason." Parker buttered his roll.

"No kidding. But I've spent twenty years wasting it on putting all my effort into looks. I feel like Shallow Hal."

"Even he figured it out."

"Why did it take me so long?"

"Because…"

Mason waited, his spoon hovering over his bowl.

"You hadn't met me." Parker chuckled and stuffed a piece of bread in his mouth.

Mason reached across the table to brush an imaginary crumb off Parker's cheek. "Yeah. 'cause I hadn't met you."

Parker blushed and they stared at each other affectionately as they ate.

## CHAPTER 16

Parker stepped out of the restaurant into the cold air. He walked to the rail at the pier edge and looked down at the spotlight lit beach. A few people were walking on the sand, but because of the cool dark evening, the area was scattered with people coming and going. Very few lingered in the wind.

"Ready for that beach walk?"

"It's pretty chilly."

"Are you kidding me? You lived through New York winters." Mason rested his elbows on the rail beside him, leaning on his shoulder.

"I wasn't stupid enough to walk barefoot in the cold darkness."

"Up to you."

Turning around, Parker leaned his back against the railing and looked at the Ferris wheel and the few attractions that were open. "Got a better idea."

"What's that?"

"How about doing it tomorrow, after breakfast."

A sensual gleam came to Mason's eyes. He stood in front of Parker and touched his waist. "Deal."

"Take me home, Mr Bloomfield." Parker cupped his jaw. "Have your way with me."

"Don't tease me." Mason made a face of agony.

203

"I'm not." Parker tapped him to begin walking back to the car.

Mason went for his hand and held it. It made Parker smile. After the walk to the parking garage, Parker sat beside Mason in the Audi. Mason took out his phone as if he felt it vibrate. Sitting behind the wheel, he looked at it.

Parker frowned but didn't say anything. His was turned off.

When Mason handed it to him, Parker took it and looked at the picture on the LCD screen. It was of Dack, singing, without his shirt, joined by older man with gray hair, at the karaoke club. It was from Sigourney who wrote, '*You ain't missin' much!*'

"Oh Christ," Parker said, shaking his head.

"Shut it off."

Parker did, handing it back to Mason. Mason stuffed it into the glove box and slammed it shut.

"Nice one!" Parker loved it.

Mason put his hand on Parker's leg and squeezed it. "I know a good thing when I have it."

"And you know I'm a good thing?" Parker rested his hand on top of Mason's.

"I do. Man, do I." Mason shook his head. "You're the one who's the loser in this deal."

"I'm not so sure of that." Parker used Mason's hand to rub his thigh.

Mason peeked at the act and squirmed in the seat as he drove. "Damn."

"Are you prepared to give me a good fucking, Mr Bloomfield?"

"Fuck!" Mason went for Parker's crotch but Parker wouldn't let him, teasing.

"Jesus, I'm about to come in my pants." Mason appeared to struggle to focus on the road leading to the highway.

"That would be a waste of good spunk."

"Do you trust I'm clean? I can print up the test results for you." Mason peered at him while he drove.

"No need, but I'll still use a condom."

"I mean for…" Mason shut up.

Parker knew he meant a blowjob. "Uh huh. I'm good."

"I'll bet you fucking are." Mason broke free of Parker's hand and went for Parker's crotch, giving it a hot squeeze.

Parker's skin lit on fire and he straddled his legs and sank into the leather bucket seat. "You better give me a good fucking, Mason."

"Don't you worry. I will."

~

Mason parked in his assigned underground parking spot, holding onto Parker's waist, as they made their way to the elevator. They didn't speak, just held close and enjoyed the contact.

After the elevator ride, the walk down the hall, and Mason opening his condo unit, Parker entered first.

Parker took off his jacket and had a look around. "Very nice, Mason. Beautiful."

"Thanks."

Parker toed his shoes off at the door respectfully, since Mason didn't like wearing shoes in the house. Dack never bothered to pay attention to small things like that.

Mason hung up both their jackets in his hall closet and kept his eye on Parker who wandered the room inspecting the titles of books on a shelf and artwork that he had hung on the walls.

When Parker turned around, and they faced each other in the dim flattering light, Mason didn't want to wait any longer. He closed the gap between them and stood nose to nose with him.

Reaching up, Mason caressed Parker's cheek, seeing if he was receptive. Parker released a soft breath and lowered his eyelashes.

205

It was all Mason needed to let loose on him. Letting go his passion, Mason grabbed Parker's jaw and drew him to his mouth. Parker moaned in pleasure and rested his hands over the top of Mason's, opening his mouth to Mason's aggressive tongue.

Mason's body went into hyper-drive, his cock thick, his muscles tensed and his desire for this intelligent man skyrocketing.

The kisses were rough and Mason sucked Parker's tongue into his mouth then nibbled his lips and chin. Parker whimpered and surrendered completely to his power.

Deep in the back of Mason's mind was the concern that if he did indeed date a man older than his twenties, a power struggle would ensue. Mason loved to dominate, and one of the reasons he resisted men over the age of thirty was the concept in his mind that an older man would battle him for that dominance.

He didn't mind a struggle, but he wanted to win.

He pushed Parker against a wall and started undressing him, staring at Parker's chest as it was exposed. Hair. Chest hair. Mason didn't realize just how much it turned him on. He spread Parker's shirt wide over his chest and ran his mouth against it, making for one of Parker's nipples. Parker's chest was rising and falling rapidly, his arms hovering in the air, letting Mason do as he wished.

Mason stripped Parker's shirt off his body and it dropped to the carpeted floor soundlessly. He opened Parker's belt and zipper, then went back to Parker's mouth to suck on his lips and tongue.

Parker moaned against his mouth as Mason exposed Parker's cock from his pants. Parting from the kiss, Mason had a look at that cock. It was fabulous, cut, straight and accented by a brown bush of pubic hair. The contrast to Dack's shaven, emasculated look was more of a turn on than Mason expected.

He could barely get his libido under control as he nudged Parker to the bedroom. Parker backed up, looking over his shoulder to avoid colliding with the wall, allowing Mason to do anything he wanted.

Mason dug his fingertips into Parker's pants and briefs and tugged them to his ankles, helping Parker step out of them. After he did, Mason backed up to admire him.

Parker removed his socks and stood still, giving Mason the chance to take him in.

As Mason enjoyed Parker's trim, tightly packed physique he removed his own clothing, dropping it on a pile on the floor.

Parker had his chance to take a look at Mason, slowly lowering his gaze down to Mason's crotch. The inspection was both intimidating and thrilling. Mason tugged at his own cock as it throbbed and couldn't wait another moment. He went for Parker and held his head in both hands, bringing his mouth in contact with his own. Parker ran his hands down Mason's back to his ass, cupping it and pulling it tightly against his crotch.

Mason persuaded Parker to lay back on his bed, crawling between Parker's legs, their mouths still in contact, making small noises of pleasure.

Parker's jaw was silky smooth as if he'd just shaven before their date, but Mason had not, and knew his dark shadow was coarse and rough on Parker's skin. He began chewing Parker's earlobe and neck, working his way to his nipples.

Parker spread his legs and caressed Mason lightly as Mason began to devour him.

After teething both nipples erect, Mason made his way to the floor in front of where Parker's legs were resting. With a hand on either knee, Mason opened Parker's legs wider, meeting Parker's eyes and watching his expression as he panted in excitement and his chest rose and fell quickly. Mason look at Parker's engorged cock and the two globes under it which were tight to his body in the cool room. He went for those balls first, opening his mouth and engulfing one, rolling it on his tongue. Parker tensed in reflex then relaxed opening to an even wider straddle.

~

Parker floated on a cloud of lust.

His eyes closed, he rested his arms to his sides and just allowed Mason to do his thing. It had been a long time since Lee had made love to him. A long time to be on his own and try to recover from that relationship, and he didn't even count the one quick blowjob from Claudio as a blip on his sexual radar. Contacts like that meant nothing to Parker. Mason, on the other hand…

As his second ball was enveloped into Mason's hot mouth, Parker's cock throbbed and leaked pre-cum. With his saliva Mason used his thumb around Parker's rim, stimulating him to a heightened state. Older men. The consummate lovers. He wasn't stupid—he knew where to get a good partner. And a forty year old man? Perfection.

Mason lapped under Parker's balls and spread his ass cheeks. When he went for his rim, Parker opened his mouth and gasped in pure heaven. He looked down between his thighs to see Mason's eyebrows knotted and his hands on either side of Parker's erect cock, also holding his balls in his grasp.

"Oh, fuck…" Parker's craving for a climax grew and he wanted Mason inside him.

Mason moaned, obviously enjoying himself, dipping his tongue into Parker and chewing the root of his cock and his inner thighs gently.

In reaction Parker raised his hips off the bed, longing the close union of making love.

Mason stared between Parker's legs as he used the wetness from his mouth to push into Parker's ass with his thumb.

A shiver raced up Parker's spine and his entire groin tingled in anticipation. Mason was panting for breath, hard, as if he were going crazy as well. He kept massaging Parker's ass and leaned over his cock, taking the head into his mouth.

Seeing Mason envelope his seeping cock between his lips made Parker's skin prickle and he began to edge the climax. The blowjob was so intense, Parker tried to hold back.

Mason didn't seem to want him to. He was drawing hard suction to the tip, deep-throating Parker, and pushing his wet finger up Parker's ass while he rubbed the base of his cock.

"If..." Parker's throat felt dry and he was struggling to talk as he came close to a climax. "It you're trying to...oh God! Make me come...oh, Jesus!" Parker gripped the bedding in both fists and thrust up into Mason's mouth deeply. A rush of pure pleasure hit Parker's balls and he clenched his jaw.

Mason amped up the action, swirling his fingertip inside Parker's body and using his tongue to do the same on the head of Parker's cock.

"Fuck! Fuck!" Parker could not hold back and his body jerked upward and he arched his back. He threw his head against the mattress and choked on his gasps the climax was so intense.

Mason kept up the pace until he felt Parker slow down his ejaculating, massaging him more gently and removing his cock from his mouth to gain air.

Parker touched his own chest, feeling his heart pounding. All contact stopped and he watched Mason go to the nightstand for a condom and lube.

So satisfied he could weep, Parker waited as Mason rolled a condom onto his fabulous blushing cock. Instead of coating himself, he used the lube on his hand and pushed his fingers into Parker, stretching him out gently. Parker held his knees and relaxed every muscle in his body in preparation.

Mason physically shifted Parker so they were lying lengthwise on the bed then he knelt between Parker's legs and lowered his cock on target. Parker stared at Mason's handsome face, the dark hair on his chest leading to a black treasure trail and dark bush. As Mason pushed inside him, uniting their bodies as one, Parker once again floated. *I love you. Oh, holy crap, to get fucked by you in my bed every night? Yes. Please.*

~

Mason was high on the oral sex. He loved both giving *and* receiving and Dack was only keen on giving, not receiving. Of course after learning what Dack was up to, he was grateful. But he had been missing that treat for a long while.

He loved eating between a man's legs, and could enjoy it all night. Seeing Parker's willingness and pleasure in everything he was doing to him was such a bonus.

Mason stared at their connection as he pushed inside that tight hot opening. Parker moaned sensually and released one of his legs to rest on the bed, while he held the other. Mason loved this position and helped Parker keep his right leg suspended. He drove in as deeply as he could, shivering at the contact and closeness.

Closeness.

Something lacking in all his previous relationships.

Why did it always seem like an 'act' before, when this felt more like a bond? A mutual meeting of mind, soul, and body.

Preventing himself from going into a furious internal battle about how stupid he had been by dating young models, Mason kept looking at Parker's fabulous body, his masculine attributes—hair on his chest and groin, long lean muscular runner's legs, and the taste and scent of pure testosterone.

"How you doin'?" Mason figured he'd ask out of concern.

"Waiting for you to take me like a man."

At the surprising comment, Mason shivered and gripped Parker tightly. Getting in a position to do just that, Mason stared at Parker's light blue eyes and began thrusting his hips.

Parker's sensuous snarl appeared and he closed his eyes at the pleasure. The sight of Parker's lusty appetite for being the recipient of rough sex set Mason on fire. With Dack it had appeared as if the airhead was bored, waiting for it to finish so he could get back to his text messages. Intercourse without connecting mentally was a vacuum—yes, for men as well as women.

At least for him.

As he felt Parker letting go, and enjoying the penetration, Mason began to move faster, staring at his cock as he hammered into Parker like he wanted to. Sweat began dripping down Mason's temples and pits as he worked hard on the friction, wanting to edge the climax and wanting to dive over the edge simultaneously.

A loud masculine grunt from Parker created a wash of pre-orgasmic chills in Mason. Seeing Parker fisting his cock, his abs tense and the lines of a six-pack and his tight chest becoming visible as he did, Mason came. He drove in deep and opened his mouth for a low groaning whimper of ecstasy. Making sure Parker had his second climax, Mason kept fucking him, rubbing over that internal G-spot until Parker's cock sprayed ribbons of cum all over his chest and his hand slowed.

*Thirty-six and two climaxes—impressive, Mr Douglas.*

Though Mason wanted to say that out loud, he didn't. The last thing he wanted was to sound patronizing. He pushed in once more and pulled out, catching his breath.

"Kept hard after you came…" Parker huffed for breath as well. "Not bad for a forty year old stud."

G. A. HAUSER

Hearing similar thoughts to his own, Mason laughed softly as he recovered. "Yeah, I was impressed with your two climaxes, Parker. Believe me."

"It's not about age. It's about being in physical shape, and having the fucking drive of an eighteen year old." Parker stretched his right leg out, resting on the bed.

"Got that right. The secret is out." Mason stared down at the condom. "Let me get rid of this."

"I'll come with you."

"Yeah. You did." Mason grinned and hauled Parker off the bed to head to the bathroom to wash up.

~

Parker used a wet washcloth to scrub up as Mason removed the condom and did the same. After the sex, Parker was feeling very sated and affectionate. For a first romp, it was damn good. He caught Mason's hazel eyes in the mirror's reflection and smiled.

"You're one hell of a fuck, Parker." Mason used a towel to dry himself.

"Thinking the same thing, Mason."

"Do you have to rush off?"

"No."

"Excellent." Mason gestured for Parker to leave the bathroom, taking a good grab of his ass as he did.

It made Parker chuckle as he returned to the bedroom and got cozy under the blankets. When Mason joined him, they lay on their sides, face to face, the pillow crushed under their heads.

Parker stared at the golden ring around the iris of Mason's eyes in the dim light of the table lamp. "What are you looking for, Mason?"

"In...?" Mason interlocked their legs under the blanket. "In work? Life?"

"Love?"

212

Mason ran his hand over Parker's exposed shoulder. "I don't know, really. I've been asking myself that for a long time."

"Do you want a loyal partner? Or just to enjoy yourself?"

"I want someone loyal. In theory that's what I've been trying to find."

"In theory?" Parker knew what was coming but wanted to hear Mason say it.

"I have always wanted a partner, not just a playmate. But I don't make good choices."

"Until now?" Parker scooted closer, using his legs to tighten his hold on Mason.

Mason raised one eyebrow. "Is that cocky? Or...?"

"Or." Parker shifted on the pillow. "You're used to cocky. Just checking if you still need some of it."

"Uh. No."

"So where are we in this discussion? Too soon to consider 'the talk'?"

"Not really. At my age, I prefer upfront honesty to lies and creeping behind my back."

"You do realize forty is not old, right?"

Mason appeared to think about it. "It is to some."

"Yes, to twenty year olds." Parker tried not to sound too sarcastic. "Look at you, Mason." Parker deliberately raised up the blanket to expose Mason's gorgeous build. "You do realize that handsome men want you for your body, not just your wallet."

"Yeah. Right." Mason tugged the blanket to cover his body.

"You think you have a bad build? Are you kidding me?"

"I'm not twenty anymore."

"No. Thank fuck you're not. And I don't want to be twenty either. I was a stupid schmuck who had no clue about life and what I wanted to be when I grew up."

Mason said nothing, but the intensity of his stare communicated a lot to Parker.

Parker caressed Mason's hair gently. "You do know you're absolutely gorgeous, right?"

As if he were modest, Mason looked away, lowering his eyelashes.

"Mason." Parker nudged him until he gazed into his eyes again. "And your beauty isn't just skin deep."

It was like an ice sheet had melted in Mason. He reacted and embraced Parker, holding him close under the sheets. Parker smiled and held him tight. *I got a good one. I'm not letting go.*

## CHAPTER 17

Mason dozed on and off with Parker in his arms. He didn't know what time it was and wasn't sure he cared if it was an hour after they made love, the middle of the night, or near morning. He moved on the bed to come in complete contact with Parker's hot body, resting against his side, his right leg over Parker's thighs. Parker shifted in his sleep and cuddled close.

While Mason hovered between sleep and wakefulness, he began to think about his life.

The triumphs were few, and the heartbreaks had been many. He didn't set out to fail in relationships, but inevitably he had.

Even as a young man he liked younger partners. When he was seventeen he'd enjoyed the fifteen year old neighborhood boy, sharing a mutual jack-off session behind the school and kissing.

Age twenty-one he was on the hunt for seventeen and eighteen year old boys...in his mid-twenties? Mason craved nineteen year old men who were insatiable, and incredibly beautiful.

He went to college for journalism but ended up setting up his own modeling agency in an effort to keep himself surrounded in pretty boys while living in LA. Being self-employed had benefits until the recession hit. The job was his access to gorgeous men to fulfill his fantasies, but inevitably he went bankrupt when bigger agencies took over, able to withstand the drop in business. He couldn't.

Although he had kept his contact book of his handsome clients, and used it like a list of prospective first dates to choose from, in the meantime Mason went in search of a job. Luckily he discovered *Judas' Rainbow* when it was just an e-publication. He and Sigourney hit it off in the interview, and he was hired, having the work explode when the magazine found the right niche market.

He got Dack the job at the magazine. Dack had been a model for him when Dack was only eighteen. They had a brief fling—more like a one-fuck-stand in his office the first day they met, and then years later when Dack was twenty-six, he contacted Mason for help since he was financially drowning.

Since Dack had a passion for photography, and a decent portfolio, Mason got him on the payroll. As they began dating, Mason assisted Dack in acquiring an apartment, helped him pay for his car, his clothing, his personal trainer...

Parker shifted against him and Mason felt a kiss on his neck.

With the light beginning to filter into his window, Mason realized it was indeed morning. He had slept very well, when normally he tossed and turned.

Mason was so accustomed to having men in his life who were dependant and needing help, he wondered how he would manage a man who was more like a peer. If he was honest with himself, he was nervous. With Parker's maturity came emotional power and control.

Though as he thought about it, it hadn't given him any control with Dack. Thinking at the time that Dack was dependent on him for his bankroll, Mason now knew Dack had many sugar daddies to tap into. *Dack—the escort to the aged*.

A hand cupped his crotch.

216

"No morning wood?" Parker asked with a slight comic lilt, massaging Mason's soft cock.

"It was there a minute ago." Mason rolled over to face Parker, eye to eye. "Did you sleep well?" He caressed Parker's hair.

"Oh? Looked at me and the wood vanished?"

"No. Thinking of what a fuck-up I've made of my life and it vanished."

It took Parker a second but he leaned up on his elbows and gave Mason a closer inspection. "He's one idiot. Why are you beating yourself up?"

"He's part of a long line of idiots I've managed to date."

"Mason. Don't dwell on it. I've made bad choices too. We all have."

"What bad choices have you made?" Mason shifted on the pillow so he could relax as they spoke, keeping in contact with Parker under the bedding. Parker rested his hand on Mason's groin but was not massaging it any longer.

"You want a list? Come on, Mason. Everyone who came before you."

"Everyone?" That surprised Mason.

"Well, look at it this way. Did I learn something from each one? Yes. But inevitably I was either hurt, or hurt the other guy."

Mason knew that pain. "Nothing lasts."

"Not forever, no. But some relationships have a good run."

"I suck at them." Mason rolled to his back and put his arm over his eyes. "I really haven't had any long term partnerships."

"That's because you pick pretty boys who are not long term material."

"And you?" Mason peeked at him.

"I've fallen into that trap. But I did have one long term relationship. He ended up cheating on me." Parker shrugged. "Not a lot I could do about it when I found out. I couldn't forgive him. I felt very betrayed."

217

"How long did it last?"

"Five years."

"Wow." Mason relaxed his arm along his side and stared at the ceiling fan.

"Yeah. Wow." Parker lay on his back too, but they were connected down one side.

"I barely managed six months. At least you had something."

"We never moved in together. It was as if he knew it was going to end and I was the oblivious one."

"I'm sorry, Parker."

"Live and learn."

"What did you learn?" Mason tilted his head to look at Parker's profile.

"I don't know." Parker laughed sadly. "Not to trust anyone?"

"Yeah. I learned that lesson too. Too many times."

"I suppose it's all about taking chances. If you don't try, let it go a little, you don't gain anything either."

"I am so sick of it." At Parker's silence, Mason leaned up on his elbow to check his expression. "What?"

"Nothing." Parker appeared angry.

"No. What?" Mason nudged him.

"If you're sick of it, am I another one fuck and untrustworthy?"

"Did I say that?" Mason tried to think of his own words.

"You implied it."

"Parker, you are nothing like the men I have dated. Nothing." He touched Parker's chest. "And I mean that in a good way."

"I know you've just come out of a crappy relationship. I have too. But at least I'm willing to try."

"To try…" Mason nudged the sheet down and touched the light hair that was on Parker's sternum. "To try and do a one on one thing with me?"

218

"Yes. But we work together, so I just don't know how this will evolve."

"It wasn't working with Dack that fucked us up. It was Dack's infidelity."

"What if we hate each other after a few months?"

"I love you, I hate you. What's the difference?"

Parker's expression became unreadable, then he cracked up with laughter, making Mason smile.

"There is a difference, you nut!" Parker shifted so they were facing each other on the bed, his head propped up on his hand. "Don't believe what you've heard about them being alike since they are both strong emotions. Believe me. They are polar opposites."

Mason smiled. "I know. I just am tired of trying for the real thing."

"You can't get the real thing with a guy who takes pictures of his dick in public places and then emails them."

"Aw, no. Really? You won't send me cock shots?" Mason kept moving the sheet down.

Parker helped him, exposing his groin. "You won't need a photograph. You can have the real thing."

Mason liked that idea. He scooted down on the bed and took all of Parker's soft cock into his mouth.

"You're going down on me again?" Parker chuckled. "Wow. I just won the jackpot."

With Parker's cock getting hard in his mouth, Mason smiled. *So have I, ya gorgeous hunk. So have I.*

~

Parker closed his eyes and relaxed. Yeah they'd both had some bad luck in the past, but that didn't mean they couldn't try. Did it?

As Parker's cock grew, Mason held the base and leaned on his elbows, drawing hard suction to the tip.

"I wouldn't mind a taste of your dick, Mr Bloomfield."

Mason sat up, spun around and spread his knees over Parker's face. "Be careful what you ask for."

"Ha! Love it." Parker caressed the semi-erect dangling cock in front of his face as his was engulfed into Mason's mouth again. Smiling, Parker held Mason under his balls and opened his mouth to bring the head against his lips. He ran the tip along his tongue and tasted a drop of pre-cum at the slit of Mason's cock.

Parker wet his finger and made for Mason's rim. He gave it a good rubbing and Mason's cock grew thicker as he did. Just because you like to top, doesn't mean you can't enjoy a good prostate rub. Parker glanced at the nightstand and reached out for the lube. He used a tiny bit on his fingers and felt Mason hesitate as if he were waiting to see what Parker would do.

"Ever bottom, boy?" Parker slapped Mason's rump with a crack.

"Yes. It's just a preference."

"Mm." Parker pushed his slick finger into Mason's ass and went back to sucking.

A low long groan came from Mason in pleasure, sending Parker's cock thicker.

"God." Mason stopped sucking to speak. "Now I know what I've been missing."

Removing Mason's cock from his mouth, Parker said, "No!"

"Don't stop."

Parker sucked it as deeply as he could while massaging Mason inside and out.

"Oh my God." Mason stopped sucking and seemed to be enjoying the attention his body was getting.

Parker wondered if not only were these pretty boys emotionally vacant but perhaps they didn't know how to make love well either. It was about experience and Parker had a lot of it.

He closed his eyes and focused on pleasing this man, who, apparently, hadn't been pleased well in a while.

Parker tasted more pre-cum and moaned in anticipation as Mason had stopped everything he was doing to enjoy.

~

*You have to be kidding me!*

In all his sexual experience, Mason had not had anyone service him quite this well. Had he given this kind of pleasure to the young studs? He assumed so, since he too knew the tricks of the trade, but had any of them ever bothered to really think about his pleasure in a partnership?

*Obviously not!*

Mason wanted to continue sucking Parker's cock but what was happening to his own body was so damn good, he couldn't function. "God! Parker! Holy shit!"

Parker groaned in agreement and sucked faster, pulling at the base of Mason's cock while rubbing delicious friction on Mason's prostate.

"Damn! Damn!" Mason came and shivered, nearly landing on Parker below him as his arms shook and his knees quaked.

"Mmm." Parker milked Mason's cock and withdrew his finger.

"Oh fuck...Damn." Mason enjoyed the aftershocks of a very strong orgasm. He rolled to his side to recuperate. "Sorry. Holy shit."

"You act as if you've never come before. And I know you have. You did last night in my ass." Parker rested his hands over his head and smiled.

"Fuck." Mason wasn't used to *that* kind of loving.

"I need to wash up." Parker held up his hands.

"Shower with me."

"I can do that." Parker smiled and rolled off the bed, landing on his feet.

As Mason watched Parker's ass as he walked to the bathroom, he stared at his own dick in awe, then up at Parker. *I want you. I want you very fucking much.*

When he entered the bathroom, Parker was at the sink washing his hands and face. Mason turned on the shower and then removed a new toothbrush from out of the medicine cabinet, handing it to Parker.

"Keep a steady supply on hand?" Parker grinned like a mischievous boy and peeled back the cardboard.

"Ha ha." Mason slapped his rump with a crack. "Tight as a snare drum."

"Running does it."

"Yeah. I'd love a partner to run with." Mason stuck his hand under the shower to feel the temperature, then loaded a toothbrush and climbed in, brushing his teeth while he wetted down.

After scrubbing his teeth, Parker said, "I can do that." He rinsed his mouth and then poked his head into the shower stall.

"Can do what?" Mason spat out the toothpaste and rinsed his mouth under the spray.

"Run with you." Parker took his spot under the shower head.

"When?"

"After work. That's when I go. If you want, we can bring our gear to the office and figure out a route." Parker put shampoo into his palm and washed his hair.

They swapped spots as Mason thought about it. "We could try it, but there's no shower at the office."

"Then come to my place after, and we can...shower together." Parker used soapy hands to pull Mason's cock, fist over fist to stimulate it.

Mason stopped what he was doing to watch.

"Love how that feels." Parker ran his hand under Mason's balls to his ass.

Mason couldn't get enough of this attention. He grabbed Parker by the shoulders and brought him under the shower head, saying, "Rinse off."

Parker did, hitting everywhere to get rid of the soap and shampoo.

Mason began to get hungry for him, to do things to him he craved doing with Dack but never did. Once Parker had washed off the soap, Mason sat in the tub, turned his back to Parker, and leaned backwards between Parker's legs.

"Wow." With one foot on the side of the tub, Parker held onto the sliding glass door to keep his balance as Mason rubbed his face against Parker's wet balls, then advanced hungrily towards his rim.

While he enjoyed Parker's clean body, Mason rested against the back wall of the shower and spread Parker's ass cheeks, using his thumb and tongue in tandem to stimulate Parker's ass.

Parker grabbed his own cock and began fisting it, panting loudly in the wet stall.

Mason's moans of pleasure echoed with Parker's gasping breaths, and he felt the base of Parker's cock thicken up, using hard friction behind his balls.

"Fuck!" was yelled loudly and Mason shivered at how much Parker was enjoying the sexual play.

Parker began leaning forward, reaching for the far wall under the shower head, spreading his legs as wide as he could in invitation. Since Mason did not have a rubber, he grabbed the soap and caught his breath as he lathered up. With slippery fingers, Mason first made rings around Parker's rim before he penetrated, wondering just what this man liked. Mason loved to play rough, and with Dack he hadn't. Dack was a prima donna in many ways, and that included not allowing them to become mad dogs in the bed.

Parker, as if he was overwhelmed by the sensation, stopped jacking off and held onto the sliding door and tile wall while bent over. His whimpers and moans were making Mason's cock swell.

In the steamy heat of the hot shower, he and Parker were making their own boiling heat.

With one hand on Parker's balls and the root of his cock, the other pushing into his ass, Mason's teeth were on edge he was so hot watching.

Parker let out a growl-like groan and Mason wondered, good or bad? He suspected a man like Parker would say something to stop him if it wasn't good, so he kept going.

~

Parker was in heaven.

Nothing was hotter to him than having a man enjoy his ass. And Mason was certainly doing that. Lee had had moments of timid fun, but seemed reluctant to go as far as Parker wanted him to go, even when Parker asked him to.

Mason had no reservations. And Parker liked it rough. Very rough. But it wasn't something he felt comfortable about mentioning to a man he'd only just fucked.

As the internal pleasure grew and the stimulation to his prostate became enough to orgasm, Parker said, "Yes!" loudly, so loud, it even surprised him.

"*Oh* yes!" Mason seemed to agree and used the shampoo to keep the contact slick.

"Mason! Oh fuck yeah!" Parker closed his eyes and braced himself, feeling his cock pulsate as Mason pushed his fingers deep and full into his ass.

"Come, you fucker! Come!" Mason rubbed hard friction on the base of Parker's cock and Parker nearly passed out from the intensity.

His cock began spraying cum, bobbing as it did with every pulsating beat. The waves of pleasure overwhelmed Parker. He nearly sobbed as he groaned it felt so good.

Mason slowed his motion down and massaged both inside and out of Parker gently. "Man, I want to fuck you."

Parker panted and knew they needed a condom. He wasn't quite that sure of Mason's test results that he would allow bareback. "Get a rubber."

Mason scrambled to his feet, threw open the sliding door and Parker felt a gust of wind from the cool air.

Still holding the shower door and wall, Parker hung his head and staring at his cock which had gone soft but his breathing was still heavy as he recuperated.

Mason returned, shut the shower door and pushed into Parker's ass, holding his waist as he hammered.

Parker gasped at the power but loved it, grinding his jaw and letting Mason manhandle him.

"You fucking doll! Holy shit!" Mason piston-fucked Parker, his vocalizations loud and sensual as if the act of them making love was pure heaven.

After a few minutes of allowing Mason to hump away, Parker felt Mason's cock shiver inside him as he came and chills washed over Parker's skin listening to Mason's orgasmic cries.

Mason wrapped his arms around Parker's body and rested on his back, his cock still deep inside Parker, as he too recuperated, catching his breath.

"Holy shit, Mason." Parker looked up at the shower head and allowed it to splash his face.

Mason pulled out and Parker was able to turn around. He watched Mason remove the condom and Parker washed himself off as he did. Mason met his gaze and they stared at each other as if they were stunned the sex could be that good.

And reading each other's minds, they began to smile, then laugh.

Mason shook his head. "I must be crazy, but Jesus, Parker. I want more of that."

"Shit. No kidding." Parker let Mason clean up and stood by as they finished in the shower.

The water shut off, each of them drying themselves with big fluffy cotton towels, they kept giving each other adoring looks as if they knew a secret.

And maybe they did.

## CHAPTER 18

Parker had Mason stop by his apartment so Parker could get a change of clothing and a few toiletries before they took their walk on the beach. When Mason reached into his glove compartment for his phone and turned it on, Parker could hear it vibrating and chiming with missed messages. He couldn't be upset, he had to turn his on as well and see what was going on in the 'outside world'. They parked and climbed out of the car.

As Parker led the way to his apartment unit, Mason walked with him scrolling through his messages and texts. Parker couldn't resist asking as he opened his door, "Any from Dack?"

"Yup." They paused just inside Parker's door. "One from last night with a picture of him naked kneeling in front of someone else, who is also naked. Dack is about to suck him. The caption reads, 'I hate you.'"

Parker shook his head and thought Dack was a total jerk. He kept walking to his bedroom to change clothing and pack a small bag for tonight.

"Then," Mason stood at the doorway of Parker's bedroom, still reading messages. "He sent me one an hour later, obviously drunk because I can barely read his text…" Mason struggled to decipher it, Parker could see him squint and tilt his head. "Oh. It says, 'sorry, now that my cock is better you can suck me.' But it's practically hieroglyphs."

227

Parker dropped the clothing he had been wearing into the hamper and put on a clean pair of briefs and jeans, thinking about having someone like Dack to deal with.

"Then he sent one at about three am," Mason said, "That text had him back to hating me. It shows him flipping me off."

Parker laughed as he put a shirt on over his head and then said, "Sorry. Maybe you don't think it's funny."

"I do now." Mason kept reading. "Then one last one. It says 'fuck you, when I'm rich and famous I'll forget your name'."

Parker started laughing again, then cleared his throat to stop finding too much humor in it as he folded clothing to pack into a small backpack.

Mason said, "Delete, delete, delete," as he pushed buttons.

"He's a real piece of work, Mason." Parker headed to his bathroom to pack his shaving kit.

"I'm the piece of work. I turned a blind eye to all of that just because he was pretty to look at." Mason kept scanning his messages. "Christ, I need glasses." He held it out at arm's length.

"Get them. You'd look geek chic."

"No. Just old and stupid."

Parker frowned at him for his self-depreciating words. "Right. Ready to go."

"Got a suit?" Mason gave him a wicked smirk.

"Yeah? I'm staying until Monday?"

"Wouldn't kick ya outta my bed, hot stuff." Mason reached out to grope Parker's crotch.

"Damn! You're a fast mover, Mason." Parker set his pack on the floor and investigated his suits.

"Up to you. I'm not trying to push you." Mason pocketed his phone and walked up behind Parker, holding him, kissing his neck.

Putting on a fake southern belle accent, since he knew Mason was from one of the Carolinas, Parker said, "Why I do declare!

228

You are sweeping this lady off her feet!" He batted his lashes playfully.

"Grrr." Mason reached both hands around Parker and cupped his groin. "Good. I want to sweep you off them. You're amazing."

"Lil ole me?" Parker chose a suit and held onto it as Mason played.

"You get me hotter than hell."

"Hotter than Dack-in-the-Box?"

"Dack who?" Mason spun Parker around in his arms and kissed him.

Parker moaned in pleasure and tossed the suit, on its hanger, onto the bed, embracing Mason. Between kisses Parker said, "How could anyone take you for granted?"

"Don't. Stop."

"You're so fucking fabulous." Parker licked Mason's mouth and rolled tongues.

"Don't. Stop." Mason laughed. "Don't stop!" He ground his cock against Parker's. "I swear, all I want to do is rub against you. We'll never get to the beach at this rate."

Parker held Mason by the hips and they rolled their stiff erections over each other, getting off nicely. "Yeah. I could do this all day."

"And all night." Mason looked down at their bodies touching in the perfect spot.

"Bed or beach?" Parker didn't care at this point.

"Beach. Bed. Beach. Bed," Mason said as he laughed and ground harder against Parker.

Parker closed his eyes and got lost in the fantastic sensation. "Let me suck you off."

"Let me eat you up." Mason began chewing Parker's neck.

Chills rushed over Parker. "Damn! We're like animals. What the hell?"

"You smell so good." Mason inhaled him and ran his hands all over Parker. "I have to fuck you."

Parker leaned back to see Mason's eyes and with as serious an expression as he could muster, he said, "I'm afraid you do."

"You sore?" Mason began stripping.

"Nope. Not enough to say no!" Parker laughed at the absurdity as they raced to get naked.

"Is this crazy? We're acting like eighteen-year-olds." After nudging the suit onto the floor, Mason flung his socks into the air and jumped naked onto Parker's bed with a bounce.

Parker removed lube and condoms from the nightstand. "Yeah, so what? We can be obnoxious eighteen-year-olds for an hour."

"Let's." Mason reached out his hand.

"I can do the honors." Parker tore open the package and rolled the condom onto Mason's stiff cock, then he slathered lube on it. He straddled Mason and sank his cock inside him.

Mason appeared enthralled at the act and said, "You are unbelievable!"

Parker was going to ask why, but then reconsidered. *Sheesh, Mason, did you and Dack actually ever make love?*

Once Parker felt comfortable, he braced his hands on either side of Mason and fucked him, riding up and down.

After he coated his palms in lube, Mason reached for Parker's cock and ran his palms over it, getting a good grip.

Parker stared at Mason's hands working his cock, then up the treasure trail of Mason's body to his chest, which had dark hair in an inverted triangle on it. Parker's gaze moved up to Mason's angular jaw, his full salmon colored lips, then his hazel eyes.

That was all it took. Parker began going into a climax. He made a deep low noise and Mason got the hint. He thrust up into Parker at the same time as he increased the speed of his hands, jerking Parker off.

Parker's cum sprayed out of his cock onto the hair on Mason's chest. In response to the heightened state, Mason came, squeezing Parker's cock as he did, clenching his teeth and snarling like a fabulous big cat.

Parker hung his head and panted in exhaustion, sweat dripping down his pits and neck. He disconnected their union and caught his breath.

"Christ, I can't get enough of you." Mason cupped Parker's cock gently, then left it alone to recover.

"Jesus, Mason. I want you for the sex alone, fuck the great conversation."

Mason laughed tiredly and looked down at his sticky chest. "You are a stud, make no mistake, Parker."

"Look who's talking." Parker struggled to get out of the bed and to his feet, holding onto the wall.

"Christ, I need a nap."

Parker cracked up with laughter as they headed to the bathroom to clean up. "Me too. See? We're both old."

Mason grabbed a handful of Parker's ass and nudged him playfully.

They stood at the sink, giving each other adoring glances in the mirror as they washed up. *I fucking love you! Shit. I am so in love!*

Parker leaned back and kissed Mason.

Mason held onto him tightly and gave him a smooch worth remembering, making Parker's toes curl it was so passionate.

~

Mason felt his heart burn with affection towards Parker. Maybe he'd felt lust for Dack, but he never felt like this! *I love you, you fucking stud!*

Parting from the kiss, Mason smiled sweetly at Parker. "Beach?"

"Who you callin' a beach?" Parker winked.

231

Mason cupped both hands over Parker's soft cock and balls, nuzzling his neck from behind. "You wanna be my beach?"

"Maybe." Parker leaned against him, rocking gently.

"Be mine." Mason nibbled Parker's shoulder.

"Be my Valentine?" Parker laughed and caught Mason's eyes in the mirror over the sink.

"Yeah. Why not?"

Parker shrugged, repeating, "Yeah. Why not?"

Mason spun Parker around with both hands on his arms until they were nose to nose. "Mine?"

"Sure." Parker teased, shrugging like it was meaningless, all the while giving Mason a tongue-in-cheek smirk.

Mason held Parker's ass and pulled him close so their crotches were tight together. "I'll treat you like gold."

"Nah. I'm easy. Silver will do."

Mason smiled and pressed his forehead against Parker's, happy. Very happy.

"Beach?"

"Beach."


Parker's clothing packed in the trunk of the Audi, Mason held his hand as they drove to the seaside, the sky bright blue, the temperature in the lovely high sixties, perfect for February. Mason's phone hummed with a text, making him groan pathetically.

"May I?" Parker asked comically.

"Yup." Mason removed his phone and handed it over as he drove.

Parker read it out loud. "It says," Parker added out of the side of his mouth, *"from you know who"*, then read, "'Moved into…'"

Mason glanced over as he slowed for a traffic signal. "Moved into?"

"Hang on. Wow, is he drunk all the time or illiterate?"

"Both."

"Uh, I think he wrote, 'Moved into new hose'? Hose?"

"Oh. The reality show. They moved him into the house."

Parker snickered. "Okay. 'Moved into new house, hot...'"

Mason tried to read it over Parker's shoulder. "'Hot dudes.'"

"Oh. He wrote 'dides'." Parker kept working on deciphering it. "I think he's trying to make you jealous."

"I need to block his number." Mason continued driving when the light turned green.

"Hell no. This makes for high comedy."

Mason smiled and rubbed Parker's thigh, thrilled he was not only not jealous, he was hilarious.

"Okay. 'Moved into new house, hot dudes...cook everywhere'?"

"Cock everywhere." Mason started laughing.

"Sure it's not coke? He's, like, so incoherent."

"Could be coke. Could be crack. He's totally into anything anyone offers. But, most of all, money."

Mason hit Highway 10 and relaxed since there wasn't too much traffic on a late Saturday afternoon. "That it?"

"No. He wrote, 'miss me?' with one 'S'."

"What did I see in that dick?" Mason felt embarrassed for his attraction to a guy like that.

"Okay. Confession time." Parker put Mason's phone into the cup holder on the console.

"Uh oh." Mason wasn't sure he wanted to hear it.

"Okay," Parker repeated, as if telling the tale would be hard. "Last Saturday night..."

"Yes?" Mason cringed.

"My cousin Claire set me up with a model who is one of her clients."

"Your cousin is an agent?"

"Yes."

"Here?"

"No. In New York."

"Who does she work for?" Mason had been in the business a long time, and well, it was a small world. He pulled off the exit for the Santa Monica pier and began trolling for a parking spot.

"She owns Spencer and Epstein."

Mason whipped his head around. "Are you kidding me?"

"No. But that wasn't the point of the story."

"That's the biggest male modeling agency in Manhattan. *That's* your cousin?"

"You haven't heard what I wanted to say yet."

Mason tried to fathom Parker being related to Claire Epstein. "Sorry. Go ahead." He found a parking spot on the street and parallel parked into it.

"She set me up last Saturday night with a real pretty boy. Claudio from Brazil."

"Last Saturday?" Mason shut off the car and gave Parker his undivided attention.

"Yes. I just wanted to tell you, you're not the only one lured by pretty bait. The fucker was so damn gorgeous I felt like a real ug next to him. But..." Parker stopped Mason from interrupting. "I felt as if I was with a cardboard cutout. We had nothing to talk about. Nothing."

"Did you fuck him?"

"No."

"Did he fuck you?" Why did Mason feel jealous?

"No. He sucked me off, and I had to think of you."

"What?" Mason laughed, the jealousy vanished. "Me?"

"You!" Parker poked him in the arm.

"You were with a supermodel from Spencer and Epstein and you had to think of me to get off?"

"Honest truth."

"That is so hot. If it's the truth." Mason raised one eyebrow skeptically.

"I am not just stroking your ego. But I wanted to let you know you aren't the only one who falls for the pretty smokescreen." Parker stepped out of the car.

"Huh." Mason did as well, checking to see if they had to feed a meter or were in a restricted zone.

"We're good." Parker pointed to a sign, which showed they had a two hour limit.

Mason joined him on the sidewalk and held his hand. "You had to think of me, while a model gave you head."

"Yup."

"No one has ever said that to me. Wow." He squeezed Parker's hand tightly.

"Honest."

Mason couldn't believe it. Then again, he could. Maybe some men didn't lie for a living. And maybe Parker was one of those men.

## CHAPTER 19

Monday morning, Parker sat at his desk in front of his computer. He sipped his vanilla flavored espresso and although he had a number of ideas for his blog and column, he kept thinking about his weekend with Mason.

It was glorious.

A walk on the beach after hot sex on Saturday, Mason making him dinner Saturday night, Sunday, a lazy day cuddling in bed and talking...talking about their childhood their past relationships, their favorite movies...

More incredibly hot sex Sunday night, and then they arrived together at work, still brushing against each other in the elevator and on the walk to their prospective places in the office.

Parker set his mug down and began typing.

*'The theory is that a princess must kiss a lot of toads before she finds her prince. There is some truth to that philosophy. All right, a few men and women meet their ideal mate young, latch on, hold on for dear life and stay married for sixty years, only to die within a week apart in their nineties.*

*'But for the real humans out there who actually have to work for a relationship? We lip lock with so many toads, it's amazing we aren't all covered in warts. A game of hit and miss, time and again. Trying to attain the balance between sexual attraction and emotional bonding. It's a cosmic joke at times.*

*'We are hot for pretty boys and compatible with nice guys. Do the two ever overlap? Maybe. But in his writer's experience, it's a coin toss, either or...until...'*

The door opened behind him and Parker stopped typing. A hand brushed through his hair from behind, sending chills over his skin. Parker watched Mason walk to the lounge, holding his coffee cup. Beside Parker was still an empty desk as Sigourney scoured the state looking to lure someone in to replace Dack-the-dick.

Once Mason vanished into the employee lounge, and Parker stopped being mesmerized by his ass and bold strut, he kept working.

*'Until...the right combination smacks you silly. Will it work? No one knows. Will he cheat? Grow bored? Get angry and fight with you all the time? No clue.*

*'But at least when you meet that one guy, or gal, who checks all those pesky boxes you have created in your head, you have a tendency to dream.'*

Parker stopped again as Mason emerged, a steaming brew in his hand, his gaze on Parker. That sensual leer made a tent in Parker's trousers. A quick glance around the room and yes, everyone noticed. How could they not?

Henry was smirking knowingly, Dixie had a smile on her lips, and Morris, Saul and Milly had their jaws hanging open as if this were big news to them.

Parker grew hot under the collar with both the approach of the hottest fucker he'd ever bagged and the knowledge that Mason and he were a 'thang'.

Mason paused behind him.

Parker looked up.

"Can't wait to read it." Mason touched Parker's shoulder.

Under his breath, Parker replied, "Can't wait to fuck you again." He caught Mason glance up as if to see who was paying attention. They all were.

Henry sent Parker an instant message which popped up on Parker's screen. *'You boys are so cute!'*

Parker blushed even hotter.

Sigourney's door opened and she announced to the group, "Two things, troops!"

Parker felt Mason directly behind his chair, his body heat mingling with his own.

"One—I have lined up several people to interview for Dack's job, and of course, once I have narrowed it down, I want everyone to have an opinion, that includes you, Mr Douglas, and you, Mr Bloomfield."

Parker nodded casually but the sense of Mason so close behind him was making him an inferno. Images of Mason hammering his cock into him were causing his cock to throb and there was nothing Parker could do to stop it.

"And second, I just spotted the first trailer for the new reality show Dack is on, on YouTube. What a crack up."

Morris yelled to her, "Send the link!"

"I will." She smiled and ducked back into her office.

"Ya got a minute?" Mason ran his hand through Parker's hair.

"For you? A got a lifetime." Parker laughed and as he stood he said, "Sorry, that was too corny even for me."

"Love it." Mason carried his coffee cup into his office and said, "Close the door."

Parker did. "I'm about to kneel behind your desk the way Dack did."

After putting the mug down, Mason craned his finger. Parker drew closer and Mason tugged him to sit on his lap, going for his lips.

Parker kissed him, sitting across Mason's legs, then smiled at him. "We'll never get any work done."

"I wanted to watch that YouTube clip with you." Mason reached around Parker and used his mouse to open the link Sigourney had sent. Parker relaxed in Mason's arms as it loaded and music began.

In bold letters on a backdrop of a group of young men and women it read '*Celebrity Get Off My Island Fitness Stars*!' at the same time a male announcer with a deep, overly dramatic style to his voice said the same words.

'*In the latest reality show series we pit men and women against each other for you—the viewer—to vote off!*'

Parker spotted Dack, shirtless, flexing both arms like he was in a Mr America competition, only he looked absurd. "It's like watching circus freaks," Parker said.

"I know. Look, the tattooed man, the bearded lady, the monkey boy…"

Parker cracked up. "And the narcissist with his head up his ass."

'*…strength, daring deeds and a battle of wills, who will be your favorite Celebrity Get Off My Island Fitness Star?*'

"This is by far the stupidest thing I have ever seen." Parker shook his head sadly.

"It's an embarrassment."

The video finished with each 'celebrity', which was silly since Parker had no clue who any of them were nor why they would be called 'celebrities' in the first place, being paraded nearly naked, with their names written on their chests in black paint. The video ended with a small credit roll and the premier date.

"Dack's wet dream come true." Mason clicked the mouse and the page vanished back to his work screen of advertising clients.

Parker faced Mason for a kiss before he stood up and got back to work. "A pleasure viewing with you, sir."

"Lunch together?"

"Done." Parker stood and winked as he returned to his desk, back to his column. Smiling and avoiding the gazes of the staff who may or may not assume there was some hanky-panky going on inside the office, Parker read where he had left off.

*'And dream we do. We dream of the perfect life, the perfect job, and of course the perfect partner. But perfection itself is what digs us that hole. There is no such thing.'*

Parker glanced at the office behind him.

*'But there are some men who come pretty damn close.'*

~

By noon Mason had arranged for few long term advertising contracts for the magazine, and began to screen and check the submitted files to send to his art director. Another new luxury car ad with the top male supermodel featured had arrived in his inbox. Mason opened the file to see Mark Richfield's body and extraordinary face being flaunted shamelessly in tight white skintight-see-through workout pants. Mason got lost on him. He couldn't help it. The guy was absurdly handsome.

A knock at his door drew his attention. "Come in."

Parker entered and smiled. "I'm starving."

"What do you think?" Mason waved him over and pointed to the computer.

Parker stood beside Mason's chair. "Oh, you have to be kidding me!"

"Look at the size of the outline of his cock in his pants."

Parker studied it closer. "That can't be real. It's gotta be photo-shopped."

"I don't think so. You saw his nude spread in the UK magazine, right? Dack made sure he emailed it around."

"Yeah but..." Parker pointed to a very huge outline of an erect cock under the model's tight white leggings. "No way."

"Wouldn't want a partner with a dick that big." Mason shut his computer off so they could grab lunch. "Too much of a good thing."

"They stuffed his trousers in the last one, believe me." Parker headed to the door. "I don't even know what car company that was."

"Car? What car?" Mason laughed and followed Parker out to the elevator.

"Christ. Wish I won the genetic lottery like that." Parker pushed the call button as they waited. "That guy is making millions on that face and body of his."

"Yeah, but even he will get old." Mason stepped back as the elevator opened.

A fantastic looking young male was getting out at their floor. Dressed in a very expensive designer suit, his hair, dark and thick, his eyes piercingly blue, he looked first at Parker, then at Mason.

"Do I have the right floor? Is this the right place for *Judas' Rainbow*?"

Mason was dumbstruck as Parker said, "Yes. Just through those doors."

Mason met the man's eyes, got one hell of a sexy smile from him, and watched the man's ass and legs as he entered the office.

He felt a hard punch on his shoulder and flinched. "Ouch!"

"Put your tongue back into your mouth, Mason." Parker grabbed Mason's sleeve and dragged him into the elevator.

"You think he's interviewing for Dack's position?"

"I'm going to kill you."

Mason glanced at Parker. "What?" When he realized what Parker must be thinking he laughed. "No! No way! Come on, Parker. I learned my fucking lesson."

"You nearly swooned at his feet!" Parker tapped the ground floor button, appearing annoyed.

"No way! Parker!" Mason kept laughing.

Parker stormed out of the elevator when it stopped at their floor. Mason sprinted after him and pinned him against the wall near the exit door. He made Parker meet his eyes. "I know what you're thinking."

"Do you?" Parker snarled.

"Yup. I love you, I hate you."

Parker's hard expression softened and he started to laugh.

Mason held his hand and led Parker out of the building and into the cool February day. "Not going to cheat on you, Parker. No way. Especially not with a man like that."

"Promise?"

"Hell yeah. Cross my heart." Mason drew a line over his chest. "Believe me. You can teach this old dog new tricks."

"Then don't go into a trance when you see a guy like that."

"Hey! I'm not dead! I can look!" Mason opened the door of the tiny café he always bought his sandwich at.

"No. You can't!" Parker obviously was trying not to laugh as they bickered.

"Yes, I can!"

"No!" Parker punched Mason's shoulder again, making him wince and hold his arm.

"Damn! You possessive, dog."

"Damn straight." Parker stood in line with Mason.

A small commotion occurred at the door to the café.

Mason spun around to see why.

Two men entered the crowded coffee shop—one macho, brown-haired and blue-eyed, totally jock All-American male, the other...

Parker choked audibly while the patrons waiting for their coffee and lunch began to whisper. The air instantly was charged with electricity.

Mason watched Parker's expression as he ogled the fabulous supermodel, Mark Richfield, and his partner. He was aware Mark lived in LA and worked around the area, but had never run into him before.

Seeing Parker's enrapt expression, Mason punched *his* arm.

"Ouch!" Parker spun around and held his shoulder.

"See? I love you, I hate you." Mason stuck his tongue into his cheek.

"Well, Mark Richfield is the only exception to the ogle rule."

Mason took another glance at the long-haired god.

"Okay. Deal." He held out his hand and Parker shook it.

They smiled wickedly at each other as they clasped tightly.

"Gonna fuck you so hard later." Mason made a growling noise.

"Gonna love it."

"May I help you?" the woman behind the counter asked.

"Yes, Mason said, "Get this man anything he wants," he pointed to Parker, "Except the supermodel." Mason tilted his head to Mark.

The woman giggled and blushed.

Parker put his arm around Mason's waist affectionately. "Don't worry. I want you."

They pecked lips and smiled.

## *The End*

# About the Author

Award-winning author G.A. Hauser was born in Fair Lawn, New Jersey, USA and attended university in New York City. She moved to Seattle, Washington where she worked as a patrol officer with the Seattle Police Department. In early 2000 G.A. moved to Hertfordshire, England where she began her writing in earnest and published her first book, In the Shadow of Alexander. Now a full-time writer, G.A. has written over ninety novels, including several best-sellers of gay fiction. GA is also the executive producer for her first feature film, CAPITAL GAMES. For more information on other books by G.A., visit the author at her official website. www.authorgahauser.com

www.capitalgamesthemovie.com

G.A. has won awards from All Romance eBooks for Best Author 2010, 2009, Best Novel 2008, *Mile High*, and Best Author 2008, Best Novel 2007, *Secrets and Misdemeanors*, Best Author 2007.

# The G.A. Hauser Collection

## Single Titles

*Unnecessary Roughness*

*Hot Rod*

*Mr. Right*

*Happy Endings*

*Down and Dirty*

*Lancelot in Love*

*Cowboy Blues*

*Midnight in London*

*Living Dangerously*

*The Last Hard Man*

*Taking Ryan*

*Born to be Wilde*

*The Adonis of WeHo*

*Boys*

*Band of Brothers*

*Rough Ride*

*Code Red*

*I Love You I Hate You!*

*Marry Me*

## G. A. HAUSER

*The Farmer's Son*

*One, Two, Three*

*L.A. Masquerade*

*Dude! Did You Just Bite Me?*

*My Best Friend's Boyfriend*

*The Diamond Stud*

*The Hard Way*

*Games Men Play*

*Born to Please*

*Of Wolves and Men*

*The Order of Wolves*

*Got Men?*

*Heart of Steele*

*All Man*

*Julian*

*Black Leather Phoenix*

*London, Bloody, London*

*In The Dark and What Should Never Be, Erotic Short Stories*

*Mark and Sharon*

*A Man's Best Friend*

*It Takes a Man*

# I Love You I Hate You

Blind Ambition

For Love and Money

The Kiss

Naked Dragon

Secrets and Misdemeanors

Capital Games

Giving Up the Ghost

To Have and To Hostage

Love you, Loveday

The Boy Next Door

When Adam Met Jack

Exposure

The Vampire and the Man-eater

Murphy's Hero

Mark Antonious deMontford

Prince of Servitude

Calling Dr Love

The Rape of St. Peter

The Wedding Planner

Going Deep

Double Trouble

Pirates

G. A. HAUSER

*Miller's Tale*
*Vampire Nights*
*Teacher's Pet*
*In the Shadow of Alexander*
*The Rise and Fall of the Sacred Band of Thebes*

## The Action Series

*Acting Naughty*
*Playing Dirty*
*Getting it in the End*
*Behaving Badly*
*Dripping Hot*
*Packing Heat*
*Being Screwed*
*Something Sexy*
*Going Wild*
*Having it All!*
*Bending the Rules*
*Keeping it Up*

## Men in Motion Series

*Mile High*

*Cruising*

*Driving Hard*

*Leather Boys*

## Heroes Series

*Man to Man*

*Two In Two Out*

*Top Men*

# G.A. Hauser

# Writing as Amanda Winters

*Sister Moonshine*

*Nothing Like Romance*

*Silent Reign*

*Butterfly Suicide*

*Mutley's Crew*

G. A. HAUSER

# Other works by G.A. Hauser:

## *BOYS-BOYS WHO LOVE BOYS WHO LOVE GIRLS*

Twenty-five year old Jag Huntington loved straight men. He couldn't help it. Something about their macho-allure intrigued him. But Jag had never even managed to have a straight man as a friend.

His best friend Tyson Hopper, and Tyson's boyfriend Howard Steinman invite Jag out for a night with the gay-boys and Howard's sister, Virginia.

When Virginia brings her straight boyfriend, Carson Phelps, Jag's attraction to the thirty year old stud was instant. But there was not mutual attraction, not even curiosity.

It wasn't until Virginia insinuated that Jag and Carson should be friends, 'close' friends, that Jag began to wonder if he had a chance.

Carson liked hanging with gay men. They were fun. His straight buddies didn't get into dancing, music, or anything he really wanted to do. The idea of having a great gay friend appealed to Carson. Self-assured, Carson didn't flinch at the racy conversation nor sexual overtones of his gay companions' conversation. He liked it.

There was something which intrigued both men into crossing the line of friendship into a physical relationship, but for Jag, it was devoid of any emotional attachment, which he craved from Carson.

Would Jag and Carson's friendship ever evolve into anything more than a couple of friends; one gay and one straight?

Or was there really something extra special about a boy who loves boys, who loves girls?

## BAND OF BROTHERS

Two young men in their early twenties, Austin Shelby and Henry 'Woody' Woodcliff, had somehow lost their way. Living in Albuquerque, petty thieves, neither man had family or hope of becoming anything more than inmates in the county jail.

Orlando Ancho had other plans. Working in his family restaurant, going to med-school, Orlando meets the two young men one night when they come to the restaurant for a meal. Immediately Orlando suspects they are living on the street, and may dine and dash. But what Orlando doesn't expect, is to find a common bond with these men.

Being deep in the closet, living with a brother who was a harsh critic of Orlando, and extremely homophobic, Orlando had no intention of coming out. Hiding from intimacy, Orlando led a lonely life. When Austin and Woody, exchange a 'blood' vow with him one night, Orlando admits his sexual attraction to the fair-haired Austin, craving his love and touch.

But jealousy and violence becomes inevitable, and disaster strikes one of the trio.

What had begun as a friendship between three very different men, turns into a journey for this Band of Brothers; blood brothers…who are put to the ultimate test of trust and loyalty.

# COWBOY BLUES

Gay cowboys? Gay rodeos?

*Rainbow Rough Riders Rodeo*, is a small, newly formed group made up of a diverse selection of gay men who each have their own reasons for wanting to compete in the rodeo challenges and enjoy the fun of the celebration of the wild west.

Follow three couples; Ken Marsh, the forty-one year old founder of the group, his forty-five year old country music singer lover, Lyle Jackson; the two bearded cuddly bears who are the perfect couple, Rob Grafton and Victor Sarita, and the youngest of the bunch, Mike 'Clint' Wolcott and the object of his desire, Cheyenne Wheeler.

Six men, three complicated relationships, and all the thrill and hardship that goes with life on the road, moving town to town, riding bareback and enjoying a good hard buck! And that doesn't even include the rodeo competitions!

Cowboys. The new macho sex symbols, or maybe not 'new', maybe just the sexiest men around. But being a cowboy sometimes is a hard road, and even Cowboys get the blues.

## *Midnight in London*

Thirty-one year old Ted Mack, the high-school 'geek', was on the cusp of developing the next mega social-network-for-one. His group of techno-philes worked day and night to create a unique computer network that would astonish the world.

Twenty-three year old Kevin Moore, Jeremy West's straight roommate from the novel 'Teacher's Pet', has graduated college with honors and is now working on his own creating websites. His idol? Ted Mack.

When the two meet during an IT convention in London, the connection between the handsome college jock and the geek is electric. With the chiming of Big Ben signaling the midnight hour in the background, Ted and Kevin kiss, altering their lives from that moment on.

Can that one moment in time make a connection that will last a lifetime? Or will their colliding worlds pull them apart?

Both Ted and Kevin knew their relationship would not be easy. And if it fell apart? They always had Midnight in London.

## *Happy Endings*

Twenty-seven year old, Kelsey 'Kellie' Hamilton was caught up in the economic housing disaster. Losing his home, his job, and having to reinvent himself, Kellie went back to school for his certificate in massage therapy and is hired by an elite spa in West Hollywood. Though Kellie had experienced 'happy endings' in the past while getting massages from older men, he was going to abide by the rules and not get sexual with his clients.

Montgomery 'Monty' Gresham, ex Navy SEAL plans to open up a SEAL training boot camp for civilians, and decides getting referrals from a celebrity club in LA would be a perfect idea. While Monty recruits members to his military training center, he meets the handsome massage therapist, Kellie Hamilton.

The contact between Kellie and Monty while Monty is on the massage table instantly sends both men into a state of pure sexual arousal. In this heightened state, where two opposites certainly are attracted, Kellie needs to decide if the tough thirty-eight year old ex-military man will be his Happy Ending, or if living happily ever after is just a fairy tale.

## *The Crush*

Straight thirty-two year old Cooper McDermott knew marrying an eighteen year old pageant queen was a mistake. And after two years, his young wife began a spree of cheating on him, breaking his heart.

Newcomer from New York City to the Los Angeles area, Blair Woodbury joins the staff of the law office where the stunning Cooper McDermott works. Blair considers himself 'bisexual', but has just ended an affair back in New York with a man. It didn't take long for Blair to get a full blown crush on Cooper, especially when he was asked to represent Cooper in his divorce. Blair knew getting emotionally involved with a man on the heels of a bad breakup was bad enough, not to mention the object of Blair's desire was straight-

As their friendship grew and they became best buddies, Blair's crush on Cooper became extreme. When Cooper agrees to go for a 'boy's' weekend in Las Vegas, as his sexual curiosity began to emerge, Blair knew he was in for a wild ride!

Can Blair convince Cooper that his feelings for him are real? Or will this fantasy of Blair's be simply just a crush on his co-worker. All Cooper kept hoping was that what happens in Vegas stays in Vegas!

## *Lancelot in Love*

Still working through an upset of a romance gone bad, thirty year old Lancelot Sanborn escapes to an old haunt; the bungalow colonies of the Catskill Mountain Resort. As a child Lance remembered the comfort and simplicity of his summer vacations, lazing by the lake and enjoying everything upstate New York had to offer. A stark contrast from his hectic life in the Big Apple.

Twenty-three year old Keefe Hammond and three of his friends from Rutgers decide to rent a cottage at the resort for a Labor Day weekend of non-stop partying. Keefe was deeply in the closet and had no intention of stepping out. Until…

The two men meet as they became temporary neighbors in the bungalow resort and soon Keefe began testing his own desires for sex with a man, against his terror of revealing who he is to his friends.

One place Lancelot never expected to find true love was during a retreat to escape from it.

In the end, love always finds a way and for Lancelot, he finds the love of his life in a young man named Keefe.

## *Capital Games*

*Let the games begin…*

Former Los Angeles Police officer Steve Miller has gone from walking a beat in the City of Angels to joining the rat race as an advertising executive. He knows how cut-throat the industry can be, so when his boss tells him that he's in direct competition with a newcomer from across the pond for a coveted account he's not surprised…then he meets Mark Richfield.

Born with a silver spoon in his mouth and fashion-model good looks, Mark is used to getting what he wants. About to be married, Mark has just nailed the job of his dreams. If the determined Brit could just steal the firm's biggest account right out from under Steve Miller, his life would be perfect.

When their boss sends them together to the Arizona desert for a team-building retreat the tension between the two dynamic men escalates until in the heat of the moment their uncontrollable passion leads them to a sexual experience that neither can forget.

Will Mark deny his feelings and follow through with marriage to a woman he no longer wants, or will he realize in time that in the game of love, sometimes you have to let go and lose yourself in order to *really* win.

**CAPITAL GAMES THE MOVIE coming soon to LGBT and Independent film festivals.**

*If you like this novel you may also like:*
*Silver Ties, by Patricia Logan*

*Synopsis:*
A serial killer is preying upon gay men in Los Angeles. Detective Cassidy Ryan of the LAPD is out to stop the monster before more mutilated corpses turn up. The victims have one thing in common and it leads back to an infamous online club called DOMZ.com. The website owner, Zachary Teak, is stunningly gorgeous and infuriatingly uncooperative. Having spent years in vice, investigating crimes fueled by pornography, Cassidy hates the Dom on sight.

Zack Teak is a wealthy man and a popular Dom with a long waiting list of subs who beg to lick his boots. The moment he meets the detective, a former Navy SEAL, he is determined to help the handsome, blond hunk explore his own submissive nature but Cassidy is having none of it.

As Cassidy closes in on the killer, he succumbs to Teak's charms, finding that it's okay to give up control and let Zack take charge. Join the men as they flush out a killer while trying not to become victims themselves.

**Now available on Kindle!**

Made in the USA
Middletown, DE
18 April 2021